EUROPA

BY TIM PARKS

Fiction

Tongues of Flame
Loving Roger
Home Thoughts
Family Planning
Goodness
Cara Massimina
Shear
Mimi's Ghost
Europa

Non-Fiction

Italian Neighbors
An Italian Education

Europa

TIM PARKS

ARCADE PUBLISHING
NEW YORK

FIRST NORTH AMERICAN EDITION 1998

First published in Great Britain by Secker & Warburg 1997

This is a work of fiction. Names, places, characters, and incidents are either products of the author's imagination or are used fictitiously.

Library of Congress Cataloging-in-Publication Data

Parks, Tim.
    Europa / Tim Parks. —1st North American ed.
      p.   cm.
    ISBN 1-55970-444-6
    1. Man-woman relationships—Europe—Fiction. 2. College teachers—Italy—Milan—Fiction. 3. Europe—Economic integration—Fiction. 4. Divorced men—Italy—Milan—Fiction. 5. British—Italy—Milan—Fiction. I. Milan
PR6066.A6957E97   1998
823'.914—dc21
                                            98–24718

Published in the United States by Arcade Publishing, Inc., New York
Distributed by Little, Brown and Company

10 9 8 7 6 5 4 3 2 1

BP

PRINTED IN THE UNITED STATES OF AMERICA

Europa (in Athens) does business
at truly reasonable rates.
You needn't fear interruption
or the gainsaying of whims;
also, she offers irreproachable
sheets, and – in winter –
a coal-fire. This time, Zeus,
come as you are. No bull.

Antipater of
Thessalonika

Love's night & a lamp
judged our vows:
that she would love me ever
& I should never leave her.
Love's night & you, lamp,
witnessed the pact.
Today the vow runs:
'Oaths such as these, waterwords.'
Tonight, lamp,
witness her lying
– in other arms.

Meleager

Part One

'My dear girl, where there are women
there are sure to be slaps. It was
Napoleon who said that, I think.'

Zola, *Nana*

CHAPTER ONE

I am sitting slightly off-centre on the long back seat of a modern coach crossing Europe. And this in itself is extraordinary. For I hate coaches, I have always hated coaches, and above all I hate modern coaches, not just because of the strong and nauseating smell of plastics and synthetic upholstery, but because of the way the supposed desires of the majority are now foisted upon everybody – I mean myself – in the form of videoscreens projecting from beneath the luggage rack every six seats or so, and of course piped music oozing from concealed loudspeakers. So that even as we pull out of Piazza dell'Università into the morning traffic on Corso Vercelli in this strange city I have lived in for so long of stone and trams and noble façades and Moroccans selling boxes of contraband cigarettes laid out on the pavements under propped-up umbrellas – because it's raining, as it will in Milan in May – even now, before the long trip has hardly started, we are having to listen to a smug male voice singing with fake and complacent hoarseness about *un amore passionale*, which he cannot, he claims, forget, and which has *destroyed his life forever*, a theme, I suspect, that may be the very

3

last thing one needs to be subjected to at only shortly after eight on a Monday morning, and not long after one's forty-fifth birthday. Though many of the younger travellers are singing along (the way fresh recruits, I believe, will sing along on their way to war).

Yes, that it was a mistake, I reflect, sitting slightly right of centre on the long back seat of this modern coach setting out across Europe, that it was a big mistake to have come on this trip, I have never doubted from the moment I agreed to it, and perhaps even before, if such a thing is possible. Or let's say that the very instant I took this decision was also the instant I recognized, and recognized that I had always recognized, that coming on this trip was one of those mistakes I was made to make. You were made to make this mistake, I thought. By which I don't mean of course to put it on a par with the grander and more spectacular mistakes that have given shape and structure to what one can only refer to as one's life, just that, upon having agreed, in answer to a request from a colleague, to sign my name at the bottom of a list of other signatures of other colleagues, I immediately appreciated that this was precisely the kind of squalid, absurd and wilful mistake that somebody like myself would make. This is the kind of thing you do, I told myself. You agree to travel for twelve hours on a coach in one direction and then, two days later, for twelve hours on the same coach (a modern coach to boot, with piped music and videos and synthetic smell) in the return direction, in order to lend your name, for the very little it is worth, to a cause which not only do you not support, but which from a purely intellectual point of view, if such a miracle exists, you oppose, you oppose it, and this, what's more, through an appeal to an institution which again not only do you not support, nor subscribe to in any way, but which you frequently feel perhaps should not exist at all. This is the kind of person you are. And trying to find a comfortable position for my head on a brushed nylon headrest at the back of this big coach presently jammed at a crossing despite the green light, I reflect once again that when, and this would have been early April, Vikram Griffiths said to me, clearing his throat and rubbing his fingers across a polished Indian baldness, as he will, or in his sideburns, or in the down of hair behind his thick neck, and then adjusting his spectacles, as he is doing at this very moment some way up the central corridor of this hideous modern coach, leaning stockily, dog nipping his ankles, over the shoulders and doubtless breasts of a young girl, gestures one presumes he makes out of nervousness and a desire to give people the impression that what he is saying is important and exciting – a dramatized nervousness is perhaps what I mean, a nervousness become conscious of itself and then tool of itself in a never-ending and self-consuming but always coercive narcissism – when Vikram Griffiths said to me, swallowing catarrh, though without his dog that day, Jerry, boyo – because Vikram is not just an Indian but a Welsh Indian, the only Indian ever to speak Welsh, he claims – Jerry, boyo, we are going to appeal to *Europe* – clearing his throat again – and we would *much appreciate your support*, what I should have done, of course, was to laugh in his face, or produce some more polite gesture but of similar subtext, as for example enquiring, Europe? or just, Where, sorry? as though genuinely unaware that such an entity existed.

I should have refused. It surely would not have been impossible even for a man who is known to be living alone and enjoying a life of very few *professional commitments* to have found some kind of excuse relative to one of the three designated days when this particular modern coach was to be speeding up interminable kilometres of *autostrada* and *autoroute* to *present our case to Europe*. It should not have been impossible. Yet not only did I not refuse, but I actually leapt at the chance. I said yes immediately. Not only did I not look for an excuse to avoid this tiresome and I suspect hypocritical pilgrimage, but I actually overlooked the perfectly good excuse that did present itself, to wit my daughter's eighteenth birthday, the party to celebrate which will take place tomorrow in my no doubt much-censured absence. And not only, I reflect, as the coach's big engine vibrates beneath my seat – and what I'm trying to do I suppose is to grasp the nettle, all the nettles, just as firmly as ever one can – not only did I accept immediately, by which I mean without a second's mental mediation, on reflex as it were, but I then went out of my way to make my acceptance affable and even friendly. I said, Why surely, Vikram, of course I'll come, and I signed my name immediately and immediately, without mediation, I reached into my pocket to pull out the new wallet I had recently bought, as I have bought so many new things of the small and vaguely intimate variety of late, and paid immediately (which was quite unnecessary) the two hundred and twenty thousand lire the trip is costing, a sum which frankly, given the present state of my finances, I can ill afford. You can ill afford it, I told myself. Though I must say that money for me of late has been taking on the feel of a currency one is eager to be rid of before moving on to some other country, a currency, that is, that will not be current for much longer, and which it does not even occur to me might be exchangeable.

I paid my money to this Vikram of the dark skin, deep Indian voice and incongruously Welsh accent *immediately* and in order then to explain a readiness which I feared would not be understood (since when have you ever shown any inclination to *fight for the cause*?), I actually went so far as to say that since others were making the very considerable effort to organize this trip on everybody's behalf, the least somebody like myself could do was to *show solidarity* and come along. I could read a book, I said, during the long journey, I had a lot to read for work, for prospective work, or I could just think (just!). And standing there in the spare because institutional room where our encounter took place, amongst graceless office furniture on a stone-patterned linoleum floor indifferently cleaned by a pampered and unmotivated menial staff, standing there talking to this man whose fecklessness rivals even my own, whose only stable relationship appears to be his passion for the mongrel dog whose hairs smother all his shabby clothes, I was trying to reassure him that there was nothing peculiar in my so rapidly subscribing to his *courageous initiative*, that there was nothing peculiar in my eagerly adding my name to his list of scrawled signatures. I was almost apologizing, for God's sake, for enrolling in his expedition. Or rather, I was already concealing what I already knew in my heart to be the real and only reason for my behaving in this extraordinary and inconsistent fashion, for my agreeing, that is, to come on this ridiculous and pointless trip; the same reason, it should be said, why I have now, even as I sit here churning these thoughts on the back seat of this coach as it inches its way out to one of those nodal points where the motorway system plugs into the city so that one can be sucked off at tremendous speed to some other and in every way similar city – the same reason why I have now suddenly buried my face in a book the words on whose pages I not only do not see but do not even really want to see. For *she* has just stood up to get down her dark leather document-case from the overhead luggage rack. She is in the third seat from the front on the left.

And to think, to think that for more than six months now, or is it a year? I had been speaking of myself (to myself) as a man healed, as a man emerging once and for all from the throes and miseries, and I suppose it has to be added ecstasies, of what I can only refer to as the great crisis, the great adventure, the great collision of my life. Yes, I had begun to look upon myself as that person who has been through it all and emerges the other side 'a happier and a wiser man', who glances back at others crossing life's rapids with a sort of affectionate and satisfying irony. And chattering to myself in my mind, as one does, or buying furniture for my little flat, or purchasing all those little things – my new wallet – that I suddenly felt it sensible to replace, so that life could start anew, free from every encumbering reminder, I would tell myself: Splendid, not even a whiff of albatross, not a hint of that weight and stench you have carried around with you for so long! Yes, the road to excess, I would quote to myself, and I remember doing this with a cheerful complacence that it is embarrassing to recall, the road to excess – perhaps I would be putting on a CD of Handel or of Mozart (I had been keeping very strict control on my listening material) – truly does lead to the Palace of Wisdom. Though one might have quibbled over the word 'palace', I suppose. But even if designations along the lines of 'service flat' or 'hovel' or even 'bunker' would perhaps be more appropriate for the species of wisdom I had arrived at, the point I'm trying to make is that prior to meeting Vikram Griffiths, our Indian Welshman, in the English Institute staffroom that day, I had felt I was cured. No, better still, I felt I had cured myself. There was pride involved. For at no point had I sought help from anyone, had I? No, I had fought my own way out of the flood, born up by the scraps of reason and self-respect one inevitably clutches at once it becomes clear one has no stomach for the darker option. And if, after what seemed a very long time at sea, the surf had set me down at the last in a place that was far away from where I plunged in and quite unknown to me and above all lonelier than any other place I had ever been before, all the same it did give me every impression once I got there, once I closed the door on my tiny apartment, of being *terra firma*, of being, that is, a place of arrival, the kind of place to which the words 'home and dry', or at least 'dry', might be applicable.

Yes, for six months, I reflect, sitting slightly right of centre on the big back seat of this powerful modern coach setting out across Europe, for six months you have been telling yourself that you are out of the woods, safe, even happy. Not to the point of clapping your hands and stamping your feet, perhaps, but happy enough, happy enough. Until a man for whom you have no particular respect approaches you in your loathsome place of work, an occasional drinking companion, affectedly shabby, determinedly Indian, though brought up entirely Welsh, with a clipboard and a pen in his hand and a nervous over-excited coercive manner manifested above all by his constant throat-clearing and catarrh-swallowing, his constant fingering of sideburns and baldness, and this man explains to you an *ambitious initiative* for saving the very job you have been trying for years to find the courage to leave, a job that is the source perhaps, when looked at from one angle, of all your woes, and what do you do? What do you do? In the space of a very few seconds you forget the resolve, for such it had seemed, of the last six months and you offer, promptly, immediately, without mediation, your – and these were the very words you used – *personal contribution to the group effort*. And then because you have never, but never, shown the slightest interest in the past in saving this miserable but of course well-paid, fatally well-paid job which has kept us all hanging on here in a limbo without future or return, trapped us in a stagnant backwater where the leaves of falling years turn slowly on themselves as they drift and rot, and because you are sure that this man with the handsome sideburns and balding nervousness never for one moment imagined you would *lend your support*, and in fact only really asked you because you both happened to be in the same room at the same time and he with his clipboard in his hand, you start

9

to make all kinds of affable apologies of the variety, If others are doing so much, the least I could do, etc. and even explaining to him that you won't really be wasting the time because you can take books to read. I have plenty of work I can take, you said in a ludicrous pretence of having *pressing outside interests*, and Vikram Griffiths said: Oh, no need to worry about entertainment, boyo – because Vikram, who has no official role in the foreign teachers' union, yet appears to be the only person who is capable of getting anything done, has this way of calling all males of whatever age 'boyo', as indeed he has of calling all females of whatever age 'girlie', which is part and parcel of declaring his Welshness, his incongruous Welshness, which of course draws attention to his Indianness, his un-Welshness, and also his matey, alcohol-fed nervousness and above all his *alternativeness*, his belonging to that *révolution permanente*, as the French like to say, or used to, that army of special and enlightened people, who are now so much an accepted and uninspiring part of our shadow establishment – No need to worry about entertainment, boyo, Vikram Griffiths says, clearing his throat and rubbing his hands together, because almost all the students coming along will be *girlies*, of course. At which point this man, no doubt delighted to have found such an unlikely supporter for his *imaginative initiative*, gives you the kind of wink which is also a leer, the kind of facial contortion, I mean, that a stand-up comedian might wish to cultivate so that not a single member of a huge theatre audience could misunderstand his insinuation. Because part of Vikram Griffiths' manner, I reflect, is to assume, ostentatiously, provocatively, a renegade complicity even with people whom he suspects may be on the other side. In fact, he said, his face still untwisting from its leer, the boys are already calling it The Shag Wagon, and he laughed a throaty, smoke-and-whisky laugh, and sucking in catarrh repeated, *The Shag Wagon*, still laughing, and then was giving me some statistics on what he expected to be the breakdown between the students, mostly girls and numerous, and the foreign teachers, ourselves, mostly men and few, and true to the totally inconsistent and I think I ought to recognize shameful way I was behaving, I am behaving, I laughed too. The Shag Wagon! I shouted with a quite unforgiveable mirth. The fucking *Shag Wagon*, who thought of calling it that? It's brilliant! And Vikram said, Georg thought of it. You know what Georg's like.

Which I did. I do.

And he picked up his list, which already had *her* name and Georg's name signed on it, and, smelling of dog, dog hairs on his shabby jacket, though he can hardly bring the creature into the University, he went across the room to talk to another of my colleagues, while what I was immediately trying to remember was whether their names, *hers* and Georg's, had been one above the other or one below the other on that list I had just signed and whether they had been written in the same colour and hence perhaps the same pen. And I couldn't remember. As even now, sitting on the back seat of this modern coach setting out towards the putative heart of Europe and forcing my mind's eye to open once again on the moment when I saw that list on his clipboard, the moment I so precipitously and it has to be said pathetically added my name to it, even now I cannot recall whether their names were together, or far apart, and not remembering, but trying so hard to remember, I am obliged for it must be the millionth time to acknowledge how humiliating it is to be throwing all my mental energy at a matter which is of absolutely no importance, and not even pleasurable in the way that so many other matters of absolutely no importance but to which one regularly gives one's mind, as for example billiards, or TV documentaries, or even, though more rarely, one's work, can be, if nothing else, at least pleasurable. Why does a man feel he has to take his dog with him everywhere?

I ask myself. Why does a man have to *put himself so much in evidence*? An ugly dog at that. And how could it possibly matter whether *she* and Georg signed the Strasbourg list with the same pen and hence were perhaps together at the moment of signing? How could such a trivial coincidence signify anything at all?

But now I am interrupted by an Italian voice that asks: What are you reading?

For it has to be said that I am very far from being alone on the back seat of this coach. Indeed, if one could be alone, or even hope to be alone, hope that other people would leave one alone, in a modern coach then I would not hate them quite so much, since perhaps what I hate most about coaches is that they imply groups, and one's forced or presumed participation in a group for a given period of time, in the way that, for example, buses or trains or even aeroplanes do not imply such scenarios, since in those cases everybody buys their tickets separately and separately minds their own separate business. Yes, coaches, I understand now, make me think of groups and the tendency groups have to operate at the level of the lowest, and perhaps not even common, denominator, and what I'm thinking of I suppose is parties of people singing together all in the same state of mind, a church outing perhaps, or old people embarking on package tours to pass the time, or adolescents on the way to support a football team, and, in general, I'm thinking of all the contemporary pieties of getting people together and moving them off in one direction or another to have fun together, or to edify themselves, or to show solidarity to some underprivileged minority and everybody, as I said, being of the same mind and of one intent, every individual possessed by the spirit of the group, which is the very spirit apparently of *humanity*, and indeed of that *Europe*, come to think of it, to which this group is now hurtling off to appeal. Whereas if I recall

12

correctly, and it was from a book *she* once made me read or rather re-read, for she was always making me read books in the hope that I might recover my vocation, might truly become that person, that man (this was important), I had once shown promise of becoming — if I recall correctly, then the first mention of Europe as a geographical entity (was it Theocritus?) referred only to the Peloponnese, and only in order to *distinguish* the Peloponnese from Asia, only to demonstrate that the small peninsula had *not* been swallowed up into the amorphous mass of an ever-invasive Asia. Or so I recall, rightly, or perhaps wrongly, from a book she made me read, re-read, in her insistent and one must suppose laudable attempt to have me recover my vocation, to have me become, perhaps this was the nub, somebody she could respect. It was a claim to distinction, Europe, as I recall.

In any event, I am far from alone, here on the back seat, which is to say that on my right, trapped between myself and the window, I have a rather plain young woman with somehow swollen lips who has been chattering intermittently with the two girls in the seat in front of us and, ignoring myself, with the girl, over made-up, to my left, who is dead in the centre of the coach's, one has to confess, comfortable big back seat, while to her left sits the handsome Georg, a German of Polish extraction, who is exchanging occasional pleasantries with the girl to his left, trapped between himself and the window, and again with the boy and girl in the seat in front of them, one of whom, the girl, is standing up with one knee on her seat and one very long and attractive leg out in the corridor, holding forth absolutely non-stop, in Italian, as is to be expected of a young Italian, on a variety of entirely predictable topics, as for example, the quality of different makes of jeans, including the pair she has on (allowing Georg to examine her leg and plump crotch attentively); the impossibility of finding a place in one of the smaller university classrooms when somebody 'important' (not myself) is lecturing; the credibility of astrology and numerology; the 'stupendous' sound system in a new discothèque recently opened in the small satellite town of Busto Arsizio; and the extraordinary behaviour, in love and out, of her cousin Paola, who studies law at the Cattolica and who, on being left by her boy-friend of long standing, got a friend to phone him in the middle of the night as though from a hospital to say that a girl with red hair (i.e. herself) had been found in a coma after a horrendous car crash, the only piece of identification found on her being a photo of a young man with a phone-number on the back, the boy-friend's — all this to *make him feel sorry for her and guilty about leaving her* and to have him rush off to hospital imagining he would find her dying, whereas in fact what he, the ex-boy-friend, did was to call her parents, who, and particularly the mother, went almost out of their minds with grief before Paola came in through the front door in an advanced state of drunkenness.

How adolescent that is, I reflect, watching the girl's animated face. And how attractive. You have always had a fatal attraction to adolescent behaviour, I tell myself. Most of your own behaviour, I tell myself, is irretrievably adolescent. And in the meantime this stream, indeed this torrent of juvenile and absolutely indiscriminating, but at least unpretentious chatter has, for the half an hour or so that we have been forcing our way through Milan's cluttered thoroughfares, together of course with an occasional burst of communal song when a new voice takes over on the airwaves crooning without fail of love whether happy or unhappy — this chatter and the singing, sometimes choral, of insipid songs, has so far been offering an excellent cover for what I'm perfectly aware will be perceived as my misanthropic behaviour, sitting silent and slightly off-centre in the back seat of this coach, the only place left unoccupied on my late (studiedly late) arrival, my face buried in a book, an attitude which unfortunately legitimizes the innocent question of the girl in the seat in front.

What are you reading?

This girl must be kneeling on her seat, because her arms are resting quite naturally on the top of the backrest above my face and her rather strong chin is just above her linked hands, head cocked to one side in an expression of friendly enquiry and what the Italians call *disponibilità*, meaning openness, willingness to listen and to help, amenability. And though she is perfectly aware, it seems to me, of this body language, this simple friendliness she is communicating, there could be no question of her having deliberately and carefully adopted it, which is exactly the opposite of so many adults, I reflect, who are often amazingly unaware of what they have indeed been meticulously scheming, as when *she*, I am bound to remember now, told you that though she loved you dearly she felt she needed a little breathing space on her own before making the kind of decisions that would upset the *vie tranquille* that she and her young daughter had been enjoying since her painful separation from her husband. And her face as she said this had a wonderful warm poignancy about it, yearning would be an appropriate word, an expression I still remember very clearly, as if gazing at a loved one through prison bars, or in fading twilight, with all the intimacy of a love that cannot be, but an expression that time would all too soon reveal as entirely false and hypocritical, knowing what she knew then, as so many of the expressions, I reflect, that you yourself have adopted with your one-time wife and indeed with all those people who at some time and for whatever reason have become important to you and whom at some point in your life you could not have done without, have been entirely false and hypocritical.

I am not reading, I tell the girl in front of me.

But you have a book.

I insist to the perhaps twenty- or twenty-one-year-old girl that though this is self-evident, the fact is that I am not reading the book which, admittedly, I am holding open in my hands.

Why not?

Already, during the course of this brief exchange, I am aware of smiling wryly and generally sending out the kind of friendly, apparently avuncular social messages which I know are expected of me. It's as if I had indeed been reading the book, but had now chosen to say that I was not reading it in order to tease and prolong the conversation, rather than just giving the girl the title of the thing and having done. Indeed it would not greatly surprise me if before very long I weren't telling this pleasant young *studentessa* some small sad half-truths about myself merely in order to appear, as they say, interesting.

I explain to her that I am not reading the novel I hold in my hands, because I already know it to be a tiresome thing written by a woman who can think of nothing better to do with her very considerable talent than prolong a weary dialectic which presents the authorities as always evil and wrong and her magical-realist, lesbian, ethnic-minority self and assorted revolutionary company as always good and right and engaged, what's more, in a heroic battle where *LIFE* will one day triumph over the evils and violence of an uncomprehending establishment.

Again I smile, warmly, to show that I am perfectly aware that this fierce demolition will seem pompous and presumptuous and even fascist, whereas what I really feel is that my criticism, far from exaggerated, is, if anything, inadequate, since what needs to be said is that people who do nothing more than analyse the world in a way in which it has grown used to being analysed, offering their readers the illusion of participating in a movement that gives them a sense of moral

16

superiority with regard to a society they have no intention of ceasing to subscribe to (as indeed why should they?) – people, whether writers or not, of this variety deserve nothing better than scorn and perhaps a good deal worse.

But it would be unwise to say this. It would be, I have discovered, and indeed it generally is, unwise to say almost any of the things one feels most moved to say. Unless you can somehow present them as a joke.

So why are you reading it? she asks me.

In a pantomime of patience I explain that, as I have already explained, I am not reading it.

But you've got it open.

It was given to me.

She looks at me with big young eyes, wondering if she can ask the question, and perhaps because we're on a coach and hence all part of the same group supporting the same cause, my cause, she feels she can. Who by?

I tell her: Somebody who wanted me to read it.

Clearly she is being teased, and clearly she enjoys being teased. She bounces up and down on her knees, she is young, she smiles, she raises an eyebrow (endearingly bushy), she cocks her head to one side, smooth cheek for just a moment against the synthetic stiff blood-red of the upholstery. Immediately I'm thinking that if I don't tell her who gave me this book, with all that the two words involved would imply, perhaps *I'll have more of a chance* with this young student, a thought which equally immediately short-circuits to have me thinking, uncomfortably, of Georg and of *her*, so expert in the withholding of information, so that in the kind of reflex that isn't so much a decision as a small convulsion of self-recognition followed by fearful rejection (as of one throwing away a cigarette after the first puff), I decide I will tell her who gave me this miserable novel. I will tell her so as to save myself from all equivocation. Just as I open my mouth, she asks, Your girl-friend?

What?

Was it your girl-friend gave you the book?

She smiles warmly. She is being bolder now. She has noticed – I saw her eyes – that I don't wear a ring. I close my mouth, hesitating again, when our conversation, if such we are to call it, is interrupted by an announcement. Vikram Griffiths is standing in the aisle of the coach up front by the driver and he has a microphone in his hand and his mongrel dog at his feet. His voice is harshly, electronically deep, and deeply Welsh: Welcome to y'all! he begins, *benvenuti, bienvenus, wilkommen, croeso*, good t'see ya!

CHAPTER TWO

When Vikram Griffiths begins to speak, the girl in the seat in front of me, whose great brown eyes are of course like those of a million other Italian girls, not to mention Spanish and Greek and doubtless other races too, by which I mean to say, unique, splendid, eminently replaceable, swivels on her seat to pay attention, and what I'm telling myself now, slightly right of centre in the back seat of this packed coach, assailed by Vikram Griffiths' efficiently amplified, demotic voice, what I'm telling myself is that *I truly am in this now*, in this coach I mean, like it or not, for twelve hours and then the two nights in Strasbourg and then twelve hours in the coach again on the way back, not to mention the danger that it could well be more than twelve hours, depending on traffic and circumstances beyond your control, since of course the moment you set out on the road with other people, the moment you undertake a trip together in a coach, the moment you commit yourself to some joint project, some communal enterprise, circumstances are always well and truly beyond your control.

I'm in. Deeply, inescapably in. We've already left Milan behind, we're on the *autostrada*, speeding along, a solid group of us, so that, as when they bolt the doors on the plane and it moves out onto the runway, there can be no more getting out now before the other end, no more splitting us up into separate sovereign urges and desires. You're in it now, I tell myself, with all these young students, girls for the most part, to either side and in front, beautiful and plain, and Georg next-but-one to my left, plus your other colleagues, liked and disliked, but mostly the latter, from France and Germany and Spain and Greece and God bless us even Ireland, and with *her* in the third seat from the front, with her dark brown hair and dark brown document-case that she just took down from the overhead rack, the same case where she used to keep such things as her train timetable and the rubbers we used and the photographs we took of ourselves with the time-delay, and then miscellaneous memorabilia of the air-ticket and hotel-bill variety, the receipts for meals I always had to be careful not to put in my own pockets, and my letters of course, my many many letters, some of them ten or even twenty pages long, some of them no more than fragments of poor poetry I had written, or better poetry I had copied out for her but which she never recognized, and later an aerosol can ·of ammonia spray, as is the way with things that are intense and have to change, things that start well but can't stand still and end badly, very badly, though now no doubt she will have nothing more in there than notepaper for the reflections she is gathering and will be using this trip to gather further, for her research into a possible constitution for a *United Europe* which is part of a competition she has enrolled in to win a *Euro scholarship* for a year's work and study in Brussels, or so I heard from my daughter, a move that she sees as the indispensable next step in her career, for she still thinks of life in terms of career and self-realization, she is still at that stage.

Yes, I am in this now, with all the singing and the toilet stops and the making friends and the exchanging of addresses and the boredom and doubtless the confabulation, as some try to grab more power and responsibility in our little group and others (myself) to refuse it, and the enormous waste of time it will no doubt be going through the bureaucratic procedure of presenting our petition to a European Parliament whose exact functions and powers and suffrage none of us understands, except perhaps *her*, perhaps the Avvocato Malerba, perhaps Vikram, and on the way back we will all have to discuss the importance of what we have achieved and mythologize it and tell ourselves we did well to come and that now we are safer, meaning that we can feel more secure that we will continue to receive our salaries for some time to come.

Yes, I am caught now, I am not in my small flat where the answering machine vets all the calls and where no photograph, ornament, poster or object of any intimacy whatever dates back before 1993, not in my own private space so dear to me and so dull, but here in the thrall of forty or fifty people. You are caught, I tell myself, trapped. And despite my late arrival, due mainly to a half-hour spent in a café on Corso Sempione debating all the reasons for avoiding this ridiculous excursion (without ever for one moment believing I would avoid it), despite my late arrival and all my misgivings, I must say that the thought that I really am *in this* now is beginning to get me rather excited, it's cheering me up, so that already I am considering indulging in a little fling, an *avventura* as the Italians say, with one, with any one for heaven's sake (for they are all the same to me – how could it be otherwise?) of these young women. You should have an adventure, I tell myself, looking around at the fresh young students, a little fling, in full visibility of everybody, flagrant. By which of course I mean in full and flagrant visibility of *her*. As if such a gesture could in any way upset her! As if she would care, which I know perfectly well she wouldn't. On the contrary she would probably say, if we were to speak to each other at all on this trip, which frankly I doubt, she would probably say how pleased she was that I was having *a healthy sex life*, a notion this, whatever it might mean, that she always advocated and indeed used, as a *precept*, to excuse almost any behaviour, and by any behaviour what I mean I suppose is betrayal, which is surely the most terrible behaviour of all, and the most inevitable it seems sometimes. And this reminds me now how, with her historical studies, so similar to my own, and her desire for sophistication, or at least to be seen to be sophisticated, she liked to say that European hegemony in the world began with a woman's betrayal, and she meant Helen, Helen's betrayal, which prompted the Achaean triumph and the shift of civilization's centre from east to west, Troy to Athens and thence of course further west to her beloved Paris. Another protagonist. Every epic adventure (I remember her saying this and myself thinking how intelligent she was and how well-read and articulate), every epic adventure turned on a woman's betrayal, of father, family, or husband – Medea, Antigone, Ariadne – and she would laugh her laugh, her liquid French laugh, and whenever history's wheel began to move, she said, it was betrayal set it in motion – Hitler's of Stalin, De Gaulle's of Britain – and she said that so long as we saw our affair in *the wider world perspective* I need never worry about feeling guilty or justifying myself.

She laughed her very French laugh. And if I mention that a second time, the Frenchness of her laugh, it's because I've just remembered that I found her laugh special and I'm trying to remember exactly what it was like, because so often one remembers that something is, was, wonderful or special without being able properly to recall it, or properly to savour it, or understand exactly why it was so. One remembers that one would like to recall it. One remembers in order to be frustrated, in order to savour not the thing itself but its absence, the shape of its absence. And thinking of this while

22

sitting slightly right of centre on the big back seat of this big packed coach with Vikram Griffiths launching into his amplified speech somewhere on the *autostrada* north of Milan, clearing his throat, his ridiculous mongrel dog Dafydd snuffling round his legs, grizzly wet nose patted by all the girls, it occurs to me that one of the main things I fell in love with when falling in love with her was her *foreignness*, and the remarkable thing about this is that I had already fallen in love with foreignness once before, of course – my wife – with hardly spectacular results, and here I was doing it again, so that you might well suppose that if I were to go to live in Africa or Asia or Russia or the far north or the polar south, if I had the energy, that is, or the courage or optimism to move around like that, as some people so amazingly do, I would probably fall in love with foreignness over and over again and be at the mercy of every different cut of female lips, eyes and nose, every different cadence of female vocal cords, every language, gaze and gait, since quite probably it is foreignness and only foreignness that is capable of making me fall in love, lose control, approach a state of adoration – except of course that I'm perfectly aware that I shall never fall in love again.

Nor would I want to.

Nor am I remotely interested in thinking about such matters, or in reading about them, or in talking about them, so that if I do think and read and talk about them incessantly, then it is presumably because I am compelled to do so. Presumably.

I'm at sea again, that's the truth, clutching the very bad book my eighteen-year-old daughter gave me, sitting amongst a coachload of sirens and ne'er-do-wells, while at the front, microphone in hand, Vikram Griffiths – and apparently he explained to the coach driver that he absolutely had to bring his dog along, because if he left it with the wife he is sepa-

23

rating from she would never give it back to him – is explaining in a surely exaggerated Welsh Italian (but he knows how much people love his quaint, or as they put it *folkloristico* incompetence, his extraordinary mixed-ness and minority-ness) the reasons for our trip, *id est*, the unlawful, on the part of the University, reduction of our salary, the attempt to limit to four the number of years we can renew our contracts, the threat of firing, the misrepresentation under oath of the nature of the work we do (i.e. our professors' work), the refusal to comply with court orders, even orders emanating from the European Court, the arrogance in short of the Italian state in its dealings with us through the University and hence our decision to take a petition to the European Parliament and to insist that pressure be brought to bear to reinstate those of us who have been fired, return our salaries to what they were and pay damages for lost salary and likewise for the psychological distress brought about by this illegal and disreputable way of treating us.

Am I right or am I right? Vikram Griffiths shouts (in Italian, demotic), upon which everybody claps and cheers, the dog Dafydd barks and is made a fuss of, since women so love to make an exhibition of their affections, chasing his tail wildly, and now Vikram, sucking in catarrh, thanks the students who have come along for their solidarity and he says how impressed officials at the European Parliament will be by this *broadly-based support* since it indicates that the students have *a rapport* with their foreign-language teachers and are aware and care, and the press will surely notice this and hence the University will be forced to take note too, since the last thing they need is for the classrooms to be occupied.

Is he right or is he right?

There is another loud, mainly feminine cheer with canine echo and Vikram Griffiths, stocky, charming, brilliant, makes a mistake, whether of grammar or of stress, or of both – of both – with almost every Italian word he utters, though apparently he speaks Welsh perfectly, and what he is not saying of course to these students who have come along to support us, and in some cases one imagines with genuine altruism, sacrificing precious hours and days that they could have used revising for the exams that are to be held immediately upon our return – what he does *not* say is how little work we foreign lectors do for our living, how long and lazy our summer holidays are, how little some of us are qualified, how many of us got our jobs because we just happened to know the professor with the gift in his hand, and one of us is having a lesbian relationship with her professor and another is taking money together with his professor to fix exams on behalf of rich and incompetent students, and many of us worked for our professors privately in language schools and translation agencies before we got our jobs, so that getting them was just an extension of an already established *collaborazione*, as the Italians like to put it, and he doesn't say that many of us have been deeply corrupted by receiving an easy and not ungenerous salary for work that nobody checks or even remotely cares about, and that most of us are terrified by the idea of having to go out and find other work and actually make our money in some way that corresponds, however remotely, to the amount of effort we put in. You yourself are terrified, I tell myself, by the prospect of having to find other work. Why else would you have stayed for so long? And Vikram Griffiths, with his handsome sideburns, his subcontinental charisma, and his dog named after the great (apparently) Welsh poet Dafydd ap Gwilym, a man who revolutionized forever the metrics of that language now spoken by so few, Vikram does not say that when we arrived at the University long ago each one of us signed a contract in which we accepted that the maximum duration of our job would be five years, because of course we imagined that we would use this time to become something else – a writer, a painter, a mother, a professor, an entrepreneur – but that by the end of those five years, our various private projects having failed, or not having satisfied us as we expected, we couldn't leave, we could not give up our empty jobs.

We are lost, I reflect, this is the truth about my colleagues and myself in this coach, we are lost in this foreign country that isn't ours, this Europe that may or may not exist, and we wouldn't know what to do if we had to go home. To a man, a woman, we are scared of going home, because most of us are forty and beyond and trapped in this place where life once deposited us, this backwater where autumn leaves circle slowly as they rot, and the unmarried women amongst us are scared of losing their one pillar of security, their state salaries and later of course their pensions, and the married women with families are scared of losing their one outlet from their claustrophobic domestic lives, and everybody is scared, I tell myself, as Vikram Griffiths talks on and on, scratching his sideburns, then his dog's ears, of the loss of identity that would be involved in not being able to say, I work for the University, this is my reason for being where I am, in this foreign country, and not at home in Paris or Athens or Cologne or Dublin or Bruges or Madrid, though most of us frankly have forgotten what home was like. When it suits us we idealize home, I reflect, and again when it suits us we demonize it, and we say we could never have gone on living under Thatcher or under Kohl, or with our parents, or near our ex-wives, or in the intellectual climate in Greece or in Glasgow. Vikram Griffiths doesn't say to these thoughtless, though for the most part charming students, that many of us dream of returning home, but with someone we love, from a position of strength (as they say), as I was obsessed for a long time by the idea of returning to England with *her*, and she I believe, or so she told me, by the idea of returning to Rheims with

26

me, and indeed we did return there, to Rheims, or at least it was a return for her, and that was a week of such love, such pleasure, as I shall never forget, though she became restless towards the end, complaining how cold her city was and how provincial and narrow-minded its people. She would rather have been in Paris, she said. We must go to Paris together next trip. But we never went to Paris, we never will go to Paris, and it is quite ridiculous, I tell myself, that you are thinking about all this now with Vikram announcing that we shall be stopping shortly for people to pee and announcing that he will be arranging for us all to go for a dinner tonight in Strasbourg, and that rooms in the hotel are double, with two single beds that is, although beds can always be put together, can they not? Ha ha. Even if there is always the risk of someone falling down the gap in the middle at an embarrassing moment, and hence we should choose our partners now without delay or *shame*, ha ha, and he produces his theatrical wink, exactly the same as I got in the corridor when he told me that Georg had christened our coach *The Shag Wagon*, and frankly I must admit that it hadn't occurred to me I would have to sleep with somebody else. Who shall I sleep with? Who shall I ever sleep with?

CHAPTER THREE

Freud ironized when people superstitiously ascribed meaning to the casual repetition of a number or a word, when they wanted the contingent world to mean and be more in their regard than it possibly could, or were afraid that that might be the case, afraid of some conspiracy between psyche and everything other. So that when I read *Das Unheimliche* in the ridiculous period when I supposed myself an interesting subject for analysis, I imagined that perhaps like me Freud suffered from the opposite problem, that the more some word or number or name was repeated the less it began to mean, the less anything means. Far from being portentous, the words dissolve to mere sound. Hence, for example, if I never say *her* name, although I think of little else but her, it is partly because that name is still so powerful that its very articulation causes an emotional seizure, an immediate tension that I feel physically, but also and perhaps more importantly, because by never saying it I keep it that way, I prolong its power, I prevent its dilution in repetition, the way a word like *Europe* has been diluted into thin air with all the times everybody says *Europe* this and *Euro* that, though once it was the name of a girl a god became a bull to rape and half the heroes hoped to find.

In any event it then turned out, when *she* gave me his, I mean Freud's, biography to read during that, as I said, self-analytic, euphoric, and above all infantile wallowing that was the first splendid year of our relationship – it then turned out that Freud himself, though he never publicly admitted it, had become fascinated by the repetition in his life of the number 62 – on a coathanger, on a hotel key – so that he began to believe he must die at that age. And sitting slightly right of centre in the back seat of this coach, having successfully kept my head down and options open throughout the frenetic discussion when everybody was trying to get the bedfellow they wanted, or perhaps trying not to get the bedfellow they didn't want, or alternatively insisting that they have a private room so that they could then introduce into it, should the occasion arise, the bedfellow of their choice, I'm surprised when the wide-eyed girl in front suddenly turns to ask all of us behind to guess what our seat numbers are without turning to look at the plastic tags on the headrests, to guess the number and to scribble it down on a piece of paper. And while everybody else is wildly out, I guess, with a sudden perception of its obviousness, 45, which is my age of course, as 045, I see, when I write the number down on the back of this morning's café receipt, is the phone code for Verona, where *she* lived until so recently. Four five. I remember Freud, and it occurs to me, as these things unfortunately will, that perhaps I am going to die this year or even this week, for tomorrow will be the fourth of the fifth. Though Freud did not die at sixty-two.

How did you guess? the girl asks, and she is doing that business of cocking her face to one side again, bouncing slightly on her knees, rocking, so that her head bobs up and down above the back of her seat.

I just felt the number 45 come to my mind, I explain. Then

not wanting, from sheer vanity, to say it was my age, nor to appear ridiculous by speaking of intimations of mortality, I surprise myself by adding and at the same time in a way discovering: Perhaps it's because I live at number 45, Via Porta Ticinese. From the corner of my eye I can see Georg smiling wryly, and naturally he thinks I looked at the number tag some while ago and am lying now, and rather pathetically, in order to get the girl's attention, whereas in fact I am telling her *the truth* to get her attention. For I did have this intuition, there's a part of me is genuinely alarmed. I do live at 45 Via Porta Ticinese and no longer at number 7 Via delle Rose as for so many years. The number 45, I tell myself, did simply come to you, invaded your mind, uninvited. That's frightening. Which then reminds me – but I wonder if there is anything now that will not remind me – that all in all this is not so unlike the way I drew *her* attention when first we met. I mean, I told her, as now, the truth about something which wasn't really explicable, an intuition that invited ridicule, but that proved to be an important discovery for me. I said – and in the sudden awkwardness and intimacy that can come with the closing of lift doors I was trying to explain my lack of enthusiasm for a job that I had had for years but to which she had only just been appointed and was excited about – I said I somehow felt that the University and indeed the whole city of Milan had been a kind of trap for me, a kind of spell, and that what's more I had the feeling, insistently, that there was another place where I was meant to be, or perhaps a whole other life I was meant to be leading, a different destiny.

I remember laughing, embarrassed, as the lift doors opened again on another floor, and it's easy to imagine, looking back these four and more years, that this embarrassment, this sense of having said a puzzling and disconcerting thing that I hadn't meant to say, made me attractive, in the way vulnerability is attractive, if only because it invites the exercise of power.

But what makes this moment here now in this speeding coach with this pretty girl so different from that moment then in the lift four-and-a-half years ago, is that I was unconscious of it then. It was a delicate and unconscious seduction then, without any studied effects, just two people with no idea at all of the adventure they were about to embark on, an immensely precious moment precisely because so dense with consequence and so blind (so that if the encounter were depicted on some vase of ancient Athens or of Crete, there would be all sorts of mythical animals round about, scaly, hoofed and horned, and a seer looking on who foresees everything, who knows everything that must happen, but who also knows he must not speak and will not be understood if he does, since foresight, and indeed wisdom in general, can never be passed on, only memories, only the interminable *schadenfreude* of narrative). And I shall never be able to do that again, I tell myself here in the coach. Never again such a blind seduction, such a blithe leaping into the dark, as if doing no more than stepping out of one's own front door. For everything is conscious now, everything is mapped and charted. And this is something *she* never understood, I don't think, my ingenuousness, I mean, in the lift that day, my forty-year-old boyishness, to the extent that when we first made love, and this was in the flat in Via Mazza with her daughter out at the nursery and Greta, the friend who was sharing the place, speaking interminably on the telephone which she would take out on the balcony for privacy, not realizing that her inane conversations were all the more audible through the open bedroom window – when we had finished making love she laughed saying how quickly we had ended up in bed together, and this was partly, she said, partly, because I had been so brazen, saying I was unhappy with my marriage like that no more than two or three sentences into our first conversation. And in the lift of all places.

I genuinely had not appreciated that implication in what I had said, though now she mentioned it I realized that it had indeed been there, and had been meant, for I couldn't at the time have been more unhappy, and when I spoke to her like that, complaining about what I saw as a boring job, what I had really been doing was complaining about the wife who, playing on my own weakness, my sense of 'responsibility', kept me in that job.

A different destiny! she laughed, A spell! You're so romantic!

But an hour or so later, when I was in the kitchen washing dishes I hadn't even eaten off in response to an embarrassing need I always feel to offer practical help and lend a hand and show that I am a *good modern man*, even when betraying my wife, she was suddenly at my ear whispering, Turn around, and when I did so it was to find a meat-knife at my throat. She burst out laughing, the steel was actually against my skin, then she kissed me with very deliberate passion, which thrilled and frightened, precisely because so deliberate, so knowing, and, handing me the knife, she said, *Alors*, use it! Cut yourself free! It takes more than just a kiss to break a spell, and again she burst out laughing in that very foreign very French laugh that I need only walk to the front of the coach to hear again, since she laughs unceasingly. That French laugh. She is all lightness and laughter. Only it would not quite be the same. Her voice has never sounded the same since the day I ceased to believe in its complicity.

But now Georg, tearing up the metro ticket he wrote his guess on, is saying that he lives at number 63 Viale Lotto, that his birthday is on the nineteenth of the eleventh, and that his car registration number is MI 807 653, but that none of this would even begin to lead him to deduce, or no? that he is sitting in seat number 47.

Georg is very droll and my girl and the other girls laugh at this and they begin to talk about numerical consequences and about tarot. The girl to my right with the swollen lips knows how to read cards. She will read Georg's cards, she says, if he wants. He raises and arches a very blond eyebrow, poses an expression of wry concern. The girls laugh again. Georg is deadpan. The last thing I need to hear is that I'm going to meet a handsome stranger, he says. The girls giggle. Until, with a ridiculous awareness of *competition*, of being two men among so many girls, of a bait that could only make a complete fool of me were I to rise to it, as I did rise to it so hopelessly and helplessly once before, I decide to seek refuge in my book. Read, I tell myself. I turn to my book again. Read. Do not rise to the bait, I tell myself. Do not engage in this conversation. Stop thinking of the number 45.

Determinedly, I turn the novel over in my hands, inspecting its extravagant cover, the extravagant endorsements of names one presumes are famous. And I find myself asking, Why did your daughter give you this book? Why did she do that? Presumably in the hope that her father would share her enthusiasm for this fantastical tale of five poor young ethnically mixed East End urchins who start a rock band to collect money for the Third World and are constantly cheated and done down by the forces of capitalism and in particular because the lead singer is black and lesbian and has magical powers. Your daughter must have imagined, I tell myself, trying to ignore a story from the girl with her leg in the aisle about a woman in Naples who repeatedly dreamt the number of the hotel room she died in on the day of the great *mezzogiorno* earthquake, your daughter must have hoped, expected, that you would share her enthusiasm for this book. So you should be more patient, I tell myself, more tolerant. If only out of fairness to your daughter. You should try to relax and enjoy this book, which was certainly written with the best of intentions. Now they are talking about someone who dreamt the date of his child's murder. I find my place some thirty pages in. But no sooner have I read a paragraph of this, as I said, extravagantly praised book by a fashionable woman writer, no sooner have I begun to tackle a flashback to lesbian incest between the lead singer and her twin sister, later tragically killed in a racist arson attack on a Brixton discothèque, than I remember how fascinated I was when *she* told me all the details of her lesbian affair with an Islamic girl who had been her housemaid and who the monstrous (but wealthy) husband had slapped round the face when he discovered them in bed. Why didn't he slap *her*? I wonder now. Until suddenly it occurs to me – and at last this is a new thought, the first for many days if I am not mistaken, and for that reason alone electrifying – it occurs to me, as the narrator returns from the flashback to resume interracial love-making with the ruthless record producer's neglected wife, that given this tendency on *her* part (and now the girl on Georg's left is talking about a pilot whose income tax code, or at least alternate letters and digits, coincided with the flight number of the plane he crashed), given this tendency, lesbian I mean, on her part, she may one day attempt to *seduce my daughter*, who sometimes baby-sits for *her* daughter. Such a thing is perfectly plausible, I tell myself. Your daughter is an attractive girl. She often goes to *her* flat now she has moved to Milan. To baby-sit. Why shouldn't *she* try to seduce her? After all, she is eighteen as of tomorrow. And I have to ask myself, is this perhaps what the gift of this literary eulogy to lesbianism is foreshadowing, or even post-dating? Could it be that your daughter is already having an affair with your ex-mistress?

Sitting slightly off-centre in the back of this coach hammering due north towards the imagined focal point of a continent whose precise borders have never been clear to me, and in the midst of this chatter of anecdotes about coincidences and intuitions notoriously catastrophic, I suddenly find myself bound to consider as lucidly as ever I can this new and increasingly shocking thought, this hypothetical lesbian relationship between my ex-lover and my daughter, a relationship, I reflect now, which would in no way be *a crime under the law as it stands*, as so many of the most terrible things we do to each other, I tell myself, are not even misdemeanours, in legal terms, are they? since we are all free agents, so called, I tell myself, except where property and money and the most basic aspects of physical well-being are concerned. Yes, I try to consider such a relationship – *her* and my daughter – in its practical, erotic, social and spiritual aspects, with all the awful and fascinating images such an eventuality conjures up. And I'm appalled. Partly by the idea itself, but mostly by the thought that I have had this idea. Why do you have ideas like this, I demand of myself? I'm furious. Though at the same time I can't help wondering at the astonishing fact that after eighteen miserable months I am still able to formulate a new thought, however unsavoury, however unwanted, about a situation whose exotic and squalid permutations I imagined I had already shuffled and re-shuffled in every possible self-destructive combination.

Such, in any event, is my state of mind when Vikram Griffiths appears at the back of the coach together with his dog, snuffling and wagging, to say in a low but excited voice, squatting down, to myself and to Georg, and hence inevitably to the girl between us, that he is convinced there is a *spy* amongst us, a turncoat, a scab, someone who, in return for guarantees that they won't lose their position, is keeping the University informed as to our every move and who, when we arrive in Strasbourg, will be behind the scenes putting the University's case to the very important people we have arranged to meet and above all taking notes of what we say so that the University will then be in a better position to prepare a rebuttal. And the thing to do, Vikram Griffiths says in his low, deep voice that everybody can hear, all the time playing with the ears of this nondescript mongrel dog, the thing to do if we manage to find out who this spy is, would be to throw them off the coach immediately and leave them to walk back home.

Turning to look out of the window, still with my daughter's possible lesbian seduction in mind, I see the drizzle is thinly persistent as we leave the dull ribbon development north of the city for the duller reafforestation of the first hills that climb towards Switzerland, a country which despite its centrality and its admirable example of the possibility of federal coexistence between different ethnic groupings is ironically not part of that Europe to which we are appealing. Through spattered perspex I see the drizzle, the sharply rising hills, the fleeting proliferation of all those details one so pointlessly takes in each moment one travels, only to expel them a moment later, like the air we breathe, the people we speak to on the street, and I must say, looking at that glum rain, the dark gesturing of those slopes, that the idea of walking back home is not unattractive, not unattractive at all, though from further up in the mountains would be better. Yes, walking back, I reflect, as the crow flies, under rain, through wet grass, alone, sovereign, preferably with streams to wade, rocks to scale, is not an unattractive prospect. I can imagine bruising my knee and my cheeks scoured by strong winds, a half-eaten apple in my pocket, and there would be mud, nightfall and dawn, ditches and crusts. How adolescent and attractive that is! But I say this of course because I'm already remembering how I once thought, indeed how I once wrote, in a letter to *her*, though whether it was one of those I sent or one of those I destroyed or one of those I neither sent nor destroyed, I cannot recall – how love (I meant our love) might be likened to some exotic holiday location where you arrive by plane with a pocket full of credit cards and an immense and criminally complacent smile on your face, only to find when the

36

statutory fun is over that there is *no flight back*, you have to walk back home. And somehow you have lost everything, your ticket, your Eurocard, even, worst of all, your *carta d'identità*. You have to walk back, no planes now, alone and barefoot, over the wildest terrain, crossing angry seas on makeshift rafts, without any sense of direction, without even looking forward particularly to the arrival, without even knowing perhaps what home would look like when and if you got there, for somehow you have no memory of what it might feel like to say to yourself, Now I am at home, now I am back. Until, caught deep in the forest, or exposed on a rocky hillside under a twittering of unseen birds, the obvious finally occurs to you: you're not even on the same planet. That plane you boarded flew you to a different world. The love plane. Thus my scribblings in a letter to her, remembered now on the swaying coach. It was a miracle of science, I wrote. I don't know whether I sent the thing or not. As for walking home, you might as well set out for Andromeda on foot.

A spy! Vikram Griffiths repeats, clearing his gravelly throat.

But Georg, to my left, is wry. Georg has an immense capacity to be composed and to be wry, about which much, very much could be said. On the other hand, who would want to take this quality away from him? Who would not envy him? To Vikram's Welsh-English, Georg replies in German-Italian. How does Vikram know there is a spy? he asks. Has he found a cigarette packet with a radio transmitter inside? A bug taped under the collar of his dog? Or a false moustache? Has some top-secret document gone missing?

But at this point both Colin and Dimitra come down the aisle to join us, for with the kind of postures Vikram has been assuming, bending down, loudly whispering, scratching in his sideburns, adjusting his cheaply framed glasses always askew on a somehow exotic stubbornness, a nervous intellectual charm, set off and thus enhanced by this shaggy, nondescript

37

outdoors sort of dog he has, and smells of – with all this posturing it is perfectly obvious that the trip's first serious confabulation has begun, the first council of war. So now there are three people plus the animal crowded into the aisle where it meets the big back seat and of course the girl on the seat in front of me turns round again, kneeling, and she smiles, and noticing her Vikram Griffiths ruffles her jet-dark hair with great familiarity, much as he does with his dog, and calls her Sneaky and asks her how she's doin', without a 'g', because it ought to be said in Vikram's defence that he knows the names of all the students, whereas I can never remember any of them, and if he can't remember their names, he gives them nicknames like Sneaky, or Sly, or Boris, so it's as if he knew their names, and understandably this makes him popular, the way clowns are popular, and renowned for finishing sadly and badly.

I'm all right, thank you, Dottor Griffiths, the girl says, in English. Her strong chin dimples in embarrassment when she speaks, but with his fingers scratching at the back of his neck, Vikram has already turned away. He is saying excitedly: Dimitra, Dimitra, come here then, you tell them.

Dimitra is a Greek woman. She begins to explain. In her role of *presidente* of our union it was obviously her task to inform the head of the language faculty that we had voted to abstain from our duties for a period of three days in order to take our case to Europe. Right?

Dimitra has this manner of interrupting herself to demand consent, as if always ready to hear an unvoiced chorus of bloody-minded rejection. Her most characteristic gesture in our long, tedious and above all contentious meetings is to offer her resignation so that she can then be begged to withdraw it, and she invariably is begged to withdraw it, not because any of us loves her or wants her to stay or even remotely likes her, but because none of us is sufficiently dedicated to the notions of justice and solidarity we all talk about to take upon ourselves the onerous job of president, excepting of course Vikram Griffiths, who cannot be president, because too conflictual and too crazy, but who nevertheless, despite holding no official position in the union at all, is effectively our leader anyway. Or at least, the only person who does anything.

Right? Dimitra demands.

Georg quickly agrees that of course Dimitra had to go and see Professor Ermani.

It was my job, she adds, never satisfied with mere consent. I had to go and see him. Otherwise we might have put ourselves in a position of illegality.

Quite, Vikram says, rubbing his sideburns. God save us from illegality. And having been to prison twice and proud of it, he winks, which Dimitra chooses not to notice.

So, while waiting for Professor Ermani, she says, to finish a phone-call in his office, she, Dimitra, noticed a memorandum on his desk on which she managed to read, albeit upside down and in her second language, the results of the vote taken only the previous day and only after a long and fraught debate (in which Dimitra herself had actually opposed Griffiths' plan, or at least its timing, had said that it would be provocative and dangerous and all in all sheer folly to go to Europe during term-time). Crucially, she had been able to see on Professor Ermani's memorandum that the names of those who had voted for and against were clearly indicated.

Which can only mean, Vikram Griffiths butts in, that some shit at the meeting went straight to Gauleiter Ermani afterwards to report. There is clearly a traitor among us, a spy.

Who is it? He covers both nostrils with thumb and forefinger and sucks hard to clear his sinuses.

Who was at the meeting? Colin asks in what is a Brummie Italian now, and he gives me a little wink of hello from above a facile moustache, too neatly trimmed, because Colin is the person with whom I occasionally indulge in *tottie-talk*, or *pork-talk* as he calls it, a supremely blokish recounting of our various amorous adventures.

Everybody was at the meeting, Dimitra says, and even anybody who wasn't could have found out who voted for what, within a name or two, from the others.

The point is, Vikram Griffiths announces – and it's not hard to imagine, I tell myself, that he is actually quite happy to be away from the difficult separation proceedings with his second wife, the acrimonious child-custody battle with his first, and above all happy, I reflect, to find himself involved in a drama – our struggle with the University of Milan – where he is inconfutably on the side of justice and morality, since in the end this is what all of us long for, is it not, to be engaged in a drama where we know what we want and what we're doing, and are quite sure we are in the right and can feel a strong sense of purpose and identity and self-esteem and heroism even. How else explain, I ask myself, all the religious crusades and wars pursued up to and far beyond the point of madness, the environmental movements and concern for animal welfare, not to mention all the novels about the same? How else explain this enthusiasm for Europe? – The point is, Vikram says, that from now on we will have to behave as if *they* knew everything we are doing and saying. And we'll have to find out who it is. He grins determinedly, digging his fingers into his dog's fur: It's going to be a witch hunt.

But the moment he says the word 'witch' I'm thinking of *her* again. Yes, here on the big back seat of this big ugly modern coach crossing Europe, in this controlled environment, so called, of ducts and vents and conditioned air, this triumph of modern mechanics, I'm thinking of her again, as if a great divide had slid down between myself and the others, some invisible screen with enormous and surely marketable capacities

40

for insulation, or as in a dream where one is shouting screaming clawing unheard unseen only inches from people behaving politely at mundane cocktail parties.

But what do I think of when I think of her like this, suddenly isolated, shut away against my will, or in some curious perversion of the will, in this claustrophobic space, this living tomb I am inexplicably digging for myself? What do I think of? What does it really mean, I ask myself in sudden angry rebellion, to say that *you are thinking of her*? What is this relation between the enigma that is yourself, this voice of yours, and the enigma that is her, her body, her laugh, the area she occupies in space? Why don't you turn your mind inward now, I suddenly decide, to resolve this once and for all, to confront, once and for all, these moments of sudden and tremendous alienation, so that you can then clear your thoughts and turn them freely to the pressing questions of your colleagues and your job and your future and your ability to maintain in the manner to which they are accustomed the family you have left, not to mention the wider issues of Italy and of Europe and of how you should behave on this trip in this coach where you are going to support a cause that not only do you not believe in but which you do not even remotely care about, since the only thing you care about, I tell myself, quite ruthlessly now, however much you might like to care about other things, as for example the new furniture you must choose for your flat, and the small car you would like to buy, and your daughter, yes, your daughter, the only thing you care about, I tell myself, is *her*, or rather what happened to you with her.

And what did happen? Do I even know? Perhaps not. Definitely not. Perhaps I shall never know what happened to me with her. Only I know that of all people I have known she was the one I was happiest with, the person I most idealized, the person I was prepared at the last to leave my wife

and daughter for, and simultaneously, yes, exactly simultaneously, and both lines of thought are at once attached to and
separate from a thousand corroborative details (words images
songs smells moments situations), I am thinking that she is the
person who most betrayed me, who most completely and so
carelessly destroyed me, the person who most built me up and
then casually blew me away, blew me to smithereens, made a
nothing of me. Because if a man, I reflect, is already next to
nothing when he can't take his work seriously and when people tell him, albeit kindly (and one is thinking here of old
friends and family), that he has *failed in his vocation*, which was
to have been, my vocation, but here one has to laugh, to make
some sort of contribution to classical studies, so called, and
above all, or so I once wrote on a piece of paper for others
more important than myself who might have found a research
position for me, to reconstruct, so far as such things can be
reconstructed, the psychology of the ancients, to savour their
minds and the way they lived inside the natural world, at
home in it in a way we never can be, the patterned constella-
tions over their heads throbbing with deities, the deep wells
they drew their water from encircled by serpents, and not a
single holy text (I'm thinking of pre-Orphic times) or social
manifesto, or sniff of political correctness to slip a credit card
between themselves and the sacred – if, as I was saying (and
how relieved I am when I can digress a moment, when my
mind, however briefly, finds some other channel to flood) – if
a man is nothing when he can no longer follow even this
most tenuous of vocations, classical scholarship, or some
similar respectable spin-off, as for example teaching, or trans-
lating, or even writing a decent text-book, any sort of
respectable and remunerative occupation that might have
grown out of that presumptuous vocation, then he is doubly
nothing when all at once at forty-three he finds himself leaving his wife and children, he finds himself without his family,

so deeply betraying and betrayed that he himself cannot help, *cannot help*, I tell myself, committing the ultimate betrayal of all, which is not falling into somebody else's bed (how remarkable that one should ever have imagined such a thing), but abandonment, abandonment. And certainly even if one never could and indeed one never would say that this is *her* fault any more than mine, or even see much point frankly now in attributing blame to anyone, still it is inescapably true that she had to do with it, with what has happened to me, she still has to do with it, she still holds me under her spell, she is or was and I don't really know what I'm saying now or what I might mean by this, but it seems to me she is or was or might still be my access to the sacred, the irreducible element in my long negotiation with the other, by which perhaps I mean death, or nature, some part of life's interminable equation that cannot come out until this harping voice, which is my mind, or part of it, is stilled forever. So that when I think of her, as I was trying to say, it is a witch I think of, a witch I cannot stop thinking of. A witch I am endlessly hunting. And at that very moment Colin leans forward and says *her* name.

It could be her, he says in his execrable Brummie Italian that makes the students smile. His moustache is the kind airmen used to wear. It could be her, the spy. She's after that scholarship business they're giving away, in't she? He switches to English. And old man Ermani's something to do with that. She's in with Ermani.

There. He said her name. Because this is the kind of person Colin is, I reflect, the kind of person who immediately names names of colleagues, speculating without a moment's hesitation on their betrayal, and also of course he is the person I sometimes spend whole evenings with, talking tottie over glasses of beer and billiards, talking nipple-hue and pubic-definition over cigarettes burning in ashtrays, because one of

43

the things that has come out of all this, this débâcle, this retreat from Moscow, is that I have no self-respect. You have no self-respect, I tell myself, the way you talk about sex and women now, with Colin. And when I think of who I was, what I was, at thirty, at thirty-five, and of the airs I put on, discussing matters social, political and moral in appropriate tones of earnestness and concern, and then of what under those airs was really in my mind, that groping after something darker, that strange waiting as if for life to begin, or end, or begin to end, in an explosion of denial of all one imagined one had been, if I think of that then I have to laugh, a long and mirthless laugh, and in the billiard hall with Colin we discuss our most recent conquests and what we have done with them, and we refer to them by some easily distinguish-able characteristic, as for example where they live or what they do or what they're like, so that they might be called Bologna-tottie, for example, or Opera-tottie, or in one case Psycho-tottie or even Armpit-tottie, because it is forbidden to mention their names, since this would suggest involvement and respect, which are taboo for those of us who have decided that boorishness is our only hope, that sex is purely physio-logical, with the result that the only thing I cannot, I must not, I do not, and I will not tell Colin, is how everything I do with them, with these women I find, or who find me, from time to time – and particularly most recently with one I call Opera-tottie – how everything I do with them is an attempt to *make them repeat* what I did with *her* and she with me those halcyon days of three years ago, and I'm talking of course about the fourth floor of the Hôtel Racine in Rheims where we did everything and said we would love each other forever. Yes, yes, we went that far, and the curious thing was how we both really meant it and knew it meant nothing. All this must be taboo between Colin and myself, indeed is the difference between Colin and myself, is what is left of my self-respect.

At least we could ask her straight up, Colin says determinedly. I mean, ask her if she told him anything.

Vikram Griffiths has his fingers behind his neck, rubbing up and down intently. Dimitra turns to look up the aisle to check that *she* is still in her place, and I'm struck by how completely unpleasant I find Dimitra, unpleasant in her busy busyness, the denim jeans, denim jacket, and in a sort of righteous truculence that glowers even under the brightest Greek smile and lipstick. What would it be like to fuck Dimitra? Daffy-dog has his wet nose in her crotch now. And why do you always ask yourself this question even of a woman you find so unpleasant? As if you were under orders somehow. As if in this controlled environment you had no control at all.

Then with that extraordinary smoothness he has, Georg says, lightly, that all this is distasteful and that it is a mistake to start naming names. What sort of example are we setting for the students who have come to support us and who want to see us united and helping each other, and showing group spirit, not fighting amongst ourselves? If there's a spy, then let him or her be, there's only so much harm they can do. Isn't there? We have nothing to hide.

Georg is right, or at least extremely persuasive, and above all *pacato*, as the Italians would add, which is as much as to say even and reasonable and calm, such admirable qualities. As *she* too was *pacata*, I remember, when saying almost the same thing to me: what did it or could it matter if there had been a betrayal, so long as we were so happy together? What difference did it make, what harm could it do? she demanded. Why should she tell me who it was? Why should I care to know the name? So that it wasn't so much the fact that she confessed, quite unnecessarily, what had happened that bewildered me, as that *she didn't see it as a confession*, she didn't perceive it as a problem. She was principally mine, she said, as

45

I well knew, it was only – and really she was just trying to explain, not to apologize – only that there had been all those times, hadn't there, when she hadn't been able to see me because I was married and had a child and had insisted for so long on keeping up appearances so that inevitably . . .

She said these words to me in French, but I recall them now, and have recalled them if once a thousand times, in English, suggesting how quickly one makes things one's own, how everything that is said to you is as much your hearing of it as their saying. For indeed everything she said to me she said in French, or Italian, and ninety per cent of it I remember in English (though I believe it is what *she* said that I remember).

But what galls me now is that perhaps she was right about this. Perhaps she was right and had I behaved differently, one way or the other, I could at least have had something, or perhaps everything, I wanted, if only I had known or decided what that was (unless it was the not knowing that I wanted, the delirium of the impossible decision?). Yes, had I left home immediately our affair began, I could surely have had her, and had I let things ride a bit more and not been so intense and jealous, then I could still perhaps be married, even happily married, or at least pleasantly, and still be seeing my mistress too, and fucking her and telling her I loved her and cared for nobody else, and perhaps occasionally fucking others too just for good measure and generally living a life of *perfectly manageable hypocrisy* to the benefit of everyone, and one thinks particularly here of my eighteen-year-old daughter whose coming-of-age party will be held tomorrow in my no doubt much censured absence.

She said my terrible problem was my mulish Anglo-Saxon Protestant absolutism, extremism, so mulishly absolute and so extreme that I was atheist without my atheism bringing me the slightest of benefits, so absolute and extreme that I attached such ludicrous pluses and minuses to words like *sincerity* and *hypocrisy*, not understanding that those two ideas were never truly incarnate but in constant negotiation, a fusion you could never separate out, and if only I would loosen up and become more *European* and appreciate that while it was important, supremely important, to have values and ideals, it was a halfwit's mistake to insist anybody live by them – as I myself hadn't lived by them, had I? – then everything would be okay. Everything was okay, she said. Because nothing had really happened. Had it? She laughed and said not to worry, everything was okay, *nothing had really happened*, and I hit her, perhaps to show that something had happened, I hit her, hard, and that was the beginning of the end for me. The moment I hit her, I tell myself sitting here slightly right of centre on the long back seat of this coach, was the beginning of the end for me. Something shifted, something *had* happened. And I wouldn't be at all surprised if Colin were not right that she is the spy, and I say this not because it would suit her personal interests, which of course it would in a way, but because she probably would not even bring the whole thing to consciousness unless someone challenged her about it, the way I challenged her earlier that fateful day, though only very casually, just wishing to be reassured, about the receipt from a café in Varese being between the pages of the book she had lent me, and even then, even when she brought it to consciousness, she wouldn't really feel it was wrong talking to Ermani, as she never really felt it was wrong fucking Georg. She wouldn't feel it was wrong telling him which lectors were in favour of what and which against, since Ermani is friendly to her and went to school with her ex-husband and is helping her with her Euro-scholarship application, her essay on a constitution for the whole of Europe which should win her a year's paid research, so called, in Brussels. I wouldn't be surprised in the least. After all, we're

47

talking about someone who throughout a long and, if it was nothing else, torrid adultery not only continued to go regularly to Sunday morning mass, but even to help at church functions and encourage her young daughter to participate in every way and to take her first communion in a beautiful lace-trimmed dress that *she* made herself and frequently showed me and discussed the details of, the lace, the trimmings. We laughed together, I remember, thinking how similar those trimmings were to the laciness of her underwear. She laughed her French laugh. So no, I wouldn't be at all surprised if she were the spy. But clearly Georg, who of course lives in Varese (and who, she says, though she never actually told me the name, *insisted so much that what could she do*? phoning her every day like that and even sending her flowers), Georg is right that it would be a mistake to suggest to the students that we are divided, though of course he is saying this in front of the girls in the back and next-but-back seats and in rebuke, though *pacato*, of Vikram and Colin and Dimitra, all seething, you can see, for drama and vendetta, all feeling personally injured by what has happened, the presence of this spy, the evidence of this betrayal, and thus in many ways not unlike myself. You are not unlike your colleagues, I tell myself, however much you may choose to despise them. What did she mean, *what could she do*? How could she imagine you wouldn't feel betrayed?

I say: Wouldn't it be more logical for me to be the spy? Shouldn't you perhaps be throwing me out of the coach?

The girl Vikram called Sneaky immediately smiles intensely at me, and just as her lips part and I think, Now she is going to speak to me, I see that she is not smiling at what I said at all, but mouthing the words of a song which has begun to come over the coach stereo in a low throb. It's the song has made her smile at me, one of those songs one hears everywhere and pays absolutely no attention to, so that you only recognize the refrain as a kind of distracting bleep in the background noise. And the refrain is *Sei un mito, sei un mito* – You're a myth, you're a myth – meaning no more in Italian than 'something wonderful' on the lines one supposes of 'fabulous' in English, which I always take as meaning 'too good to be true'. *Sei un mito*. She mouths and smiles at me.

It would be much more logical for me to be the spy, I insist.

Why? Colin is chewing gum.

I've always thought our demands were over the top, you know that, and then I've never believed in Europe anyway. It's a myth.

I say it with a coy smile on my face.

Vikram Griffiths laughs and the girl next to Sneaky, who can only be described as prettily made-up and entirely uninteresting, very belligerently asks why, why is Europe a myth, on the contrary a united Europe is our only hope for the future. Unity in Europe is our only hope for keeping the fascist nationalists out long-term, she says. Dimitra agrees. You have no sense of history, she tells me, still caressing the dog's snout in her crotch. So I ask, jokingly, if others present are aware what the divorce rate is in marriages between people from different European countries, and when of course they don't know, as why on earth should they, of what use are statistics to any of us? I tell them fifty per cent higher than an average of the average in each of the countries concerned. Fifty per cent.

Vikram is looking at me with curious red eyes as if at some oddity he has just remembered never having properly explained to himself – my eager participation in this trip perhaps. He clears his throat and grins: You're talking about yourself, Jerry boyo.

And about you, I tell him.

Twice fuckin' over, Vikram laughs.

And me, Georg admits happily.

49

So that in the space of a moment three men in early middle age have managed to tell a number of twenty-year-old girls that they are divorced and ergo available, though in Georg's case this is something of a simplification. Rather than mentioning her own separation, Dimitra has got up to return to her seat. You are rather beginning to like Vikram Griffiths, I tell myself. Quite unexpectedly, you are beginning to like him.

Then Colin brags that he doesn't know why we bothered getting hitched at all. He never has. He wriggles his moustache. Know the word 'hitched', love? he asks, turning to the girl with the long legs and quality jeans. Know it or not? Where is your English in the end? Don't you girls study English? What's going to happen to you at the exam, I don't know.

This is Colin's way.

Let me teach you my favourite words, he insists. The girls giggle. Sneaky is still mouthing *Sei un mito*, and still, quite ingenuously, she smiles at me, bouncing on her seat, and her smiling again makes me ask, What are you going to do about such a young woman who will keep smiling at you like this from great brown eyes (a sort of bright vulnerability suggests contact lenses), who will keep bouncing on her chair and resting her long neck and strong chin on the crinkly white headrest cover – jet-black hair just trembled by the air from her ventilator – and then letting her head cock slowly to one side while the bright eyes hold yours. How am I to behave?

Cuddle, Colin says ominously. Anybody know what 'cuddle' means?

He hams his Brummie accent, I tell myself, the way so many ex-pats ham their lost identity. The moustache is a pose. Yes, he hams this unpredictable matey belligerence, this curiously Midlands attitude. Colin is home away from home, I reflect, even if not the home you ever really liked.

'Cuddle' is p'rhaps my most favouritest word, Colin says. He overdoes it, pouting, twisting his chin from side to side in his collar. You know what 'cuddle' means, girls?

The girls, the two in front of me, the two each side of me and the one in front of Georg, all say no, they don't know. What is the word again, please? Thus the girl with the swollen lips.

'Cuddle!'

They shake their young heads.

I'll show you then, Colin says in his Brummie swagger, funny and frightening, and, grabbing the girl Vikram called Sneaky, who is closest, he pulls her to his chest. Then exactly as he makes that gesture, that coercive embrace, I feel a pang of jealousy, I feel that somehow this girl (who has been exchanging smiles) *belongs. to me*, than which nothing could be further from the truth, of course, and sitting here slightly off-centre on the big back seat of this racing coach with the stocky Vikram Griffiths up against my knees winking his comedy-hall wink again, and gorgeous Georg laughing his cultured German laugh, and then Vikram shouting (now Dimitra's gone), Ask 'em if they know what 'shag' means, Colin boyo, give 'em the direct method on that one! I wonder, Why, why this pang of real jealousy for a girl you met only half-an-hour ago, and young enough to be your daughter? Why are my emotions so inappropriate? I ask myself. Because it's propriety that we're talking about in the end. I must remember the word propriety. Why am I reading the slightest signs of complicity as if they were the hallmarks of a fairy tale in the making? What is this immense promise I am always imagining in every woman I meet, as if the girl and I were already in league in a refined and tender and emotionally sensitive way against the Colins and Vikrams and Georgs of this world, the boors the libertines the rakes. And I am reminded, instantly, and with an almost overwhelming sense of derision and loss of faith, of how *we* used to lie in *her* sheets Friday evenings feeling deeply in love and infinitely superior to those who *just screwed around*, and the irony must surely be that with all that happened afterwards, the complicity betrayed and the determination to beat her betrayal out of her, or out of me, yes, out of me perhaps, the irony must be, I tell myself, that I still feel superior, and my superiority lies in the violence of my reaction, which is ugly, in the depth of this obsession, which is crippling and exhausting. Yes, your superiority, I tell myself, if such it is, lies in the fact that all the women you've seen since, you've seen not for their own sakes but only in order to repeat every gesture and caress you enjoyed with her, which is unspeakably ugly. Your superiority actually lies in your self-derision, your rancour, your inability to stomach yourself, which is ugly and unhealthy. So that in my superiority, if that is what it is, I am uglier and unhealthier still than Colin, who is now saying that his next favourite word is 'squeeze'. 'Sque-ee-eeze', he repeats, drawing it out quite obscenely, rolling stale chewing-gum along his lips as he does so. Do they know what 'squeeze' means? But before they can say no and hence give him his chance to demonstrate I ask the young girl Sneaky what her real name is and she smiles. Nicoletta.

I'm Jerry, I tell her. Then at my prompting everybody on the back two rows of this coach announces their names, and so we have Margherita on Georg's left by the window, and Bruna the heavily powdered girl between myself and Georg, and Veronica, tiny, generous lips, to my right, and in front, going from right to left, Maura, belligerent, politicized, and Nicoletta, whose friends call her Niki, and the other side of the corridor Monica of the long legs in quality jeans, and Graziano, a tall lean eager boy with acne and a copy of the communist, ex-communist, newspaper, *Unità*.

'Squeeze', Colin repeats, who is nothing if he is not stubborn.

Know it or not? Again he shows his chewing gum. Come on, 'squ-ee-ee-zah!

Georg leans forward, Means *stringere*, he explains.

Georg's accent is German, very correct, very proper, and this fits somehow with the way he holds himself, with the straightness of the back of the neck, which makes the face tilt down a little, a little pedantically, but at the same time cool, relaxed. A man ageing with dignity, I tell myself, almost with nobility. A man who sent heaps of flowers and phoned so often that what could she do?

'Squeeze' means *stringere*, if applied to people embracing, or *spremere*, if applied to fruit. He smiles, deprecating, cool, like the pro who has just defused a bomb too primitive for him to claim glory. The girls giggle. Because Colin is mouthing, I can think of somethin' else we could *spremere*.

Georg. She was fascinated by his foreignness perhaps? Almost hourly he phoned, she said. She fell in love with that Germanic authority, that smooth Teutonic wisdom, the charmingly formal gestures, the simple assiduousness, the flowers delivered by a reputable company. I'm just about to plunge into my blind alley again, my splendid isolation, when Vikram Griffiths says, Hey up, Dafydd, what's this?

The coach is pulling off the road.

CHAPTER FOUR

In the service station I quoted Thucydides, and this is something, sitting once again on the coach, but in the third seat from the back now on the right-hand side, and so in front of Nicoletta and Maura, because Colin has stolen my place and is at this very moment (I can hear his nasal voice) proceeding with his lexicon of favourite words, cuddle squeeze rub neck (verb form) smooch pet, etc., this is something I can't forgive myself.

The actual words I quoted, I remember now, sitting beside the somewhat morose Doris Rohr, whose only exchange with me so far has been to express her concern that we, and in particular Vikram, are asking too much of the University, that perhaps we should have accepted a cut in salary in return for certain guarantees, for her terror is, she says, that we will now all lose our jobs precisely because of this asking too much and that she as a result will be left unemployed and unemployable at forty-three (so says this well-married woman who arrives at the University in one of two fur coats and whose lipstick, make-up and perfume seem to conspire to express the complacency of wealth, rather than the lure of sex) – the actual words I quoted, dredging them up from my love affair with the classics of twenty and more years ago – and it was *her* genius to realize that in reviving that love affair she was reviving my youth, she was making me feel strong and enthusiastic again, to the point that I actually began to apply for jobs and to read and think again, and even my wife cheered up at the sight of me cheering up and began to encourage me and, encouraging me, became attractive again, so that a wonderful and wonderfully inebriating equivocation developed and continued for nigh on two years, an equivocation which would only make the taste of humiliation and betrayal and abandonment all the bitterer when finally the truth came out of course, but that's as maybe – yes, the words I quoted, as I was saying, were as follows: *We believe, out of tradition so far as the gods are concerned, and from experience when it comes to men, that as a dictate of nature every being always exercises all the power he has at his disposal*, and the occasion for my quoting this portentous and unhappy credo was partly brought about by a decision taken last night by the German Bundesbank and partly by my finding myself next to the Avvocato Malerba in the queue at the till for the purchase of a *café au lait* and croissant at the Chambersee Service Station.

We filed into the Chambersee Service Station, built as was to be expected in the ubiquitous Euro-architecture of curved cement-and-glass surfaces, with a generous bristle of flag-poles outside displaying the colours of every nationality the franchise-holders hope to take money from and inside a sense of disorientation generated by flights of steps and walkways and signs that are no longer in any language but just cups and knives-and-forks and wheelchairs and crossed-out dogs all presented in stylized white lines on plastic blue squares, and in fact the moment we're through the steamy swing doors, heavy against the cold, almost all the girls, none of whom is wearing a skirt, follow the sign displaying a human figure

55

distinguishable from another human figure precisely and exclusively because it is wearing a skirt, or dress, rather than trousers, reminding me of something I read not so long ago in *Corriere della Sera* where a woman contributing to one of those *déjà vu* debates about the discrimination against the fairer sex inherent in the insufficient provision of lavatory facilities in public places remarked, against the swim of the debate, that as she saw it the queues outside ladies' lavatories were really caused by the fact that women like to go to the loo together, and to chat there for a while, which again reminded me, though how this can be I don't know (perhaps just the thought of the way women are with each other, something I have always been envious of), reminded me of a desire I frequently used to express to *her*, usually immediately after we had made love, that I myself would like so much to be a woman, just for a day, or a week, I would like to know what it feels like to be a woman, and this desire was, and sometimes is, a terribly real and intense desire and part of a sort of deep biological yearning of mine, a yearning to do and to be and to have everything. A yearning against mortality, I presume. Or ultimately, since life is distinction and choice, a death wish.

When I mentioned this to *her*, she would always reply that I wanted to be a woman so that I could make love to a man. In a very profound part of myself I was homosexual, she said, and I should try to have an *avventura* sometime with a man as part of this voyage of self-discovery that I had embarked on with her, part of this quest for *a happy healthy sex life*, as she always put it vhich would make me a profoundly wiser more even-tempered understanding fellow. But I said no, no, I wanted to be a woman for a while, only a day perhaps, or not even, so that I could have sex with another woman, so that I could lose myself in femininity, be all woman licking woman and woman licked by woman, so that I could have sex with *her*, but she laughed at my excitement and said what a profoundly male and banal fantasy that was and in the end perhaps nothing more than retrospective jealousy because she had once said that the best sex in her life she had had with her Filipino cleaning girl.

With these ideas flashing through my mind as we entered the service station for our ten o'clock coffee stop, I was reminded again of my new thought of ten minutes ago, that *she* might be having a lesbian affair with my daughter, and partly because I wanted to be reassured that this was not the case, and partly because in this way I would be able to see when the girl Nicoletta came out of the Ladies and thus to contrive to go and sit next to her for the coffee and croissant I planned to eat, I decided not to go up the stairs with Colin and Vikram and Georg in the direction of the stylized cup, but to cross a granite-tiled floor and walk past the stylized skirt and trousers to where a stylized telephone receiver pointed the way to three small booths against a cement wall, one of which, thankfully, took my Eurocard, thus resolving the problem of my not having any Swiss currency.

The phone rang for a long time, so that I began to think I would just have to hold it there ringing for four or five minutes until the girl I was interested in, or imagined I might be interested in, or might be interested in me, came out of the loo, but finally my wife did answer and, on hearing my voice, immediately asked why on earth I was calling. Yes, my wife was her busy, peremptory self. I could even hear the vacuum-cleaner booming in the background, which probably explained why she hadn't heard the phone for so long. And I have to confess that I found this cheering, this business of the vacuum-cleaner, and her peremptoriness, and the fact that although it must have been perfectly obvious I was calling from a call-box she didn't think to ask me where I was. I found it cheering because for about one second it gave me the passing and extremely rare sensation of *having done the right thing* – you did the right thing leaving her, I told myself – since I often feel that one of the reasons our marriage reached the sorry state it did was my wife's obsessive use of the vacuum-cleaner, and not only of the vacuum-cleaner but of every cleaning implement, product and aid available to modern man, or rather invented by modern man for modern woman. Simply, the vacuum-cleaner was always on, nudging round my feet when I was trying to read on the sofa or to play draughts with Suzanne, clattering against the bedroom door when perhaps I was trying to sleep late on a Saturday. And this was nothing other, I believe, than one of my wife's many ways of expressing her suffocating desire to *ripristinare*, as the Italians say, to be constantly returning things to their pristine state, or more particularly in my wife's case, her desire to have everything remain exactly as it was the day we were married and moved into the new flat which I had made the terrible mistake (in this case absolutely formative, one of the grand structural mistakes of my life), the terrible mistake of letting her parents buy for us and of living in ever since, or at least until about eighteen months ago, which means I was there nineteen years, nineteen years, and every year the shutters had to be re-varnished and the walls re-whitewashed and the window-frames re-sealed, and in our relationship too it was likewise understood that everything had to be freshly whitewashed and re-sealed, everything had to be kept in a perfectly mint emotional state, and in particular it was tacitly understood that we had to use the same love language, forever, the same cooing little terms of endearment we had used during our courtship of twenty-one years before, terms that I have absolutely no intention of evoking here and now, although I can sense their presence as I sit turning over and over my thoughts in the third seat from the back of this powerful modern coach pounding across Europe, I can sense them lurking there below the surface of consciousness, below the modulations of this voice, below the vibrations of big tyres on smooth tarmac, they are present to me, hard dark rocks I would founder on if I went that way. One uses words, love words, I tell myself, for years and years, only to discover one morning that they mean nothing any more. Not only do they mean nothing, but they are dangerous. They are frightening. And yet my wife insisted on our using them. You haven't called me *this* for ages, my wife would say, or, Why do you get so angry when I call you *that*? I refuse to evoke even one of them here and now. My wife insisted that we went on using these words far beyond the point of exasperation, words, as I said, that had meaning once but now meant only the meaning they had lost, the meaning all words always lose when you use them too much and find they mean nothing at all, not rocks then I suppose, but corpses, has-beens, different from the living, different from the never-alive, corals perhaps, sharp and dangerous, hundreds of thousands of sharp little dead creatures. Our love words.

Yes, we had to be forever in love, I remember now, my wife and I, so that one had the feeling of something that had solidified, terribly, an awful process of fossilization, a shell one had made for oneself, but that somehow wasn't the right shape any more, wasn't *appropriate* any more. Again it was a question of propriety, I tell myself, sitting beside Doris Rohr. And perhaps this was why she and Suzanne, our daughter, could never really get on together, because Suzanne would insist on growing up, on not staying the same, and hence was a constant reminder to us that we were not the same either, offering as she did that yardstick of age and of all its attendant transformations in the flesh which children must offer and parents must take note of.

I wanted to have a word with Suzanne, I said.

Her birthday's tomorrow, my wife said drily.

I told my wife I was perfectly aware my daughter's birthday was tomorrow, but even as I said this I would have liked to have added something to ease this studied and obvious unpleasantness, because it is unthinkable really that two people should live together for nigh on twenty years and then have nothing more than their mutual irritation to trade on the telephone, unthinkable, but apparently the norm, or almost (when things are not worse), and sitting here on the blood-red upholstery of this hideous modern coach, where six video screens have just been lowered in perfect simultaneity from wells fixed in strategic positions in the overhead luggage racks, and where Doris Rohr is offering me an expensive chocolate, her mauve nails turning the pages of *Marie Claire*, sitting here thinking of that phone-call to my wife conducted in the freezing entrance to the predictably and it has to be said depressingly designed Chambersee Service Station while watching for sneaky young Nicoletta to come out of the loo, and, from the corner of my eye then, seeing *her* come in from the coach and head off up the stairs to the cafeteria, perhaps the only woman on the trip to be wearing a skirt as depicted by the stylized sign, so that even from the phone-booth I could see the achingly slim calves black-stockinged above high heels scraping the stone steps like so many matches struck on sandpaper – sitting here in the coach, my mind prey, as it has been for so long, to every passing thought, but somehow not only the prey but the aggressor too, or a prey to its own aggression, self-consuming – sitting here in this parlous psychological state, it once again, I mean as a result of this phone-call, strikes home to me how much I have lost: my role as father and husband, the obviousness of my old life, the simplicity of being somebody's husband, somebody's father, the readiness of an explanation when required, being able to say, This is who I am and what I do. So that as the video two seats in front of me begins to glow and one or two people pull pink curtains against the rain outside to make the screen more vivid, it occurs to me that if I lose my job as well as everything else, this job that I always saw as a mere stepping-stone, a sensible way-station, an income to tide me over while I picked up my ticket to somewhere else (until, like my marriage, it became a desert island, a place of loathed and ultimately terrifying convenience), if I lose my job, I will have lost the last element in life, after wife and daughter and mistress, that gave me any sense of role and identity. And I begin to think, for the first time, that perhaps this trip was not a mistake after all. Perhaps it isn't a mistake, I tell myself. Perhaps I should take it seriously and work hard at it alongside the others, lobbying Euro-MPs and talking to the press and generally making every reasonable and *democratic effort* to save this last attachment I have to the common-sense world of role and identity and usefulness and source of income – myself as paid language teacher at the University of Milan – You should take this trip seriously, I tell myself, very seriously, and stop pretending to be so superior to crazy Vikram with his drink and his dog and his victim politics, and dull Doris with her chocolates and magazines, and dour irritable Dimitra with her square-jawed determination to keep her place on the gravy train. You are arrogant, I tell myself. You are irretrievably arrogant. You are obsessed by the notion that you are somehow superior to every task you have been allotted and every person you have shared your life with. This has to stop, I told myself. *You* have to stop.

But then the words *gravy train* remind me that I had vowed I would leave this job, which is a pointless and soul-destroying job. You have been doing the same job year in year out for fifteen years now, I tell myself, staring at titles on a video screen as Doris Rohr pops another chocolate in her elegantly made-up mouth. You have gone on and on doing exactly the same thing, teaching huge groups of students who are never the same from one week to the next and with whom one has no contact at all and who are only interested in passing their exams, punching their meal-tickets. Indeed many of the students on this bus, I tell myself, to whom you were no doubt hasty in your attribution of altruistic impulses, are perhaps hoping that their faces will be remembered by the foreign lectors, ourselves, and that they will thus get better grades in their oral exams. For having come on this trip. For having lent their support. For years and years, I tell myself, suddenly extremely anxious, you have gone on and on teaching students interested in nothing more than the acquisition of a convenient piece of paper, a convenient *passe-partout*, students with no interest at all in English, all the while nourishing, cherishing, defending, the initial illusion that you were somehow *transmitting culture* to these people. This has to stop, I tell myself, refusing Doris Rohr's offer of a Walnut Whirl. I should never have taken this job at all. Or never have stayed there for more than a year or two. Then reaching this conclusion, and terribly aware that only a moment ago I had reached the *exact opposite conclusion*, I am appalled at my own vacillation, at my loss of direction and purpose, as this whole trip, I'm obliged to observe, has been a terrible loss of direction for me, a deep lesion in the identity and resolve I had so carefully been constructing, reconstructing, in my little flat with all the new personal items and objects I had slowly been accumulating, to wit my wallet with its purpose-cut spaces for an Italian identity card, an Italian driving licence, my key-ring, purchased in heavy snow from a Moroccan on Via Manzoni, which has a little leather pouch the perfect size for a johnnie (it is presently loaded), my new leather jacket to replace the one *she* helped me buy, my new music collection, after I threw out the old with all the French singers she taught me to listen to and all the sixties music I rediscovered – yes, I'm appalled, appalled by the idea of being in my job for the rest of my life, and equally appalled by the idea of losing my job and being alone with nothing whatsoever to do or be for the rest of my life – I hate the expression 'the rest of my life' – and without of course, it occurs to me now, a ready supply of young women, which has been, as I said before, together with screen-based computer games and billiards and arguments about politics, an important solace for me over the last two years. But above all I'm appalled by my lack of resolve, by my not knowing what, even if I knew how, I should do. I'm appalled by my constantly being appalled.

Suzanne was out, my wife said. I could get in touch with her this afternoon.

Okay.

But then although these credit-card calls are expensive and I really had nothing to say, I made a conscious decision to stay on the phone to my wife for a moment or two longer, partly because Sneaky Nicoletta was not out of the loo yet and partly because *she* had barely reached the top of the stairs and I did not want to give her the impression that I was still at the stage of hurrying off phones to follow her about and thus still dangerous, although of course I'm perfectly aware that I came on this trip for no other reason than to follow her about, and it may even be that I *am* still dangerous, something I can hardly deny having been. Indeed, if there is one legitimate, or at least convincing thought in my mind on those occasions when I stand by the phone thinking, Now I am going to call her, now I can't stop myself calling her (so that my finger will begin to punch, or until very recently, the buttons 045), it is the desire to show, in the course of a light and relaxed conversation, that *I am no longer dangerous* and that I deeply regret having been so, the desire to end the affair well (when in fact it ended long ago and badly). And if I have learnt not to pick up the receiver on those occasions, or at least to stop dialling after the five, it is because bitter experience has taught me that the longer I go on talking the more violent and outraged I will become, the more dangerous I will show myself to be. How could she say that nothing had really happened, she who had previously insisted to me how important it was to have things happen in life? Make something happen, she said. She put the knife to my throat. It takes more than a kiss to cut yourself free, she said.

But mainly I decided to stay on the phone in the service station to my wife because taken by the idea of coming away from this conversation with something resembling cordiality, or even a deep mutual acceptance. I constantly hope that we can somehow still be friends, my wife and I, despite this terrible thing that has happened to us. It's a desire, I sense, which always seems to be the aspiration of he or she who has abandoned, but never never never of he or she who has been abandoned, as I would never want to be her *friend* (what could that mean?), but only to be her lover again, her beloved again, which is why I suppose my frequently repeated attempts to engineer a happy ending, after all was already over, were so disastrous, because the truth was I was still hoping in some part of myself deep down that it hadn't ended at all, that the discovery of a happy ending might become a new beginning. And I wonder now, could this be my wife's problem, could this be why she is so difficult sometimes? She wants a new beginning. She wants me to start using those words again. Those words that would be like spitting sharp stones. And how tedious, I think, how unbearably tedious life is to be forever engineering these same problems that everybody has written about and suffered over for centuries, for millennia: Ariadne gazing out to sea from an empty beach and Samuel Pepys going crazy for his serving maid. To mention but two.

So I told my wife, apparently by way of easing the tension, that I was reading this book Suzanne had given me for my birthday, my forty-fifth birthday, a book called *Black Spells Magic*, and my wife said, yes, Suzanne had been raving about it for weeks and had bought copies for everyone she knew, but no, she, my wife, hadn't read it. I thought how typical this was of the sublime lack of interest my wife has always shown for the lives of those around her, for the influences, adventures, friendships and agonies that are changing and reshaping those lives, and even for the simple details: why somebody is late, why somebody is calling from a phone-box; and I thought how this lack of interest had enabled me to conduct an intense love affair and to start reading and thinking and laughing and living again, without my wife's showing the slightest curiosity about what was happening to me, and later, again, had allowed me to stop living, to descend into utter mental darkness, to withdraw into the silence of complete and total alienation, so unlike my normal, talkative, and on occasion people have gone so far as to say charming self, without my wife's appearing to notice anything at all.

Well, I was a shade concerned, I said to my wife, how pro-lesbian this book was, you know? I hoped Suzanne wasn't getting ideas into her head, I hoped there wasn't any more to it than met the eye. But no sooner had I touched on this particular subject, which masked what in the end is my first new thought *vis-à-vis her* for some weeks or months, than two things happened at once: Nicoletta came out of the loo about twenty yards away, saw me, smiled at me; and my wife a hundred miles away burst out laughing. Typically then, it was precisely as I demanded to know what was so funny, winking at the same time at Nicoletta, who is rather taller than I had thought, that I appreciated that she, my wife, was right. She is right, I told myself, while she went on laughing. She is perfectly right. It is ridiculous of you to be so concerned about the sexual orientation of your daughter, eighteen years old tomorrow on the fourth of the fifth, and thus entirely beyond your jurisdiction and probably even influence, and especially ridiculous since that concern, though your wife couldn't know this, was only felt with regard to a possible relationship between your daughter and *her*, your ex-mistress, a relationship (lesbian), what's more, that in the delirious post-coital moments of three and four years ago, you had longed for for yourself. Why shouldn't your daughter at eighteen have the pleasure of a lesbian encounter? Not to mention, to stay on the subject of your being entirely ridiculous, the present instance of your having more or less decided, while worrying about your daughter, to try to seduce, on this coach trip, a girl only two or three years her senior.

How are things looking jobwise? my wife asked quite kindly, apparently appreciating and deciding to satisfy my need for cordiality, but I said my money had run out and got off the line.

I caught up with this girl Nicoletta about half-way up the cement stairs and, speaking to her in English, which I knew she would take as a compliment, I remarked with the most engaging and I suspect infectious bonhomie, that these cement stairs resembled nothing more, did they not, than those at the University, where one had to pick one's way through students standing and sitting and chatting and even *snogging* on occasion. She laughed to hear me deliberately use a word she had just learnt from Colin's favourite lexicon, and with one of those wonderful gestures that Italian girls are always making and that English girls never make, or I don't recall them making, she slipped her hand under my arm to proceed the last dozen or so stairs together in close and amicable contact, with me saying that this inflicting upon us of the same architectural pattern in more or less the same materials the world over was at once inevitable yet depressing, and her laughing and saying that that must be the third or fourth pessimistic thing she had heard me say, and then even

66

leaning slightly against me, which at once delighted me with the electric stupid and wonderful thought, *I'm on here*, but at the same time unnerved me because it occurred to me that far from feeling jealous, or even, and less interestingly, happy for me, which is not something frankly I would care for, *she* would think me monstrous to be arm in sentimental arm with a young girl after only a couple of hours together on a coach. She would think this was proof of how completely off the rails I was. She might even go and say something to her, to the girl, or to me, about my dangerous past. So that, turning the final corner of the stairs, I took the opportunity of having to push open another double glass door to disentangle myself from the young Nicoletta, and at the same time noticed, as I stood aside and ushered her through in an exaggeratedly cavalier fashion, that the anorak she was wearing was a dead dark blue and very shabby and her jeans likewise and her shoes clumpy and sensible. And while I couldn't help feeling how delightfully endearing this was, together with the fact that she wore no make-up on a tissue-pale face with that jet-dark hair above, still I immediately felt a pang of regret for *her* more flamboyant femininity, manipulative though it may have been, her sharp high heels and short skirts and suspender gear *et al.*, which she would keep on while she masturbated for me in Professor De Santis's office, or later, in the period when she still liked to think of my jealousy as something of a joke and invited me to belt her arse. I regretted her theatricality, the feeling you had with her that she would and could squeeze, as Colin would say, the very most out of life, and above all – and this was so refreshing after my wife's obsession with varnishing and cleaning and repairing – her determination to shake things up, her pleasure in seeing things change, people change. Her desire to have things happen. Whereas this little girl, this nice-mannered Nicoletta of the jolly bounce and cocked cheek, already pulling out her little black purse from one of those hideous fluorescent nylon pouches all young Italians tie about their waists, this charming young girl, now remarking with resignation that she has no Swiss francs, is clearly of the common-sense variety. At the most she will kiss and make love. I will never be able to take her through the Rheims routine.

Then in the queue with trays and a mill of people, I was just pointing Nicoletta to the small sign in six or seven languages that indicated that we could pay for our beverages in Swiss francs, French francs, Austrian schillings, Deutschmarks, sterling and, yes, amazingly, Italian lire, when the Avvocato Malerba, who was immediately in front of me in the queue, leaned towards us to say that although this was true it didn't make sense to pay in lire because the exchange rate was so unfavourable. The exchange rate was about forty lire to the franc worse than you could get at the Bureau de Change downstairs (there had been a small blue plastic sign with a white stylized image of a stack of coins on a pile of banknotes, though of course they will never change coins, just as most girls never wear skirts) and this in itself, the Avvocato Malerba went on, meaning the Bureau de Change exchange rate, was more than thirty lire worse than the exchange rate yesterday, for the simple reason that the Bundesbank had been expected to lower their interest rates at a meeting yesterday evening, but then hadn't done so, thus throwing, as it emerged from the morning paper and indeed from the chaos in the Bureau de Change downstairs (where they did not even want to see Italian lire), the European currency markets into *complete turmoil*. Yes, our dear Europe was *in turmoil*, announced the Avvocato Malerba. And he thus suggested, raising his voice now, because of the noise two loutish French schoolboys were making choosing a pastry, that we might take some Swiss francs from him, repaying him, if we insisted, in lire at the rate he had, with uncanny foresight, exchanged them at the day before, i.e. something to the tune, all told, taking into account the devaluation of the lira and the price-exploitation practised by the Chambersee Service Station cafeteria, of eighty lire to the franc more favourable.

This was my first encounter with the Avvocato Malerba, who I knew taught a course on Employment Legislation in the Law Faculty and had been encouraged to come along by Vikram to present the legal side of our case as lucidly as possible in the event of our having to talk to legal experts and above all in the event of our having to explain why, while it was perfectly normal to hire people on only a one- or two-year contract in the UK or France or Germany, in Italy, or at least in the public sector, this could only be considered as a case of discrimination against foreign teaching staff. The Avvocato was a tall, dry-looking man, not far off retirement it seemed, but surprisingly boyish in manner when he began to talk, almost childishly animated you might say, and painfully eager to please, as witness this very generous offer, made in a stiltedly correct English, to save a little money for two people he had never met before.

I immediately wondered, while we were more or less bound to accept and Nicoletta made all kinds of ingenuous murmurings, in an equally stilted though less correct English, as to how kind he was being, what on earth had prompted this elderly lawyer and university professor to waste two, no, three days in coaches and service stations and cheap hotels with a gaggle of young girls and a motley of feckless foreigners whingeing about the job they'd be lucky to lose. Did he just want to see the European Parliament, was he the spy who was keeping the University informed of our every legal move? I remembered now that both Dimitra and Georg had been against his coming, finding it strange that somebody in the employ of the University should see fit to support our cause in this open and indeed recklessly obvious fashion, and particularly someone, they were Dimitra's words, who had *no history of left-wing militancy or union activity*.

All the time I was thinking this and choosing my croissant from what looked like a very weary pile, and hearing Nicoletta introduce herself to the Avvocato and the Avvocato saying what a wonderful name she had and how Nicoletta derived originally from the Greek *nike*, victory – all the while this was going on I was growing more and more intensely aware, to my great surprise and trepidation, of *her* voice, yes, *her* voice, immediately behind me, talking to Vikram Griffiths and insisting that we have a proper meeting on arrival at the hotel this evening to decide the strategy for our approach for the following morning, to decide above all, she said, not to mince words, *who should be our representative* on this occasion.

It was the first time, I should explain, standing beside Nicoletta and the Avvocato Malerba choosing pastries from a glass case in the Chambersee Service Station, that I had heard *her* voice for some months. Despite working in the same institution, we have both gone out of our way to avoid each other since the last tremendous encounter of perhaps nine months ago when first we made love and then shouted at each other until I held a knife first at her breast and then at my wrist and then wept and hit her and finally went off to smoke cigarettes all night on the sofa and drink heavily while she slept in my bed, the first time I had heard this French voice speaking Italian with wonderfully over-pronounced 'r's and under-pronounced 'l's and its curious inversion of Italian intonations, this voice that in its time has whispered to me almost every loving word and erotic provocation one person can whisper to another and then again has shouted almost every extreme of contempt and derision. And even as I listened to the way she was rather unpleasantly hectoring the clownish Vikram Griffiths, who of course was convinced, having arranged everything himself, that he was to be the representative, but at the same time, to show off to the students, was pouring whisky from a hip flask into his plastic coffee cup and then going over to the window to wave down, cigarette in hand, to where two girls were walking his shambling dog (crossed out of the service station by a small blue sign) — even as I listened to her following him and hectoring him, *I knew that it would never be over for me*. Never. Your stupid heart, I told myself, as Vikram Griffiths, hardly helping his cause, now made a joke about the whisky being called Teachers, will always leap on hearing Italian spoken with a French accent. Always. You will never get beyond this, I told myself. Old Dafydd's a terrible shagger, Vikram laughed, given half a chance. He was waving at the window. Never. A shaggy shagger, he laughed. Then, together with a sense of resignation and defeat, I was suddenly filled with an immense and absolutely crazy desire to make myself heard, to see if *my* voice, my English voice speaking Italian in an inevitably English accent, mightn't have the same effect on her, while she argued with Vikram Griffiths, as her French voice was having on me while I engaged in a less than enthralling conversation about exchange rates with the Avvocato Malerba. So that when, a metre or two on, at the till, the Avvocato laughed and said how strange it was to have Germany playing the spoilsport in Europe, and not Britain, a real reversal of roles, the Avvocato Malerba said, I immediately and patriotically and very loudly objected that these things were never a question merely of one country or another's being more or less altruistic, but of each country always exercising all the power it had at its disposal to get, so far as was possible, what it wanted, what it perceived, that is, was in its, and only its, best interests. For this is what it means, I said, to be a sovereign individual, a sovereign state.

I raised my voice quite considerably as I engaged in this argument, surprising young Nicoletta and the Avvocato Malerba not a little as the latter paid exactly eighteen Swiss francs and forty-five — yes, forty-five — centimes for three coffees, a pastry, a croissant and a cream cake, upon which Nicoletta immediately began to fuss in her money pouch, trying to establish how much exactly she owed. Just as this service station, I insisted, still in the same hectoring tone, and thus not unlike the voice *she* had been using with Vikram Griffiths, this Swiss service station, despite its friendly display of flagpoles suggesting adherence to the current orthodoxy of some kind of fraternity among nations and the generally fashionable notion of solidarity, this service station was chiefly and properly concerned in exacting the maximum price (in whatever currency) consistent with people's continuing to purchase the optimum volume of the merchandise it supplied. No, you will never get beyond this, I told myself, but with a curious surge of elation now. As if it were pleasant to be stuck here. As if glad to know where I was.

The effect of my raising my voice was that the Avvocato Malerba now felt obliged to object — though he did so with a commendable mixture of politeness and jocularity — that this was a very cynical, typically Anglo-Saxon, and above all *un-European* way of viewing the world. There were clearly, he said, picking up what had now become, with his offering to pay, our collective tray, those in Europe, visionaries, who thought chiefly of the common good — Jacques Delors and Prime Minister Gonzalez, to name but two, and likewise the Dutch Prime Minister, was it Maartens, who . . .

But before he could finish speaking and with a quite ludicrous and shameful sense of triumph, as though of a child crushing an insect, or a Rottweiler snapping at some innocent hand that wishes to feed it, I began shouting that far from being Anglo-Saxon my views had been most eloquently expressed by Niccolò Macchiavelli and before that, and even more eloquently perhaps, by the ancient Greeks, whose culture surely lay at the heart of European identity and whose alliance of city states had quite probably been the first example of a European joint venture, though one established primarily of course against an outside enemy, not in the name of any fine principles, and always fraught by internal power games, of the kind, I insisted (aware now as we moved across the fluorescent-lit space that *she* must be no more than an arm's length away on my right), of the kind that had led the great Thucydides to say, and I quoted, speaking far louder than I needed: *We believe, out of tradition so far as the gods are concerned, and from experience when it comes to men, that as a dictate of nature every being always exercises all the power he has at his disposal.*

There was a brief silence.

The Bundesbank included, I added.

Shall we sit here? Nicoletta asked. I owe you five thousand three hundred lire. Oh forget it, the Avvocato Malerba said. No, please. But I insist. *Grazie*, Nicoletta said, blushing, it's very kind of you. At which the Avvocato Malerba looked up and, smiling at me from his somehow dusty but boyish cheeks, said, Just take it as a demonstration that not everybody is obsessed by the exercise of personal power, a statement which, on the contrary, I could have shown, only demonstrated the truth of what I had said, in that it served most perfectly to make him look gracious and myself foolish, and all the more so when, on turning round, I realized that *she* would not have heard at all. She had crossed the whole cafeteria since I last saw her and was now leaning over Georg, deep in confabulation.

CHAPTER FIVE

Robin Williams has just read *Carpe Diem* to his Dead Poets Society. How everything leads back. Does he have daughters? Lear asked, of anybody remotely unhappy. And even this unexpected analogy, Lear, Cordelia, leads me back through my own daughter's fantasticated lesbianism to *her*. She is the centre of the world and this trip a vortex, the mind channelled, like the chase of traffic through this interminable tunnel beneath the Alps, in that one direction, her slender video-lit neck just a few paces further forward, but ever distant despite the headlong flight of this coach, these thoughts, never to be touched again, or licked, or when your nail trailed the knuckles of her spine. Everything is past, I tell myself, and yet because of that more present than ever. As if the only paradise one might ever set out to explore were paradise lost.

And it is this, sitting here on the third seat from the back in this luxury coach racing on a slight downward slope beneath incalculable tons of rock through one of those engineering feats which have given us the miracle, so called, of rapid communications, it is this that I cannot understand: how presently omnivorous that past is, how Robin Williams quoting Horace in an Alpine tunnel immediately recalls Robin Williams speaking a demotic DJ Italian in *Buon Giorno Vietnam* when my wife was away at the sea with Suzanne and *she* on the red couch at home in only a silk nightdress admiring the dubbing, saying how clever it was to have matched such rapid speaking and punning, how clever dubbing was in general, putting words in people's mouths, annihilating differences, annihilating barriers – she would love, she said, to get a job in dubbing – and I can smell the sweet perfume in her hair fallen slantwise as she absently preens, I can sense the neatness of her posture sitting cross-legged, telling me in French that this Italian dubbing of American English was so good. And for all my adoration, I tell myself now, for all her complacency, the barriers between ourselves were such, though I didn't know it then, as no polyglot facility or engineering prowess could ever resolve. The words, as now on the screen, were one thing, but the gestures came from quite another language: two cultures indifferently superimposed for the convenience of apparent comprehension, the luxury of immediate entertainment.

Cars overtake in the tunnel. There are red lights and glare. To the right, yellow neon every so many metres spangles on the curved plastic of our modern coach window, flashes chemically over the deep red upholstery, altering the colours on the screen, as if through fading and intensifying filters. And watching Doris Rohr (who always votes against strike action, who openly says she would be willing to accept less money so long as she can keep her job, her precious job, she whose husband is a surgeon, she who has to decide which of her holiday homes to spend the long summer break in), watching this German woman pensively unwrapping another of her expensive chocolates in the insistent on-off of a dark underground brightness, her fingertips plucking unseeing at coloured foil, her eyes happily fascinated by Robin Williams and by the sort of contemporary pieties these films purvey and that we all identify with in opposition to a *status quo* which miraculously no cinema-goer is ever part of, yes, watching solid, square-mouthed, brick-lipsticked Doris, it occurs to me, sitting on the third seat from the back of this coach full of, to use a Colinism, shaggable young women, it occurs to me I was saying, *what an incredibly foolish philosophy the expression* carpe diem *enshrines*.

Carpe diem, yes, yes, seize the day, seize it, now, and now, and now, then to be marooned there in those few precious hours, days, months, whatever, it doesn't matter, of love, of passion, marooned for all the waste sad time that must stretch after, not shovelling shit against the tide as my wife would to keep the corpses at least unburied, our grave-clothes decent if nothing else, her impossible struggle to *ripristinare*, nor gracefully chasing about the mythical urn in the bliss of the moment anticipated – those routine or romantic relationships with intensity, with beauty – no, but waltzing, as I am waltzing, with the living dead, the memory trapped in the groove of an endlessly repeated pirouette pushed to the furthest extremes of vertigo, *she* and I here, *she* and I there and then (when the day was so fatally seized), *she* and I as we might have been, today now, side by side on this seat, in this coach at this moment, her head against my shoulder, now now and still now. Which is the worst waltz of all.

I hate myself for quoting Thucydides, for shouting at the Avvocato Malerba in the Chambersee Service Station. I hate myself for having come on this trip. My idea, when Vikram Griffiths placed his clipboard beneath my nose in the miserable and amorphous institutional space of the foreign lectors' tutorial room – my idea, or rather the idea that so seductively presented itself, was that of showing myself in public again, no, showing myself to *her* again, of demonstrating that I wasn't the least bit troubled by the sight of her or even by the sight of her confabulating together with Georg. I would show her, and myself – this must have been my idea – that these things did not touch me any more, because she had not after all, I told myself, had such a determining effect on my life. Quite the contrary. She had merely been the catalyst I needed to make a change in my life, merely the particular day I had chosen, at the last, to seize: Tuesday, though it might perfectly well have been Wednesday; *her* though it could equally have been Psycho-tottie or Bologna-tottie or Opera-tottie. Yes, I would come on this trip and be urbane and relaxed. That's what I imagined. I would watch lights flash on and off in deep Alpine tunnels and the effect would not become an image of my obsession, pulsing, lurid, unflattering. For I had left obsession behind, I told myself, when I moved into Porta Ticinese number 45, when I changed my whole music collection, when I bought a new wallet, a new briefcase, a new coat.

So I would come on this trip and I would be sensible and witty and just slightly but not overly ironic when my colleagues talked of *community spirit* and *group identity*, when they made a great show of their knowledge of the legal niceties of Italian Law and European Law, of the way in which we have been victimized and of our ultimately inevitable victory. I would be friendly, savvy, even helpful. And at the end I would return home unscathed, though perhaps with a fresh tottie or two to place on the old back-burner, as Colin puts it, one or two new phone numbers to inscribe in the old *carnet*. I would have been near her – this was my idea – for three days, and nothing out of the ordinary would have passed between us, *nothing would have happened*, and this in itself would be the beginning of the happy ending I hoped for.

But I wasn't ready for it. And had I been ready, it would never have occurred to me to do it, I wouldn't have needed

77

it. Had I been *ready*, I would have appreciated that this was not what I hoped for at all, this prosaic, sensibly cheerful fellow seeing through the world with a sort of mild, devil-may-care indulgence. I would have known that what I hoped for, what I still hope for, against all the good sense in the world, was, is, some impossible turning back of the clock, not so much a softening on her part, but on mine, on mine, since *she* has never forbidden me to speak to her, she has never said it was impossible. On the contrary, the last time we met she said she hoped one day it might be possible again, she said one day I might see things as she did.

But most of all, as it turns out, I wasn't ready for the train of thought that begins now as Vikram Griffiths, who despite the film has been walking up and down the aisle, his mongrel trotting at his heel, continuing his never-ending parleyings with all and sundry, perhaps in search of the notorious spy – as Vikram Griffiths leans over me, his breath full of whisky, his clothes of dog, and, nodding to the video screen, suddenly pale as the coach shoots out of the tunnel into a world of white mist and drizzle amid the great looming shapes the Alps are, frozen in the contortion of that last orogeny, majestic and broken – leans over, clears his throat and says low, so as not to be heard by Doris, What do you think, boyo?

This business about a meeting this evening?

No. The shagplan, man! He grins, fingers in his dark side-burns. The film! he explains. Don't tell me you hadn't realized why I chose it? Fuckin' toss in itself of course, but gets the girlies in the right old mood, you know. Love thy teacher. Thy Teachers. *Carp* the old *diem*. Can't get more fuckin' appropriate than that, can you? Without writing 'shag me' up all over the screen.

My Welsh colleague with the Indian skin puts his arm round my shoulder with what is now an extraordinary assumption of complicity, an avuncular matiness, as if to force me to declare myself in some way. The dog thrusts his snout between the seat and the underside of my knee.

Can you? he insists.

At random I agree, I laugh half-heartedly, I ask, Got anything lined up?

But he's already saying, I don't mind yours either. Lovely little girlie. And he nods back to Nicoletta.

Who I now realize I have forgotten. Astonishingly, in the space of only ten minutes of having her sitting behind me rather than in front, I have forgotten about Nicoletta, her little glow-coloured purse and sweet gratefulness, *clean forgotten*, as they say, the way I am so often forgetting the names of my tottie, so that sometimes someone you supposedly *made love to* only a day or so before, Bologna-tottie for example, will call you on the phone and you simply cannot remember the name. Or worse still, you can't remember which of two or three names. You know it's Bologna-tottie, but you can't remember whether Bologna-tottie is Francesca or Marta or Valeria, and for a moment you're desperately flustered, searching for the name, before recalling with a sigh of relief that so long as you don't care, it is perfectly possible to carry on not only a conversation but an entire relationship, or *avventura* as *she* always used to call them, without ever using the caress a woman's name is. Except that this in turn only reminds you that *her* name on the contrary, *her* Christian name *her* surname *her* second name *her* daughter's name *her* home phone number *her* work phone number *her* address *her* bra-size *her* birthday *her* saint's day *her* daughter's birthday *her* necklaces *her* earrings *her* bracelets *her* brooches *her* ankle-bracelets *her* shoe-size *her* complete wardrobe *her* favourite drinks pastas meats and sweets *her* brands of perfume of deodorant of cigarettes of tampons of chewing gum, and a thousand other details are things *you will never be permitted to forget.* You will never be permitted to forget them. So that on more than one

occasion, having got the phone down on some nameless tottie, I have found myself dialling *her* number, automatically,
without even being aware of it. 045, it begins, it began, for
Verona, for my age. Then I stop.

Nice little girlie, my colleague is saying. Sneaky Niki.

Turning my head for a moment I see that the charming
and charmingly forgotten Nicoletta is having to lean,
because of Vikram's balding head, over to the middle of the
seat behind me, in order to see, on the video screen four
places up, a cluster of boys who, under the influence of their
charismatic schoolmaster, are now, somewhat improbably,
reciting Wordsworth in a cave by torchlight. The world is too
much with us late and soon, these Americans read, badly, and
in Italian to boot: *Il mondo è troppo presente* . . .

Bit young for me though, Vikram laughs. And he whispers:
Perhaps I'll take a poke at old Doris. Because another thing
about Vikram Griffiths is that he never misses an opportunity
to remind you that his preference is for older women, even
fifty- and sixty-year-olds, and this is part again of his wilful
outlandishness, his determined declaration of difference, in all
its possible forms (the whisky flask! the red cravat!), and
simultaneous demand for acceptance. *He is different in order to
crave acceptance,* I tell myself. As if he had got himself born
half-Indian in Wales on purpose. And in the early fifties at
that. Vikram Griffiths, I tell myself, as he leans over me to
make a pantomime show of squinting down Doris's cleavage,
has made a destiny out of circumstance, has multiplied and
magnified his separateness a thousandfold, the better to
demand that we accept him. Even tossing in a shabby mongrel
dog to the bargain. An ugly dog. A smelly dog. Named after a
Welsh poet. Worth a squeeze, Vikram laughs, his arm round
me, fingers of his other hand fidgeting in his dog's prosaic
ears, and all at once I appreciate that I find all this endearing,
I find it attractive, and sad, as if, far from having put one over

on me by getting me to come on this questionable trip and by taking these little liberties of complicity – the arm round the shoulders, the innuendos, etc. – he were himself in danger somehow, vulnerable, in need of help. He cares so much about keeping this dull job, I tell myself, about leading the boys to victory, about being our misfit, alternative leader, whom we must love. It's touching.

Pouting his lips in a kiss, Vikram is saying: Anything to do a proper lady a favour, boyo. He taps his nose. Especially if she's a *frau*.

The only problem, Vikram, I warn – and how witty I can be sometimes! – is that a delicate personal kindness like that, shown towards one of our Teutonic colleagues, might be mistaken for merely another manifestation of Euro-solidarity. You know? More political correctness – Celt to Kraut – than the gesture of a sensitive, passionate man.

Ah, yes, the ambiguity of the Euro-shag! Vikram nods his sideburns, apparently pleased to be called a Celt, while on the screen a curiously sexless Robin Williams expounds to his eager class on the theme of *living one's life to the full*. I might just have to toss the old sou'wester at someone else's door then, he laughs. And then he says *her* name. He might shag *her*, he says.

Go for it, I immediately tell him.

Y'see, what I fancy there, he says, in his interminable search for intimacy, his low voice that is never low enough (and there is a positive gale of whisky on his breath), what I fancy about that, is the razzled, last-orders look, y'know, the mauve lipstick and the skirts and stockings and shoes. The gear. Very French.

Give her hell, I tell him. My voice is flat. Quickly I say: By the way, I hope you've got it all organized for tomorrow? I mean, who we meet, what we say? The great campaign. Treaty of Strasbourg.

Right enough, he laughs. Then amazingly, and with that awesome remorselessness with which things can go wrong sometimes (as when, at billiards, the white shoots *unerringly* off three cushions into the centre pocket, doesn't creep or slither down like the balls you've aimed, but slams straight home, as if nothing could be more meant, at some metaphysical level, than the unfortunate coincidence) – amazingly Vikram Griffiths announces, Oh yes, when it comes to campaigns, *fuckin' Napoleon Bonyfarts got nothing on this boyo.* This boyo just rolls on from one war to the next. I'd've stuck the old Duke's mercenaries right back in their Wellington boots.

And Vikram goes on then, after the brief interruption of a feminine cheer when Robin Williams invites his students to tear pages out of the books they or their parents have paid good money for, to explain the details: the Welsh MEP who will meet us and prepare us for our meeting with the Petitions Commission; then the presentation itself; then . . .

But I'm lost, I'm suspended between the chattering video screen and Vikram's now earnest Welsh rhythms in a world where, quite apart from the subsiding ripples of pain that fanned out from the word 'razzled', and the vaguer, deeper disquiet generated by the fact that *people don't know about us*, to the extent that this man can merrily talk about having a poke at the woman who has meant most to me in my life, apart from all that I'm suddenly riveted by the recollection of the last time Napoleon Bonaparte crossed my path, a recollection of such absurd and tangled complexity, such abject consequence, that I find it remarkable that my mind can hold it all together as a single entity, a single feeling, can say to itself, Ah, the *Napoleon thing.* For this anecdote, this little – no, not little, this *personal* – horror story, which I immediately understand I am doomed to go picking over for at least the next hour, like a ghoul over his own carrion, is the kind of improbable agglomeration of negative material that would seem to crave just one nice international word to sum it up and get it out of the way as soon as possible; the way there are convenient words like *Inquisition* or *holocaust* or *pogrom* which sum up whole epics of human awfulness so that they can be got out of the way with the greatest rapidity, buried forever in the immense sludge of world-wide buzz-words and brand names – global warming and Gor-Tex, Coca-Cola and ethnic cleansing – or rather perhaps, assuming we have a certain *level of culture*, as the Italians like to say, we may exhume such words from time to time in well-written novels, serious films, to enjoy the pang, to check that it's still there, to feel good that it *is* still there, as so we should, then to push them even deeper in the shit once again (in fact it's rather unusual, now I come to think of it, that neither *Black Spells Magic* nor *Dead Poets Society* has aired the holocaust as yet, seen fit to set its compass by that convenient lodestone of human cruelty).

Oh for just one word for my Napoleonic anecdote! To be able to say, Chaeronea, the Terror, or Waterloo, and never to have to retell the story at all, never to have to think of it or through it at all. I hate *having* to think of things, *having* to go over things. The tyranny of memory. But in the meantime, I suddenly tell myself, how remarkable, isn't it, that while listening to Vikram Griffiths, now saying that it's important the girlies are properly shown around the Parliament and hence able to feel that they have *taken part*, that they didn't come all this way for nothing, and while observing Doris Rohr, with whom I have no particular axe to grind, trying to find the space between one seat and the next to cross her thick legs in those kind of loose, too sharply creased woollen trousers (maroon) that in semiotic terms at least would surely permit her to use the men's lavatory, how remarkable that while taking all this in, and at the same time allowing once again the complex misery triggered, absurdly, by the name Napoleon to explode in your mind, you are nevertheless still able to *marvel* at the extraordinariness of a brain that can do all this *at once*, a brain that can be totally obsessed and yet totally conscious of everything that is not obsession, locked into a tremendous, perhaps *unforgivable* alienation, yet aware too of a change in the hum of the coach, a change that must be the result of switching from a smooth road surface to a rough, with some of the American college boys in this pretentious and unlikely film being punished now for having left the school premises to read their Wordsworth and Whitman in the more romantic surroundings of that underground cave, perhaps grotto is the word, and Vikram doing his whisky-inspired imitation of a plummy Queen's English to say: After which ceremony we are graciously invited to a jolly luncheon with the correspondent of the London *Times*. So that there is always Self, I tell myself, taking up pretty well the whole of the picture, but equally invariably there is always that little Brahminic bird sitting on one corner of the frame observing Self, observing everything around Self, and saying, To what end, to what end? And did you remember to pay the phone bill?

Or so I thought. I thought psychology had established this business once and for all, this doing and observing oneself doing, and some very long time ago too. Until I challenged *her* about it. Until I said: But didn't you even feel bad doing that, wasn't there a small part of you watching as you did it, or, in this case, said it, a small part, detached, smiling wryly, sad?

And what I meant was, Will you offer me nothing I can cling on to, no small sop of remorse, of the variety I have always been willing to give to my wife, to help her, if only for my daughter's sake, to believe that I'm not all bad, to help her feel the past was not a farce? Our marriage was worth something?

And she said no. There were no small parts of herself that saw or did or said anything different from what the main part of her did or said or saw. Because she was *a happy, together, integrated person*, she insisted, in French, though I remember it in English. And just at this very moment, she went on in an inappropriately husky voice, just at this moment what she was seeing was me, what she was doing was lying there spread out naked like melted butter on fresh baguette, and what she wanted to say was, Make love to me! Why bring up that whole ridiculous story again now that we've got over it, now that we are back together and with nobody between us at last on one side or the other. And she said: Who cares how this came about? The fact is, it's what we wanted!

But I was holding a copy of a coffee-table book, entitled *The Age of the Courtesan*, and inside the lush front cover of this extremely lush and doubtless expensive exercise in historically aware prurience – as gifts of flowers also are never vulgar and always expensive, as telephone-calls from charming and assiduous suitors are always welcome and all the more so if they come long-distance and cost a great deal – inside the front cover, and in turquoise-blue fountain pen, someone had written, in Italian: *The taste of triumph – how can I forget?* And there were two tiny mistakes in the way this Italian was written, one of syntax and one of spelling, as if the whole thing had been spoken-written-thought in a foreign accent.

It's not, I said, and as Vikram lurches off up the aisle ruffling girls' hair as he goes, I find myself mouthing the words now towards her back, or rather towards that sliver of shoulder and freckled neck I can see as she sits entirely engrossed in the vicissitudes of the Dead Poets Society, quite oblivious, though occasionally passing some comment to her companion, who I can't see, but I believe it must be Luìs, a Spanish teacher of quiet, reflective, unreproachable character, and what she's saying no doubt, as one of the romantic young

85

Americans under the influence of the excellent Robin Williams now argues with his parents about wanting to become an actor rather than a lawyer, what she's saying is how good the dubbing is – *un vrai miracle de la communication*, I remember her telling me – No, it's not, I mouth – and I'm repeating the words by heart almost a year after the event – it's not that he gave you the book, or even that he wrote that in it. It's not that that upsets me.

She lies there on white sheets staring at me, so beautiful and beautifully, if only one could detach oneself.

Et alors?

It's that *I said that*! They were *my* words.

At first she didn't understand. I had to point to the dedication again. The taste of triumph. Then she didn't remember. She did not remember. Whereas I will say this of my wife, that though she was/is criminally inattentive, would not notice if you were sitting in front of the TV weeping or had an adulterer's grin all over your face as you washed the dishes, she did at least remember things, she would never forget a moment that had been precious. How else would she have known in what state things must be preserved?

She, on the other hand, had *clean forgotten*. As I have clean forgotten Nicoletta. The kind of cleanliness which really is a blessing.

The name Napoleon? I said. Doesn't that mean anything to you? His letters to Josephine?

Because when I first managed to invent a fictitious conference and we spent three days together in her ex-husband's second or third or fourth house that she still had the keys to in the mountains above Bolzano – and this was the first time we had been away together, the first time we had actually spent the night together – there was no running water. The pump had been turned off, there was no running water, and though I spent hours at it I couldn't work out how to prime it. So she couldn't take her bidet. She couldn't soap and perfume herself as she so much liked to. And this worried her. She didn't want to be putrid, she said, when I went down on her, as I invariably would. I invariably go down on women. I can't understand men who don't. Life, Colin says, is a muff mountain.

So it was then, in her husband's somewhat twee ski and hunting retreat, surrounded by cuckoo clocks and stuffed birds and the like, that I told her what I was surprised that, as a Frenchwoman and indeed a student of the Revolution, she didn't already know – about Napoleon's letters, when, on return from military campaigns, he would command Josephine not to wash for at least three days before his arrival. He liked her gamey.

We laughed and hugged, thinking of raunchy Josephine, and it would be difficult to exaggerate, assuming I would ever wish to exaggerate, how much we were in love then, how much we believed we were in love then, which is the same thing, I imagine, how much, for example, we stared and stared into each other's wide eyes, how immensely gratifying it all was. And drawing on the classical education that she was so determinedly re-galvanizing in me at that point in order to stimulate my sense of self-respect and of purpose, to give me back a vocation, a sense that I could do something and be somebody, I said that returning from Marengo, from Austerlitz, from Jena, from the Europe, in short, he imagined he was liberating and uniting, returning from his military campaigns and approaching Paris and the crowds and the celebrations, the wonderful thought of how Josephine wasn't washing, of how her plump little puss was getting stickier and saltier, must have been, for the victorious Emperor Napoleon, the *secret taste of his triumph*.

We made love, our first whole night together, and though it was wild and wanton, I tell myself now, it was religious too. There was an awesome approach to the sacred, even a sense of becoming sacred oneself. It was she not me first used the word, first wept and laughed, so that it seemed and seems now here on this coach inconceivable to me that she could later have told my little expression, *the secret taste of his triumph*, to Georg, and told it without even remembering where it had come from, or, assuming she did remember, without respecting that moment's apparent uniqueness, a moment never, we would have thought at the time, to be crassly repeated or dubbed or offered in ten translations (putting words in people's mouths) to whoever happened to phone with a certain insistence, whoever happened to draw on the services of a national network of florists to send a tangible sign of his lust.

The taste of triumph, he had written, losing the classical reference suggested by the possessive, which was the remark's only wit, the only thing that redeemed it from the merest male chauvinism. And then that *How can I forget?* Well, only too easily, it would appear. And I don't even turn my head to envy his straight German nose and wryly wrinkled brow as he sits *pacato* behind, intent no doubt on a pasty-faced Robin Williams now contemplating the very bad news that the sensitive young student has killed himself over his Dead-Poets-induced actor-lawyer dilemma.

I don't believe you, I shouted. And I don't believe you could have gone to bed with someone just because they phoned so often and sent so many flowers and *insisted so much you could not refuse.* What does it mean, you couldn't refuse?

I was shrieking at her on a hot afternoon in her Verona flat. I was shrieking. First she had said she was leaving me just when I had said I wanted to leave home, for her, I wanted to be with her. Because she wasn't ready, she had said, to compromise the serenity of her young daughter in a new and perhaps risky ménage. Then I had left home anyway, too betrayed and betraying to continue with the old façade. I told my wife everything and left home. Then she had come back to me. What, a month later? She was ready now, she said. She said she just hadn't wanted to be the one who made me leave my wife, surely that was understandable, but now that I had left her of course she wanted to be with me. She came back and we were happy. We were wildly happy. Perhaps two weeks. Until, in response to the merest enquiry about a receipt from a café in Varese found between the pages of the Michelet I had borrowed from her, she told me *entirely gratuitously* (for she could perfectly well have hidden it from me) that in fact the real reason why she had hesitated before, when I offered to leave my wife for her, was not, after all, because of her daughter's psychological welfare, or her scruples *vis-à-vis* my making such a radical decision for her, but because she had just started a second affair. She was having a second affair, she told me. But that was over now, she said. Three weeks ago. So first she says no. Then she comes and says yes. Then she blows my world apart with this story, told *entirely gratuitously*, of a second affair conducted during our apparently perfect passion, during the passion where we had both stared into each other's eyes and sworn we would love each other for ever. And now, after weeks of unhappiness and confusion, just when I finally seem to be getting over this, when I have finally accepted that, given the difficulties of her affair with me, it was not unreasonable for her to have tried to dilute that intensity with a casual *avventura* elsewhere, at this very point I discover *The Age of the Courtesan*, I discover *the taste of triumph*. His triumph. Which she hasn't even tried to hide. You didn't even try to hide it, I protested. What I mean is, I discover who she is. And that the whole thing meant nothing at all. There had been no great passion.

Then, since it seemed at the time to be the only way to maintain any seriousness at all, any sacredness at all, I hit her. That was the second time. All your life, I reflect, you tell

89

yourself you are a pacifist, you tell yourself you will never hit anyone, you never have hit anyone, you can't imagine yourself hitting anyone. And then you do. When she said nothing had happened. You hit her, hard. But immediately you regret it. Immediately you tell yourself that you will never hit anyone *again*. And you feel this vow is stronger now. Because of the experience of the first time. Forewarned is forearmed, you tell yourself. I will never hit anyone again, you tell yourself. But then you do do it again. You find *The Age of the Courtesan* with that triumphant dedication, not even hidden, barely remembered, and you hit her again. I hit her across the face, very hard, I who never hit anybody, not even as a boy, and she cried and said, Again, hit me again, if it will get it out of your system. And I did hit her again, even harder, two or three times, across the cheeks and face, and I was appalled and begged forgiveness and hit her again and we made love, until she found she couldn't move her jaw properly, it clicked when she opened and closed her mouth, and I took her to the casualty ward at the hospital where we invented some story which they clearly didn't believe about her catching her chin on one of those fold-up garage doors, and even while they were shaking their heads in disbelief, all I could think, repeating it over and over to myself, was that *she was not the person you imagined her to be*. I had fallen in love with someone and she had turned out to be someone else. And already *I* was someone else. And even though that night was spent together and there was no suggestion that we were breaking up or that it was all over, still I understood now that everything was impossible, everything was past.

Dead Poets Society has reached its climax. Robin Williams has been fired by the reactionary school authorities who do not realize what a splendid life-force, despite the suicide, our million-dollar actor is. Robin agrees to go, with a certain nobility, with the wisdom of he who accepts the inevitable having *carped* his *diem* – the wisdom, in short, that I lack. But the boys in his class are challenged to show their solidarity, to show that their relationship with their teacher was a real one, of trust and complicity and mutual respect. And to do this, one by one and very bravely, they climb on top of their desks, a gesture of wilfully making oneself visible and vulnerable, for of course they have been forbidden to do so by some conservative schoolmaster eager to tidy away the whole unfortunate affair and get back to some serious teaching. The boys climb on top of their desks because they feel the need to show their love and support and affection for Robin and to show above all that *the past was worth something*, even if the future must now be different.

On six video screens speeding across a soon-to-be-united Europe a dozen American college boys stand up on their chairs and then on their desks, and I can see, sitting here on the third seat from the back, how this wonderfully kitsch scene, where we all enjoy feeling that we are on the right side and revelling in our sentiments, is actually drawing tears from many an eye in our group, and not least, amazingly, from the expensive, soft-contact-lensed eyes of Doris Rohr, whose own lessons one imagines must be the last word in the dusty formality of the day unseized, since teaching, for Doris, is merely a necessary and unfortunate corollary of having a position. Yes, a fat tear is rolling down through heavy powder on Doris's cheek. She is weeping for Robin, as others once for Hecuba, and at this point I too get up from my seat. I can't stand it any more.

I get up from my seat. But without standing on it. The coach is charging down those long curves that lead away from the Alps. Swaying up from the red upholstery, I stumble a moment, for someone has left a bag in the passageway. Head down! a voice shouts, in Italian, We can't see! I start to lurch forward up the carpeted passage, which has small rubber squares every pace or so. The light from outside comes in in chinks and slashes, since the curtains are drawn on the video, a muddled, fluid, mobile light. There's the throb of the road beneath my feet and sudden gleams of reflected daylight glancing over the seat backs.

I draw level with *her*, level with her seat, where, as expected, she is utterly engrossed in watching how even the last and weakest of the boys has the courage to climb on his rickety desk and declare his sniffling allegiance to his crazy non-conformist schoolmaster, who, intercut with the brave boys, is beaming with poignancy, his pointed nose red with emotion. And *she* too is beaming. Her face, which always had a friendly, nibbly rabbitiness about it, is smoothed out and as if polished by the soft-hued light playing over her cheeks, and her eyes like Doris's are shiny with the pleasures of vicarious emotion. I'm barely a foot away.

Then standing here, swaying in the passageway as this multi-facility air-conditioned coach abruptly changes lanes to overtake something slow, I experience an overwhelming sense of incongruity and inconsequentiality, of the unlikeliness and unloveliness of everything, both within my head and without. Here, only inches away, I tell myself, is the woman who more than any other gave you the illusion of love, who made you believe, no, who systematically undertook to make you believe, that you had taken a wrong turning in life, as she put it − your marriage − and that all you need do to feel whole and happy again was to take matters into your own hands, reverse that decision: *Be yourself*, I remember her saying; as she was also capable of saying such things as *honesty is the best policy* and *make love not war*, and even, on our return that night from the hospital, despite a heavily bandaged jaw, that there was *no point in crying over spilt milk*, an expression which exists, remarkably enough, not only in English, but in Italian and French as well, and even, I believe, in Georg's German, and is equally ridiculous in all of these languages, since what would one ever cry over, I demanded of her then, what would one cry over if not spilt milk? I wanted to hit her again for saying that. For the stupidity of saying that. Would you cry over milk if it hadn't been spilt? No, it's over spilt milk you cry, people have always cried. Nor does there need to be any point in it at all. Whoever suggested there need be any *point* in crying, I tell myself now. And sensing, with this sudden and atrocious awareness of incongruity, literally inches from this woman who fills my thoughts incessantly and to whom I have nothing to say, sensing that I am only seconds from that awful brink where I might try once again to drum some meaning into absurdity, to force a resolution that cannot be – with the back of my hand, I mean – I tear myself away to stumble forward almost to the front of the coach, where Vikram Griffiths is talking to the driver.

I stand by the front seat. There's the huge curved windscreen, spattered with spray from the road, but gorgeously clear, clearer somehow than the air it pushes before it, or giving a greater illusion of clarity. And here, standing up front while we overtake a truck from Trieste carrying two great blocks of stone up to France in that constant sorting and re-sorting of things the race always seems to be involved in so that a million Chambersee Service Stations can be built all over the world and can all look exactly the same, I'm able to overhear Vikram wanting to know from the driver how much extra he would charge for taking us into central Strasbourg tonight and what's the latest he'd be willing to pick us up on the way back, because having come all this way, Vikram laughs, appealing to that old male solidarity, we're eager to see a bit of action, aren't we, and if . . .

But I'm too agitated to hear this out. I butt in.

Vikram, about that meeting they want this evening . . .

When he turns to look at me, there's surprise on his face,

as there was surprise on his face when I suggested I might be the spy, and likewise that day I grabbed his clipboard and said, yes, of course I would come on his trip, of course I would lend my support.

You do realize it's all been set up to dump you?

The driver is saying something and Vikram with his fingers in his sideburns laughs and says eleven's okay but later would be better, and no, he won't be leaving the dog in the coach. He takes the dog with him. Everywhere.

Dimitra's in on it, I insist, and Colin and Georg and – and I said *her* name. But her surname. *She's* in on it. They let you set up the trip because you're the only one who believed in it, but now they're going to vote that you're not fit to represent us when we actually get there. Because you're too unstable. And I said: I just want you to know that I'm on your side. I'll vote for you.

Vikram fiddles in the pocket of his shabby tweed jacket. His dark eyes are bloodshot. You should have a swig of this, boyo, he says, producing the whisky flask. Because you look terrible.

I lifted the bottle to my mouth. I took an extremely long slug, and exactly as I did so a truck went past and the address of the company written on the container this truck was carrying was Stuttgart, Widenmayerstrasse, 45.

Part Two

Everything that partakes of life is, both
in the literal sense and the figurative
sense, *unbalanced*.

Cioran, *The Fall into Time*

CHAPTER SIX

I am lying on a narrow bed in an anonymous hotel room in the suburbs of Strasbourg, whether north south east or west I have no idea, nor interest, all I can see is that headlights pass at regular intervals stretching and flitting over wall and ceiling, their yellow glow softened by the synthetic mesh of the curtains, but with swift shards, as though of unpleasantly illuminating thoughts, where the material doesn't pull to at the top. Attended by a slight rise and fall in the background swell of traffic noise, the intermittent brightness passes, a split second before the auditory peak, over a reproduction of something from Picasso's blue period, a reproduction so flat in its printed melancholy, and so poorly framed in what must be extruded poly-something-or-other, it immediately makes you aware of all the other reproductions of famous paintings bought in bulk no doubt for all the other fifty or so rooms of this prefabricated, out-of-town hotel so suitable for accommodating large and unprosperous groups of coach travellers – pensioners, strikers, pilgrims – until the very subject, it occurs to me, of this reproduction hung between TV and bathroom in this room that could be any of fifty rooms in this hotel that could be any of a thousand hotels, has become, exquisitely and irretrievably, reproduction itself. This printed copy, I reflect, lying quietly in my bed, of a picture that by universal consent marks one of the supreme achievements of twentieth-century visual art is really none other than the epitome of reproduction, of reflected repeated printed-to-death sublimity, of modern myth turned motel chronicle, mass-produced and bought in bulk, as the meaning, I am now aware, of the lights that regularly slide over its textureless surface, and of the constantly rising and falling drone of traffic noise outside, must be monotony pure and simple, people following each other along the same tracks at the same speed at the same distance in the same vehicles through the night, through the day. And I realize, suddenly I know, that the couple embracing in this blue, but intermittently green landscape – beachscape – are not that intense blue couple the fabled Pablo Picasso painted, or sought to paint, or imagined he was painting, but another. They're another. They look exactly the same, I tell myself, but they're a different couple, both of whom are seeking to recapture, this must be the explanation, with no more than a stranger perhaps, or with a familiar person become a stranger, something they once felt elsewhere and with someone else, or with the same person before they became someone else. And watching them embrace there as the headlights pass again and again, each headlight different but each with the same effect, like the passing seconds, the passing hours, watching them locked in that embrace, the sea entirely flat behind them, you can see these two are at the thousandth attempt now, I mean at recapturing whatever it was, they're years, if not decades on, so that it's not really a conscious seeking they're engaged in any more, they're not expecting to recapture anything, but more a sort of mysterious imposition, this clasping, this rehearsal of intimacy, this placing of cheek against cheek, a blue and green ceremony they have forgotten the origins of, like the ceremonies Plutarch mentioned in *Quaestiones Graecae* and suggested were the most faithfully observed of all, the ones nobody could understand or explain to him any more.

The traffic is steady. The lights stretch and flit. It is past one o'clock in this cheap Strasbourg hotel and for the last ten minutes, lying in just boxer shorts on this narrow bed staring at a poor reproduction of a sentimental painting by a lecherous Spaniard, I have been quietly laughing my head off.

I am laughing my head off because I am to be the *Foreign Language Lectors' Official Spokesman* at the European Parliament tomorrow, and I am to address an assembly of the European Petitions Committee in English and another of Italian Euro MPs in Italian.

How it came about that these tasks were entrusted to me, how it came about that I, so incongruously, accepted this trust, and above all how it came about that I agreed to do so under *her* technical guidance and supervision, to the extent that *I have already talked to her for several minutes* about the exact composition and competence of the Petitions Committee and the political orientation of the dozen or so Italian Euro MPs who RSVPed our invitation to attend a meeting intended to voice our grievances to an audience who might see some small advantage in currying our favour – since EC nationals can now vote for Euro MPs in their adoptive countries – these are things that I am not sure I can fully explain, though they may have to do with the whisky I shared with Vikram Griffiths at the front of the coach as we drove across Switzerland, the exhilaration of finding a hand on my knee as the matter was discussed over dinner, my quotation, cruel but apropos, of Benjamin Constant, when Barnaby Hilson offered his own candidature as representative in a falsely self-deprecating attempt to resolve the deadlock between Dimitra and Vikram, and, last but by no means, as they say, least, my belated awareness, heightened perhaps by a disastrous phone conversation with my daughter, that I am once again on the edge of *a tremendous psychological abyss*, that the next two days, and in particular, the fourth of the fifth (though I have been unable to find the number 45 anywhere in my room), could prove fatal if I do not somehow break out of the suffocating isolation which brought me within an inch of striking the woman I love, I hate, in a crowded coach beneath the bearded smile and dubbed pieties of an American actor I have always loathed, thinking back on an incident of two years before that involved the sexual preferences of a man who appreciated that the only way to unite Europe was to run backwards and forwards across it with an army.

You should have a slug of this, boyo, Vikram Griffiths said, turning from trying to bribe the driver to take us into town in the evening of his own initiative without referring the time and expense to the coach company. You look terrible, he said, What's up? So, lying with the instinctive fluency that years of betrayal engender (and if one is lying one owes it to the world to do it well), I said the combination of the coach's movement and trying to watch Robin Williams seize the day had given me the most atrocious headache, and I told Vikram Griffiths, this feckless fragment of Empire (as he himself once described himself), this genius of broken marriages, bizarre manners and interminable good causes, this man who came to my house just once, his dog only a puppy then, and frightened my wife with his life story – told him that I had come to the front of the coach to speak to him because I had heard, in the Chambersee Service Station, Dimitra and Georg and *her* agreeing that he, Vikram, would have to be replaced, because incapable of putting a *presentable face*, I said (partly inventing, partly quoting), to our claims; he would make us look ridiculous, I said they had said, with his unkempt baldness, his bushy sideburns and wild gestures. Nobody sensible had sideburns like that, they said. Nobody drank like that!

And of course I would have passed these observations on to him a half an hour earlier, I explained, I lied, when he spoke to me at my seat, except that the appalling Doris Rohr had been beside me then, Doris Rohr who inevitably, in her constant dread that we would overstep the mark, was doubtless on their (Dimitra's) side and would have passed on my remarks (to him) to them. But the long and the short of the matter was, I insisted (partly inventing, partly not), that they were frantic; they were frantic, I said (frantic myself), and in particular they were frantic because he had started drinking in the Chambersee Service Station at only ten-thirty in the morning and getting the students to drink too, and nobody knew, I said they'd said, what state he would be in tomorrow, and people were rumouring that it had to do with the custody battle over his child, his son, which he had engaged in, they said, because of his ex-wife's, first ex-wife's worsening depressive state, but was nevertheless losing, partly because of his difficult separation from his second wife, which the court could hardly ignore, and so they felt it important, I finished, in a state of total self-loathing, staring past Vikram's mottled baldness at the great sweep of windscreen collecting filth and spray from a French truck ahead, important to replace him with someone more apparently reasonable, someone who would guarantee *respectability for our cause*.

Then to his fair question, after a slug from his flask, why was I on his side over this matter, I who had never shown any interest in any side in this affair, let alone his, I who had even been heard to speak of wanting to be fired, I replied, no doubt rather distractedly, since actually I wasn't thinking about the lectors' grievance or our mission to Europe or Vikram Griffiths at all, nothing could have been further from my mind, but simply and miserably and exclusively about *her* and about Napoleon and the taste of his cunty triumph (so that if I was talking now, and in detail, about *the lectors' crisis* and above all about *the problem of our proper representation* it was only in the forlorn hope that this would help me to stop thinking about what I couldn't help but think about, stop myself from doing something irremediable, as if I hadn't already done so much that is irremediable, surely that is the problem, that is why I am behaving in this quite absurd fashion, speaking so urgently of a subject that does not even minimally interest me) – yes, to his fair question, *vis-à-vis* my suspect allegiance, I replied that I hated it when people stabbed other people in the back. Yes, I hated that, I said, and at the same time was telling myself: You have done so much that is irremediable, and here you are now trying to stop yourself doing something else. Irremediable. That's simple enough, surely. Even reasonable. Then the fact was, I said, because it seemed important to go on speaking, that I liked the way he, Vikram, treated the whole thing as a battle. Yes, he was willing to get his hands dirty, I said, at random, he didn't whine, I invented, about *rights* as everybody else did, he didn't believe that we really deserved the salary and conditions of work we were demanding, no, he just used all these complicated laws about Europe to see if they could be manipulated in our favour in the particular dire situation we were in back at the University. Quite irremediable, I told myself, remembering the blood at the corner of her mouth. Which was more honest, I said, taking a third and very long slug from his whisky flask. Yes, altogether he was more honest. And what I meant now was more honest than *her*, who always used to try to explain everything she did in terms of *human rights* and *the need for experience* and *discovery of her inner being* and her *vraie sympathie pour les autres* and never never never in terms of appetite and selfishness and stupidity. Since quite plainly, I told myself, the reason *she* doesn't want Vikram to be representative has nothing to do with his ability or presentability or anything of the kind, and everything to do with her eagerness to grab the job herself as part of the PR operation involved in furthering her, as she sees it, *career in Europe*, which I too would have been invited to share in, I can't help thinking, if only I hadn't lost control of myself, as she always put it. You lost control, I told myself, as Vikram's dog found something to lick from the side of my shoe. You did things that were *irremediable*. The dog licked earnestly. Someone must have spilt something on my shoe. Yes, we could have gone away to Brussels together. I can see that now. I watched the dog's pink tongue against the leather of my shoe. And I could hear her saying the words: Let's go away to Brussels, Jerry. Let's go away. Except that you lost control of yourself.

Vikram Griffiths was braced between two front seats when I said what I said. He had both hands raised to grip the luggage rack, coalie sideburns bristling and eyes narrow behind the cheap lenses he goes back to the UK for, to Cardiff, to get on the National Health (as *she* always went back to Rheims to have her teeth fixed, and as Georg, it finally came out, goes regularly to Germany for the drugs *the mother of his child* needs, driving through Verona on the way). And seeing how greasy those NHS lenses were, and how red and watery and unhealthy Vikram's poor eyes behind them, as his dog's eyes likewise are red-rimmed and unhealthy, it vaguely crossed my mind, so far as anything could get across that minefield at such a moment, that my colleague would be upset by what I had just said – that he didn't believe we deserved what we were asking – he would see it as an outrageous accusation, a cynical assault on his sincerity, his credentials – wasn't he the champion of modern left-wing holier-than-thou (except where women were concerned) political thought? Yes, I told myself, you have spoken out of turn, carelessly, as you so often do, you have offended a man whose whisky you are drinking and who is clearly eager to make friends with you, in the end a charming man, a man who has overcome all kinds of disadvantages, who is dealing with all kinds of personal problems, you have insulted him blindly, at random, merely in order to drag your mind away from the vomit it will not be dragged from. You have offended him, I told myself, and now Vikram Griffiths is going to be outraged, or cold, or upset, as I have seen him be on other occasions. Of course he believes we deserve what we're asking for. Of course he believes in Europe. And instead he laughed, Vikram Griffiths laughed, happily and throatily, and clapped me on the shoulder and he said dead fucking right, if fucking Europe decided against us he would never mention fucking Europe again, he couldn't give a tinker's fucking shite for a United Europe run by the German fucking Bundesbank who raised and lowered their interest rates exactly as it suited them, plunging the currency markets into turmoil. Rather the Raj, he laughed, though he had never been south of Rome himself, of course. The German lectors were the only ones who never never wanted to strike, he said, they always toed the line, always, they had such a respect for authority, for law and order; Doris Rohr, for example, he said, was, he knew, doing library work for her professor despite the strike, she was putting in her regular hours, despite the strike, so she could claim the salary she didn't need. He put two fingers to his nostrils and sucked at his catarrh. Krauts were like that. No, he wouldn't be at all surprised, Vikram Griffiths said, and clearly he was half-drunk and they were right about his not being presentable, they were right, he wouldn't be at all surprised if Doris wasn't the spy, unless it was Heike the Dike, the Austrian lectress, or lecheress, though you had to take your hat off to dikes, he laughed, clapping me on the shoulder a second time, if only in the hope they'd let you watch someday, he giggled, though he couldn't particularly care for the idea of seeing Professoressa Bertelli on the job, despite her seminal text on Sappho – ha ha – and no, the only thing about our job, boyo, he said, since we're speaking of jobs, he laughed, and he was rubbing the whisky flask beside his mouth now in much the same way children will speak behind a hand so that everybody can see they've got a secret to tell, the only thing that made our cause just, as he saw it, though one could never say this out loud, was, why should we be fire-able when others, the Italian professors, were not, and why should people who did even less than we did get paid even more? We were the only ones in the faculty who did any teaching at all, Vikram Griffiths said, the only ones with any sense of *duty*. He himself worked far longer and far harder and far better and far more *generously* than any of the professors. He loved teaching, he said. He actually *cared* about his students' welfare. Though that was more than could be said for Doris Rohr, or Colin Mattheson, if we were going to call a spade a spade, he said. Anyway, it was a fucking battle, he finished. I was dead fucking right about that. To the death. If they wanted to fire Vikram Griffiths they'd have to walk over his dead fucking dusky body first. And Daffy's too, right? He slipped a shabby shoe beneath the animal's rump and lifted it up till it yowled. Dafydd ap Gwilym, renowned for his lyricism.

Vikram Griffiths laughed as he spoke behind his whisky flask and the coach lurched to avoid some miserable humpy machine from backward Eastern Europe where they never learnt to build cars the way we did, and clutching at a seat-back for balance as the driver switched lanes, finger-nails slipping on the synthetic red velvet that looks so plush, that promises such luxury, the way all that is modern promises such luxury, invites such complacence, such sitting back in this world of paved roads and metalled directions, gleaming surfaces, reclinable seats, this world where everything is ready for us, technically, to be happy, I was completely disorientated, as I am so again now in this narrow bed in this suburban hotel, watching the light flit over and over Picasso's lovers, completely and utterly disorientated, thinking of the *important responsibilities* I have accepted for tomorrow, and which somebody like myself should never have accepted, thinking of all the half-truths I shall have to tell if I am to do my job well, if I am to be loyal to my feckless colleagues (and really only the feckless attract my loyalty), and thinking once again of the way Vikram Griffiths so blatantly sought to establish a complicity with me, a complicity directed against Colin Mattheson, who he knows is my present drinking companion, by making this disparaging remark about Colin's not caring for his students. For Christ's sake! As if I cared for mine! And what amazes me, going back now over this conversation with my drunken but endearing colleague, Welsh of Indian extraction, as I seem to be condemned to going over and over all my conversations, so that if I'm not engaging in a conversation you can be sure that I am going over one and generally wishing I hadn't engaged in it – what amazes me is how I have never been able to be either an earnest supporter of good causes, or a manipulator, as Vikram Griffiths is somehow both, never an idealist and never a pragmatist, as *she* is somehow both, so idealistic in her love and so pragmatic in its distribution, but always as it were almost an idealist, yet not quite ingenuous enough, almost a pragmatist, yet too romantic, too scared perhaps, until at some point I fell into this role of the eternally rancorous detractor, but dreaming of some unimaginable commitment, some unimaginable propriety, which I almost achieved with *her*, but never properly believed in, until the day she made it impossible.

Then somewhere beyond Lucerne, having finished the whisky and feeling I wouldn't last much longer on my feet and with the driver complaining to Vikram over the radio, now grinding out accordion-accompanied love, in German, that somebody somewhere was smoking, definitely smoking, and if they didn't stop, he personally, the driver, would stop the coach and throw them off, because while his arm might be twisted into accepting a dog he would never let people impregnate his nice upholstery with smoke, he hated smoke, I said I would go and sort the matter out. I blundered back along the aisle, banging against the seats, remembering, incongruously, as I turned my head away from *her*, holding my breath against her perfume, how even on that trip to Rheims which remains for me, as Olympia for the Greeks, the very image of happiness (something past and distant and unforgettable), even on that trip she remembered to visit her childhood dentist for a filling she felt she had lost a piece of. Perhaps I had dislodged it with my fierce tongue, she sighed. She laughed. So that in the end I was granted two more days of paradise to lose because the man decided she needed a root canal.

At the back it was Colin, the tottie-man, smoking, holding a cigarette between finger and thumb, the coal turned inward to his palm, as if this could ever hide the smoke drifting out. I told him of the driver's threat, at which, enjoying the opportunity to impress with childish transgression, for this is what groups do to people, and above all what they do to people like Colin, who are simply begging for some formal situation in which transgression will be visible, he scuttled to the stairwell leading down to the door just in front of Doris Rohr's seat – the driver wouldn't be able to see him there, he said, as if it was a question of seeing – and poking his head round grey-trousered legs, for Barnaby Hilson was now sitting next to Doris Rohr, earnestly discussing the merits of the Dead Poets, he took a pantomime drag with pouting moustache and said, Suck. Di'n't I say suck was anuvver of me fav'rite words!

While everybody was laughing at this, I took his place, which is to say I took my own place, because it was number 45 again, as I couldn't help noticing on the oval plastic tag sunk into the luxury red velvet which must not be impregnated with smoke, and exactly as I did so and remembered once again, as if I had ever forgotten, my age and *her* phone code and my address, I heard Barnaby Hilson, who is Irish and a writer, in his late twenties, objecting to Doris Rohr, who'd felt that the nice boy's suicide was unnecessary, that the film was so good *precisely because the boy does die*, that is, it was a good film because the director had *allowed something to happen*, he hadn't shunned the obvious fact that *seizing the day was dangerous*. Aspirations are dangerous, I heard Barnaby Hilson say, as I sat down on seat 45, with no other aspiration, it occurred to me, than to get through somehow. To get through what? Just through, I shall get through, I keep telling myself, I must get through, what else can I do but get through, however unlikely that sometimes seems? Whereas Barnaby Hilson of course is a budding novelist, Irish, ambitious, Catholic, young, and he likes to hint at successes by complaining about low publication advances and literary mafias in imperialist London, and the subtext of all his conversation, even this debatable remark on the supposedly *courageous narrative structure* of a box-office blockbuster, is that he, Barnaby Hilson, a clever, clean-shaven boy from a middle-class family in County Cork, has a real vocation; for him the job of foreign language teacher at the quite atrocious University of Milan is a mere, though always properly discharged (because he has a sense of self-respect), sideline, to pay his way, while the rest of us are really rather sad cases with nothing to do but mark time and cling to our salaries; and my problem dealing with Barnaby Hilson, who has had one novel published in Ireland and more recently one in paperback original in imperialist London, is that I couldn't agree more, but I hate him for saying it, for reminding me of it, as if I needed reminding. So that when, later on, I quoted Benjamin Constant at Barnaby Hilson across the huge table of one of those irksomely German *stube*-style restaurants with their long plain scrubbed wooden *tischen* where strangers are supposed to sit elbow to elbow under hunting trophies and be jolly together, as if belonging to the human race meant we had anything in common – when I quoted Benjamin Constant to Barnaby Hilson, who was offering himself as, as he put it, *a compromise candidate in a delicate situation*, I did so entirely out of envy and rancour and not with any desire whatsoever to become the *foreign lectors' representative to the European Parliament*.

And because I thought *she* might recognize the book I had got it from.

I sat down in seat 45, wondering if the powers that be, like the script-writer of *Dead Poets*, would have the wisdom to *allow something to happen* on this otherwise preposterous and preposterously dull trip, and on my left this time, as I lowered myself on to the big back seat of this powerful modern coach crossing the Confederation of Switzerland, on my left was a new girl with a plaster-cast on her ankle who was deep in conversation with Georg on her other side, and what she was saying, very earnestly, as I tuned out of Barnaby Hilson's conversation and into hers, was that she didn't expect she would ever live to be forty. Georg smiled his mature man's smile and asked her why, and he winked at me across the girl as I sat down wishing I hadn't drunk Vikram's whisky, or that there had been more of it. These girls are so young, Georg's wink said, while she – and since I can't remember her name, can't remember whether she even told me her name, I'm going to call her Plaster-cast-tottie, as if I was speaking of a conquest to Colin, because that kind of vulgarity cheers me up, if only by reminding me how callous and downmarket I can be – yes, Georg winked while Plaster-cast-tottie, or perhaps just Plottie, explained that she would never get to forty *because there were so many diseases and wars and things*. Georg smiled again and admitted he was forty-three.

Colin was stubbing his cigarette on the fire extinguisher and with his curling lip beneath thin moustache he asks, What diseases? Wass the problem, luv?

AIDS, she says demurely.

Oh, AIDS, Colin says, climbing out of the stairs, 'ow's a nice girl like you supposed to get fuckin' AIDS, fuckin' Ada? and everybody laughs. Or perhaps around Italians one should say fuckin' Aida, he adds. And everybody laughs again. Nicoletta in the seat in front laughs and Maura beside her laughs and Georg laughs and says, avuncular, in Italian, to the girl beside him, between us, If Colin hasn't got AIDS it can't be that ubiquitous, can it?

The girl laughs.

Who says he hasn't got it? I suddenly join in. It's the whisky speaking. And I add, in English: AIDS aids for the man who's got everything, which is the kind of joke I crack when we're talking tottie over billiards.

Oh speak for y'fuckin' self, Colin says, swaying in the aisle. Oh thank you very much, Mr Jeremiah. And for stealing my seat, cunt. He winks and taps his nose. Anuvver fav'rite word.

All the girls laugh, because people in groups do laugh at this kind of thing; sometimes it seems there is nothing that people in groups will not laugh at, or rather giggle about, as on other occasions it seems there is nothing people in groups will not do to other people in smaller groups or no groups at all, and Plaster-cast-tottie, who I've now noticed has a low-cut sweater and generous breasts though on the kind of stocky body that could only make itself desirable between say thirteen and thirty, Plaster-cast-tottie says, unasked, that she doesn't believe in God, but she doesn't disbelieve, she is searching, Plottie says. This girl is very earnest, but very flirty too, with a sort of bold, glassy stare that demands to be exchanged. Perhaps she knows that her attractions are only the attractions of youth. Perhaps she knows she has to use them now. There is something very glassy and very bold and very hyper about Plaster-cast-tottie's stare and she keeps pushing a page-boy fringe from her eyes. So then I ask her, because suddenly it seems I'm talking to people, I'm talking to everybody, I've given up all hope of hiding away in books I don't want to read, I've given up all hope of cultivating aloofness and dignity, I ask Plottie, what does she mean, she is *searching*? What does it mean when people say they are *searching*? Where do they look, how do they look, what do they actually do when they are *searching*?

Nicoletta appears from above the seat-back in front and smiles at me from her big eyes and the girl is faintly reproachful, as if to ask why I have neglected her so long, staying at the front talking to Dottor Griffiths and then not even acknowledging her a moment ago when I came back and flopped into my seat. As if there were no intimacy between us. I smile back, and I'm aware that I like this girl who cocks her head to one side and smiles reproachfully, as though at a puppy that's misbehaved, I like her because she is so different from *her*, and at the same time Plaster-cast-tottie is telling me – she has a blue bead necklace she is winding round a finger – that what she is searching for is something that will give her an *equilibrio interiore*. She's twenty-one and she still hasn't achieved an *equilibrio interiore*, she says, and this time Georg lets a very broad smile cross his face.

You bastard kraut, Colin shouts. I saw that smirk. Don't laugh at the little girl as if you were so fuckin' superior. An *equilibrio interiore* is fuckin' important, Colin says, standing in the middle of the back passageway right in front of us, enjoying his theatrical belligerence.

Georg only smiles the more.

Unwisely, I throw in, I'm forty-five and I've never achieved an *equilibrio interiore*.

Colin says: Oh, aren't we *sturm und drang*! Not bad, eh, he adds, elbowing the attractive Monica of the slim jeans and the cousin who wants ex-boy-friends to feel sorry for her, Not a bad range of cultural reference, what eh? Very Euraufait, no? Euraufait. J for joke. He shakes his head. Shove up a bit, love, this sod has stolen the seat I stole from him.

Colin sits on Monica's legs even before she has a chance to move and starts to explain his Euraufait joke for the benefit of the young Italians who haven't understood, while I'm thinking, Why can't you be like Colin? Would you like to be like Colin? What on earth do the girls think of him? Beating someone across the face is irremediable, I tell myself. Much worse than anything Colin does. Until with a sudden determination to participate at all costs, to escape at all costs the Furies pressing their faces against the wet coach windows where hills are massing again now under a heavy shower surreal with doodlings of afternoon neon, I ask, Hands up those who have achieved an *equilibrio interiore*, come on, hands up! And of all those sitting in the back two rows, to wit Margherita in the extreme left corner, Georg, Plaster-cast-tottie, silent, pouty Veronica on my right, Graziano, Monica, Nicoletta and Maura, and Colin on Monica's knees, of all these only Graziano and Nicoletta half put up their hands.

Explain, I say, determined now not to be left alone with myself for one more minute of this trip, determined to talk, to be the centre of attention – so that now lying here on my narrow bed in this Strasbourg suburb, whether to north or south or east or west I neither know nor care, it occurs to me that this must have been the moment when I consciously changed plan, or rather became conscious of having unconsciously changed plan, having opted in a complete and bizarre swing of temperament, not for silent reserve, but for a virtuoso performance. From now on you will perform non-stop, I told myself. For the next forty-eight hours and with the help of a little whisky perhaps and enormous reserves of nervous energy you will be deeply ironic and sparklingly witty, and *she* will see you being brilliant and crackling like a firework and she will imagine that you have *got over her entirely* and she will be intensely jealous of the young women you're talking to and will deeply regret . . .

Explain, I demand.

Graziano, in the second seat from the back on the left-hand side, has an open, boyish face whose patchy unshavenness suggests how young he is. He shrugs his shoulders and smiles shyly. *Così*, he says.

But you feel you have achieved an *equilibrio interiore*?

He smiles.

Georg says smoothly, Leave off, Jerry.

I just want him to explain how he does it, I said. With the best will in the world, I asked the boy, What do you do? I mean, how do you fill the time? Let's see if that gives us the clue.

Wanking, Colin suggests.

Only Plaster-cast-tottie laughs. That gave a naughty little girl away, didn't it? Colin says. Don't we know a lot of naughty words?

Colin! Georg says. For Christ's sake!

So then Graziano tells us that he plays the guitar, classical guitar and folk songs, that he attends meetings of *Rifondazione Comunista* and delivers leaflets for them because he believes they're the only political party who seriously want to help poor people. He reads a lot for his exams and helps his father on their grandfather's smallholding near Lodi which they work Saturdays and Sundays and sometimes in the evenings in summer. They grow salad greens and aubergines and peppers.

Rifondazione Comunista! Maura, beside Nicoletta, protests, and it's the first thing she's said that I've registered. How can you support *Rifondazione Comunista* when it's them prevented the Left coming to power?

But I suggest we leave aside the politics. The last thing we need is an argument about politics. No, what we want to establish, I say, is whether there is anything profoundly similar to each other and different from ourselves in the lives of those claiming to have achieved an *equilibrio interiore*. Something that might indicate how the rest of us can get there. No trouble with women? I ask Graziano.

The unshaven boy smiles, embarrassed, pouts, shrugs.

Have you got a girl-friend? Monica asks. Squeezed next to her, Colin makes a face.

Graziano says he goes out with two or three girls now and then, on and off, but he hasn't got a girl-friend.

Blessed state, I tell him, but Plottie says why, she is unhappy *because* she hasn't got a boy-friend, or rather because the boy-friend she had was an *idiota*.

Exactly.

And Colin says, What's this with the indefinite article in front of boy-friend/girl-friend? The singular crap. When the girls smile, he says in his most Brummie Italian, False presumption of binary opposition.

Georg says: We can't all be as emancipated as you, Colin. Which is such a beautiful piece of hypocrisy, coming from Georg. He turns to the girls and is smiling especially warmly, I've noticed, at the small red-head Veronica with the swollen lips, though in a very quiet and correct way. Colin is *avant-garde*, he says, forerunner of the new man.

When Georg smiles his face takes on such an expression of wry wisdom, of one who's been there and come back, one who knows what he knows; it's as if in his case the whole of self had been transmuted into the Brahminic bird, not a small part of one's identity observing the whole, but the whole observing a mere shadow, an efficient routine put on for his own amusement, and it occurs to me now that when he sent those flowers, when he made those phone-calls and *insisted so much*, and later when he explained to her how *the mother of his child* suffered from *an incurable disease*, which she then explained to me as if this somehow made what she had done not only perfectly reasonable but generous, towards a man in a difficult predicament, her *vraie sympathie pour les autres*, yes, it occurs to me that when he did all these things, which he has done, I happen to know, with scores of women: the seduction, the sad story that excuses him from any involvement, and then the gift, in this case *The Age of the Courtesan* with the neat calligraphy inside to write down an expression he imperfectly remembered from her, or more likely she imperfectly remembered from me, *The taste of triumph*, it was all a game to Georg, or rather it was pure form in which he had no investment at all. Or there was investment, there is, but only in the form, the motions, the image of himself he projects, and not in whoever happens to be the object of those formal motions on any particular occasion. Which may be why he is so convincing. Certainly little Veronica is warming to him, doubtless thinking how mature he is. And he is. And the galling thing for me, one of the many galling things for me, the many many galling things, is that even now, even after marriage and separation and eighteen months' shiftless shagging around, or *amour amok* as Colin always says, even now I can't behave like this, like Georg, with the tottie I meet, I can't observe the traditional formulae, I can't tell my sad story to advantage. And somehow this makes me less, rather than more convincing. You are less convincing than everybody else, I tell myself. For example, everybody thinks now, as I ask Graziano these questions, that I am playing, I am teasing, I am being cruel. But I am not playing. I am not teasing. And I am not being cruel. I really do want to know how someone can achieve an *equilibrio interiore*. Then everybody imagines, when I can't become heated about my rights, about my salary, when I can't undertake a battle for the job that puts bread in my mouth, that I am merely flippant. Or cynical. But I am not flippant. Or cynical. I'm lost.

Your breath smells of whisky, Plaster-cast-tottie says. She looks me in the eyes, pushing her page-boy fringe from her forehead. She stares glassily at me from too close, but with youth and sex written all over her.

It must be because I drank some whisky.

Got any for us? she asks. She's speaking Italian and she has that endearing boldness of people determined to be adults for the first time, more adults than an adult, which is to say adolescent. So I say, *Non c'è più* – All gone – in the voice parents use with their tiny children.

Antipatico, she objects.

Oh, if the naughty girl likes whisky we can buy her some this evening, Colin says. Whisky is another favourite word.

And you? I ask Nicoletta, the other possessor of an *equilibrio interiore*. Tell us. Is *Rifondazione Comunista* the key?

Or have you got a dog? Colin asks.

Nicoletta isn't flustered. She's kneeling on her seat, but turning this way and that, a slim young body, though sadly flat-chested, so that if, it occurs to me with fatal inappropriateness, if I should score tonight with Nicoletta, I shall have to say that I like tiny breasts, love them, as I did once with a girl who became known as Psycho-tottie who was the first I had, or had me, after the disaster, by which I suppose I mean the Napoleonic episode. Yes, I swore to Psycho-tottie that I adored breasts that were no more than a sort of sad fried-egg with nipples, but she knew it wasn't true, and I called her Psycho-tottie, telling Colin about her, because of a way she had of bursting into tears in the middle of love-making, something that I presumed had to do with a previous lover, but I felt it wiser not to enquire. The last thing you want, I told myself as she cried, is a story like your own.

I'm not interested in politics, Nicoletta says, though I do think it's important to have ideals.

You betcha, Colin says.

Georg asks, Like?

Nicoletta puts the tip of a thumb between her teeth, smiles. She is such a *little girl*, but apparently so sensible, so genuine, with an imminent, immanent, motherliness about her.

Well, things like this trip, she says. Helping people in need, people who are being treated badly.

Dead right! Colin applauds but at the same time I feel warm breath against my ear, and Plaster-cast-tottie is whispering: Niki fancies you, did you know that? She fancies you. Though later it would be her, Plottie, who put her hand on my knee under the wooden table of the *stube*-style restaurant after I quoted Benjamin Constant in response to the sickening false modesty of Barnaby Hilson's self-candidature to the position of lectors' representative to the European Parliament: *The mania of almost all men*, I quoted, later on in the evening, leaning across the scrubbed top of the *stube tisch* – and it was my first contribution to a long discussion – *The mania of almost all men is to appear greater than they are; the mania of all writers is to appear to be men of State.* There was a short silence of incomprehension, before I added, since *she* clearly hadn't recognized it, Benjamin Constant, *De l'esprit de conquête et de l'usurpation.* Vikram Griffiths said in a loud Welsh voice, What if I propose our Jeremy as a candidate? and at the very same moment Plottie slipped her hand on to my knee and squeezed, definitely squeezed, but I was merely mortified to see that there was still no sign of recognition, or even gratitude, on *her* face.

CHAPTER SEVEN

It occurs to me now that memories act on me the way alcohol does, they excite and depress me, they inflame me, so that after all the talk in the coach about how only a sense of acting for a good cause could lead you to an *equilibrio interiore*, and after having to hear Georg agree with this and then add, along the same lines, that even when you weren't acting for a good cause *you should never act in contradiction of your beliefs*, in a negative cause as it were, since moral contradiction led to mental turmoil, he said (speaking all the while in his measured *pacato* tones for the benefit of the young Veronica), and after remembering, as inevitably I would then remember, how *she* insisted that on being invited to spend that first weekend in Varese she had not gone there in contradiction of all she had promised to me, no, since she had not gone there thinking to make love at all, but only, she said, to be close to someone the mother of whose child was in hospital, and hence the fact that they had made love in the end, she said, was just *something natural*, something that had arisen out of her *vraie sympathie*, the last piece, she said (and these were her very words), in *that complex mosaic that friendship is*, and thus not something she would, or could, ever feel guilty about – after all this, as I was saying, on the coach through the afternoon, this inflammatory cocktail of piety and platitudes spoken and remembered on top of a considerable amount of whisky, how could I be expected to conduct the phone-call I fell into shortly after checking into my room with anything like a clear head?

There was a mill of students around the reception desk when we climbed off the coach with Vikram Griffiths reading out names and handing out keys from an envelope while the sour proprietor, furious about the dog, tried to get people to be quiet enough for him to speak on the phone. Never seen a more tottie-rich environment, Colin laughed, and he had Monica's bag over his shoulder and another girl's too, because a gentleman would never allow a young lady to carry her luggage, he said, and he insisted on delivering the bags right to their rooms: I shall not let a lady carry a bag in my presence, he announced, while both girls were fighting, pretending to fight, to grab their things off him and he was shoving his way through the others with one pink and one neon-green backpack held high above his head, when Vikram called out my name, then called it again when apparently I hadn't answered the first time, and he told me I was to share room 119 with the Avvocato Malerba. We were the only two who hadn't settled on a partner.

I took the key and walked down the linoleum corridor to this shamelessly anonymous room where I now lie disorientated, unable to sleep, on a narrow bed, as yellow headlights turn Picasso's blue period to green and perhaps in the next room Mondrian's *Composition in Red*, etc. to orange, etc., or a Van Gogh sunflower to cellophane, and the first thing I did, on getting in here, and this must have been perhaps seven o'clock in the evening, was to go to the phone and call my answering machine in Milan, which told me, in Italian, that I was out and that if I left a message I would phone myself back as soon as possible. Pressing the code on the beeper to retrieve any messages, I thought of the tiny tape whirring backwards and forwards on the small shelf in the narrow passageway of my minuscule apartment, stale and dark with the shutters down and all my nice books and pens and intimate odds and ends, recently replaced, in safe and shadowy order; and I thought how only twenty-four hours before I had been safe in that room, which was my room, and only mine, perhaps the first room that has been truly and exclusively mine in all my life. I had been safe and functional and had imagined myself cured, or almost, or at least convalescent, whereas now I knew that the contrary was true and that away from that neat and narrow retreat into order and limitation I was quite lost, completely without definition or identity, and that what lay ahead of me, until such time as I could return to my small apartment, was nothing but ever more bizarre strategies for avoiding the worst. A female voice announced, Hello, it's me, and asked whether perhaps I was really at home but just not answering the phone, since it seemed too early in the morning, the voice said, for me to be up and out. No? Hadn't I said I was never up before nine? With all I did in the evenings, ha ha? The voice left a message saying it would call back later, which, after a couple of beeps, it did, now leaving another message saying it only wanted to say how much it had enjoyed the evening before, thus confirming that this was Opera-tottie, whose peculiar urinating habit I have still to tell Colin about. There was a pause, followed by a nervous, calculated, adult woman's laugh, generated in Monza, stored in my sitting room in Milan, heard, without interest, in Strasbourg, and she rang off. Then another voice announced name and time of day and said she had finished her thesis summary and would like to fix an appointment to bring it over to my flat for me to see, as I had suggested. Would Friday at five do? and this was a *mature student* who I was planning to lure into my tottie trap (Colinism). Then after another silence of beeps and scratches my daughter said: Daddy? Daddy, have you already gone? She was speaking English to please me, and since she never speaks English to anyone but myself, and then only rarely, her voice, in English, has a babyish, uncertain tone to it, an endearing childishness, so different from her adult, rather brash Italian, and she over-accents the ends of all the words: I was justt callingg to see iff you likedd yourr presentt, she said.

From along the corridor I could hear the girls refusing to let Colin bring the bags into their room and he protesting that he had never been anything but a gentleman. I phoned my daughter at once and got my wife's voice from the kitchen phone over the throb of the dishwasher. The skylight was leaking again, she said. I asked to speak to Suzanne. It was pouring, my wife said. It had been pouring all day and the skylight was leaking. Then Suzanne came on the extension, where I could now pick up the gibberish of the television. Suzi, I said. My wife rang off, taking the dishwasher with her, and I said I was sorry I'd have to miss the birthday party. I had tried to get out of this business, but in the end I felt a certain obligation when everybody's job was at stake, not just my own.

My daughter asked me had I read *Black Spells Magic*, and I said about half, and she asked what did I think, and still inflamed from all that had been said and remembered on the coach, and what's more irritated with myself now for having lied about my motives for coming on this trip, and not only for having lied about them, but for having heard in my own mouth precisely the kind of pieties I have no time for in others (a certain obligation!), I began to say, injudiciously, just as the Avvocato Malerba walked into the room with a far larger suitcase than anyone could possibly need for two nights, that although I was enjoying the book *overall* I found bits of it hard to take.

Don't you think all her magic stuff is great though! my daughter said.

I said I had only got to the bit where their love-making in the lift emanates a power that puts all the stockbrokers' computers on the blink.

Isn't that brilliant! my daughter said. It's a fantastic metaphor.

Of what exactly? I asked obtusely, and what I remember now, lying in this lurid, insomniac dark, is that although I was perfectly aware, at this point of the conversation, of the impending danger, aware I mean that I was perhaps about to argue with my daughter, or at least to disappoint her, almost the only person in the world I would rather not argue with or disappoint, I nevertheless, inflamed as I was, already knew that I would not be able to resist saying what I feel has to be said about books like this, perhaps because it sometimes seems that all that has happened to me, all that I have allowed to happen to me, has intimately to do with such books, or at least the mentality they are steeped in, which is of course exactly the mentality of the person who can pretend, on accepting an invitation to spend a weekend with a man who has bombarded her with flowers and phone-calls, that she is not going to his house to make love but only in order to add one final piece to *the complex mosaic that friendship is*. To wit Georg's no doubt considerable cock. And twisting the receiver cord round my finger, I told myself, *All her love for you was mere whorishness.*

My daughter was saying, Obviously it's a metaphor of how human emotions and sensations – I mean when two people make love like that – are stronger than electronics and money.

The Avvocato Malerba had now laid out three sober and, to my untrained eye, identical suits on the bed and was going through a pantomime of gestures to ask which wardrobe he could use when I objected to my daughter, who is eighteen tomorrow and hence at just that age where you begin not to know whether you should still be making allowances, that this was precisely the kind of comforting cliché it was so easy to sell to people, was it not? Didn't she think, I went on to ask, trying to indicate to the Avvocato Malerba that he could have either of the wardrobes, or both, since I had no clothes worthy of hanging, unless with myself in them, didn't she think that in the end this book was not unlike a narrative version of a Benetton advertising campaign, *Hands Linked Around the World* and such-like stultiloquence, *United Colours of Good Conscience*, etc., etc., while all the while the company, as here the author, sorry authoress, was sensibly pocketing the cash that came with a higher moral profile. Entirely inappropriately, I was furious. The Lira's fallen fifty points against the Deutschmark today, I said. I want to see what love-making could reverse that.

You don't approve because it's lesbian sex, my daughter said, switching to her adult Italian. And I had offended her. Your daughter, I thought, your delightful daughter, Suzanne, has given you a book for your forty-fifth birthday and you are telling her it is terrible. Your daughter is trying to establish a new relationship with you after the period of hostility that inevitably followed your walking out on her mother and herself and then again the shocking stories she quite probably heard about you from *her*. She has given you a birthday present, something she did not do the previous year. She has called you in your flat, something she has done no more than two or three times in this whole period of separation, the norm being that it is you who call her, you who visit her, engaging in conversations of an almost palpable limpness and hostility. Your daughter, I thought, has given you a present and called you. She has left a message on your answering machine.

In English. And what do you do? Rather than sharing, or at least tolerating, her enthusiasm for what is in the end no worse than another kitsch expression of present-day orthodoxies, you simply confirm what an offensive and irretrievably acrimonious person you are by judging the book according to standards perhaps exclusively your own and anyway entirely dependent on your own peculiar vision of the nature of contemporary decadence.

Why don't we talk about it when I get back? I said. Hotel calls are expensive, I said, and I wondered, Did she have lesbian tendencies, or didn't she? The Avvocato Malerba was selecting a shirt and tie.

All men are afraid of lesbians, my daughter laughed. Come on, Dad, loosen up, go with the flow. And she laughed again, rather mockingly. At which, instead of repeating that we should talk about this when we were together and could relax, I foolishly, on the line from Strasbourg, began to object that, quite the contrary, men were *not* afraid of lesbians at all, they were *fascinated* by lesbians. *Lesbianism was the only aspect of the book that even remotely interested me*, I told her. And this was the truth. But all the same, I insisted, as far as the doubtless imaginative scene in the lift was concerned, I just felt that such a prurient enlisting of fashionably transgressive multiracial pop eroticism to blow away the paper tiger of white male domination symbolized by the computer circuits of an evil stock-market could hardly represent the apex either of literary achievement or of intelligent political comment. Could it?

Was I right in imagining my daughter had begun some kind of relationship with *her*? How often had she been baby-sitting? And how was it my wife could look on with such indifference while her daughter baby-sat for her husband's ex-mistress? Was she deliberately encouraging the kind of relationship she thought would make me jealous?

I don't understand you, Suzi said, and she asked, why did I have to talk in this pompous way? She didn't understand at all. So that now, rigid on the bedspread while the Avvocato Malerba drew the curtains before removing his jacket and shirt, I recognized this as another of those increasingly frequent conversations where one feels that one must reconstruct the entire history of Western thought just to knock the undesirable parts down again, say absolutely everything in order to say anything at all. Which at the price I was no doubt paying to call suburban Milan from suburban Strasbourg, at hotel rates, would be imprudent to say the least. Such is the power of money over human relationships. And once again it occurred to me that one of the sources of immense uneasiness in my marriage had always been the growing preoccupation that both my wife and in a different way my daughter were, if not stupid, then *hardly very intelligent*. No, they are not particularly intelligent, I told myself. They don't discriminate. They don't *think*. And the agony here is that one feels presumptuous and judgemental in reaching such conclusions, in deciding that one's wife and daughter are not particularly intelligent, yet on the other hand one cannot help but be aware of the evidence that comes constantly before one's eyes. So that perhaps one of the reasons I fell so completely for *her* when I did was the illusion she managed to generate of being *deeply wise and extremely intelligent*. The illusion. Let's talk when I get back, I said to my daughter.

She laughed. Switching back to English, she said, You always back down from an argument, don't you, Daddy?

Happy birthday as of tomorrow, I managed, and finding, on getting the phone down, the Avvocato Malerba buttoning a white shirt over a grey hollow of chest hair, I asked him – I would pay the phone-bill of course, I said – if he knew what Nietzsche had once written down in his notebook as the most cogent argument against his own cherished notion of

The Eternal Return, the eternal repetition of all things?

Determined to show off his English, which it occurs to me now might be a plausible reason for his having agreed to come on this trip – seventy-two hours of free English lessons – the Avvocato Malerba said he found Nietzsche *unbearably presumptuous and judgemental*. He actually used those two words, *presumptuous and judgemental*. The world would have been a better place, said the Avvocato Malerba, without people like Nietzsche, who had been *criminally responsible*, he said, for the rise of Nazism and Fascism. He preferred Spinoza himself. So there seemed no point in telling the Avvocato Malerba, or indeed any person who could prefer Spinoza to Nietzsche, that the most cogent argument against the notion of the eternal return, for Nietzsche, was the existence of his mother and sister.

But going over all this now on my narrow bed after the extraordinary farce of the *stube* supper and the brief conversation with *her vis-à-vis* the exact composition and competence of the European Parliament's Petitions Committee, and then the absurd group walk in the wet night arm-in-arm with the long-legged, sadly flat-chested Nicoletta in search of a late-night bar – going over this and struggling to get a grip on the day's events, as I appear to be under some kind of obligation, vain as it is compelling, to get a grip on everything, which is to say on myself, I am struck by the question, How can I preserve my relationship with my daughter? How can I behave towards someone who would be deeply offended and hostile if I told her what I thought about almost any issue worthy of discussion, to whom, if I wish to keep the peace, I will always have to say things like, I enjoyed the book overall, but . . . , or, I really tried to get out of this trip, but . . . For years, I tell myself, tossing and turning in my bed – because I have never quite known what to do with my arms when I am trying to go to sleep, and particularly when I am trying and *failing* to go to sleep – for years you have sought the affections of your daughter, sought the heart of your daughter, as before for years you sought the heart and affections of your wife, only to be thwarted by your daughter's taking offence at observations so reasonable as to be self-evident, as before it had been your wife who took offence at such observations, all perfectly reasonable and even, so far as you could see, self-evident. Where *do* people put their arms when they sleep? For years, I reflect, one curries the favour of a person, one feels the need for a relationship with that person, one feels that one will be a lesser person oneself if one doesn't have that relationship, only to discover, in a trice as it were, that the chief obstacle to that relationship is the other person's *lack of intelligence and discrimination*, only to see, from one day to the next it seems, and perhaps after years of frustration, the blindingly obvious fact that you have been so desperately contriving to ignore: *this person is not particularly intelligent.*

How should I behave towards my daughter, I ask myself? Shall I lie on my right side or my left? And more in general, I ask myself, how should I behave towards anybody when almost anybody would be offended if I honestly discussed with them almost anything I care about? Or on my stomach? Which is the opposite of the illusion *she* brought, of course. The illusion she brought was that everything could be said. Every tic and quirk. Every masturbatory impulse. Every passing opinion, however extreme and unacceptable. The inebriation of total intimacy, that was what she brought, on the fourth floor of the Hôtel Racine, where everything was clear, everything was said, everything was acceptable, in a rapture of total communion, until the first piety, the first lie, not more than a fortnight later, when she said that *she did not wish to compromise the serenity of her young daughter in a new and perhaps risky ménage*, and then the entirely gratuitous revelation, not three months after that, of the simultaneous *mosaic of friendship* she had been laying down with another man, unmistakably, though never admittedly, my colleague Georg, right down to the cod-piece, the cock-piece, at the centre of that tasteless mosaic, out of *vraie sympathie*, she said, because *he insisted so much*, with flowers and phone-calls, and then worse still somehow, worse than all this, the unwillingness to retreat from what she had done in any way, the unwillingness to see it as shallow in any way, to regret having done it in any way, to regret having so gratuitously told me that she had done it, to regret having so gratuitously blown away the foundations of our illusion, my illusion, that intimacy, and worst of all, worse than everything else, my sudden awareness of her almost constant use of such expressions as *I have made my choices in life*, or *Je suis allée jusqu'au fond*, or *Je n'y suis pas allée pour faire l'amour*, or *There's no point in crying over spilt milk*, my sudden awareness, I mean, that *she wasn't wise at all*, that I had been a complete and utter fool ever to imagine her so, that I, a stupid man, had left my wife for *another stupid woman*, until the moment I shouted whore and hit her. Irremediably.

How can I discuss things with people if discussion inflames me, if discussion makes me violent? Or is violence the only proper response when you are right, for years and years you are right and others are so obstinately wrong? But then why do you imagine, I ask myself, pushing my hands under the pillow now – and if my wife, my daughter, my lover have anything in common it is that they have all asked this same question – why do you imagine that you are right and that everybody else is wrong? I can't answer. Yet that is exactly what I do imagine. Wouldn't it be madness to suppose one was wrong merely because others did not agree with you? Where would that lead? You believe what you believe, I told myself. There's no way round that. Even if you have frequently acted blindly and foolishly. And lying on my back now with my arms on my chest in this narrow bed in this

Strasbourg hotel that I am beginning rather to like, if for no other reason than its appropriate awfulness, it occurs to me that the only way for someone like me to behave is to wait for dumbshow situations like the hand on the knee from Plaster-cast-tottie, and to go for them.

The hand on my knee! I can still hear talking, laughter, glasses, distantly from the lobby, despite the protests of the proprietor, who was nevertheless ready, after our vain, drizzly search for a suburban night-spot, to sell us what Eurobooze he had (cognac, brandy, pernod, grappa – bottles of it – which people acquired quite wildly in infantile gestures of group bonhomie) before he drew his bar grille down and complained about the noise, as nations selling bombs like to complain about the noise when other nations explode them, as *she* complained when the love and dreams she nursed me on for so long came back to her in blows and ugly phone-calls. Yes, I can still hear talking from down the passageway through the thin prefabricated walls and the squeal of young girls' giggles and occasionally Vikram's Welsh voice in Welsh song, or Colin shouting his favourite words, or a sort of fruity nervous guffawing that comes I suspect from the ambiguous Avvocato Malerba. So that most probably, if I wanted to, I tell myself, that hand, Plottie's hand, could still be made to engage in something more than a caress of the knee – it's only one o'clock, or thereabouts – I could still capitalize on that promised intimacy, or at least contact, with this strange girl. And the fact that I did nothing to capitalize on that caress under the table, indeed quite the opposite, discouraged, even spurned it, is, I suppose, reflecting on it now, here in this hotel room where I have just realized that *I shall never really be able to talk to anybody about anything*, both heartening and unnerving – heartening because it suggests that you are not on for absolutely anything, you are not totally a slave to that, to sex, in the way on occasion, very many occasions, you have been; and unnerving because it may well be that you acted as you did out of an incorrigible romanticism. You are an incorrigible romantic, I tell myself. How fascinating that those two words should have wed together in standard collocation. An incorrigible romantic. For sitting on the other side of me at the massive *grosse tisch* around which, to pre-empt any formally convened meeting of the lectors, Vikram Griffiths raised, over a sort of dumpling stew, since it turns out that Strasbourg is as much German as French, the *pressing question* of our representation to the official institutions of the European Parliament, thus muting the carefully prepared attack on him by conducting the affair in the presence of the students, who love Vikram and tend to equate him, and particularly his bushy sideburns and his drinking habits and his well advertised and injudicious private life, not to mention his embodiment of two ethnic minorities, with an idea of revolution dear to their innocent hearts – yes, sitting on my right side at that moment when the hand to my left reached across and firmly took my knee under the table was the ever more engaging Nicoletta, she of the flat breasts and *equilibrio interiore*, and of course it was she, Nicoletta, who later, in the fruitless search for a bar back in *les banlieues* when the coach driver had gone to bed and the group had lapsed into that sort of wilfully daredevil sentimentality that dictates that an evening cannot be allowed to end but must be made mythical in some bar or other under a tidal wave of alcohol, it was she who took my arm and invited me, for the air was a mist of dark drizzle, to share her umbrella, a gesture I immediately and excitedly compared, even equated, with that previous gesture – the hand on the knee – from young Plottie in the restaurant, to the extent that the thought, *There must be something about me today*, crossed my mind, *Spoilt for choice I am*, I told myself, *Sneaky Niki indeed!* – the kind of presumptions you have to laugh at later, you have to mock and poke fun at, for it wasn't long after I had been drawn under the umbrella and then into a conversation which seemed to have to do with difficulties the dear girl was experiencing at home with her widowed mother, it wasn't long before I began to realize that far from being a gesture of sexual complicity, this, of Nicoletta's, this drawing me under her umbrella, was no more, no less, than *a gesture of friendship*! And decidedly not the kind of friendship whose mosaic would require the placing of my cock-piece in its centre. I had turned down Plottie's brazen advance for friendship!

The German *stube* restaurant was perhaps the fourth restaurant our group of forty and more had tried after the coach driver abandoned us at the edge of a pedestrian area in heavy rain of the same weather pattern, no doubt, that was leaking through the skylight of what was once my home in the suburbs of northern Milan. Overwhelming a dozen quiet, Monday-evening clients, silently mulling over their chunks of boiled pork beneath the glazed stares of nobly stuffed stags and owls on wood-panelled walls, we were allowed to pull two great *stube tischen* together to accommodate us all, Dafydd the dog curling up on a seat to nibble at his hind parts, while Georg and Doris and Heike the Dike negotiated the cheapest group menu with a solid proprietress, many of the students being short of cash, and particularly so after it now transpired that in the brief space of our coach journey from Milan to Strasbourg the Lira had fallen not by fifty but by seventy points against the Deutschmark, and similarly against the French franc, and was still falling, indeed *plummeting*, on the so-called *international markets*, to wit New York and Tokyo, where it seemed, or so the Spanish lector Luìs claimed to have heard on the hotel television, that people simply did not want to have anything to do with the Lira any more. And while Georg was negotiating with the proprietress in German, a language I once knew but have now forgotten, wilfully I sometimes think, Vikram Griffiths, infinitely more astute than I imagined, stood up as soon as everybody else had sat down and suggested that in the face of the present *economic crisis* the lectors could perhaps pay more for their meal in order to allow the students, who had so generously decided to *lend their support to our cause*, to pay less; we could fork out to ease the burden on them. That is, Vikram Griffiths suggested *a redistribution of wealth*, something which, lying as it does at the heart of the socialist ethos, and more in general at the core of what the Italians with technical piety and pious technicality like to refer to as *consociativismo*, the others in the group could hardly disagree with, though some wanted to, and in particular Colin, I felt, who is the tightest person with money I have ever known. And perhaps Doris Rohr. The lectors would pay half of the total between them, Vikram Griffiths suggested, and the students, of whom there were more than twice as many, would also pay half between them, meaning we would pay more than twice as much pro capita as them, Vikram Griffiths said, and he ordered ten jugs of the house wine and further suggested that before the food arrived we might as well resolve at once the pressing question of our representation at tomorrow's important encounters, since he personally had no intention of wasting the latter part of the evening at a meeting. He was going out on the razzle. Devaluation or no devaluation. If they wanted to unfrock him, he laughed, let them do it now.

The silence that followed this supremely political manoeuvre confirmed the Indian Welshman's cleverness, with the students clearly wondering what the trouble was, and what on earth 'unfrock' could mean, and those lectors who were against Griffiths finding themselves embarrassed to have to say so in front of students to whom he had just generously awarded the cheapest of meals. Then how could they speak against his drinking at precisely the moment they were so eagerly filling their glasses themselves? So it is, I thought, that one thinks all kinds of unpleasant things about a person, one denigrates that person in the urgent chatter of one's mind, or in complicity with a third person or persons, one denigrates and wholly condemns a person and draws a certain satisfaction from having done so so comprehensively, but then hesitates to say what one thinks in public, and particularly in front of that person themselves, finding quite suddenly that one is, in some obscure way, *ashamed of opinions one nevertheless still feels it perfectly legitimate to hold*. One hesitates, for example, to say to one's daughter, I think the problem here is one of your ignorance, or to one's wife, I think the problem here is your terror in the face of change, in the face of *life*. Instead one stays silent and polite. Such is the nature of *consociativismo*, the sad glue that keeps couples and countries and coach parties together. Until the day you walk out or hit someone, or drop a bomb.

But for Dimitra, perhaps, that moment had come. Or was close. Insisting on her Greek Italian, she started to say that, no offence meant, but there were those who felt that his, Vikram Griffiths', how could she put it, wildness – she tried to smile at the students she knew – might not be entirely appropriate for the kind of *interlocutori* we were likely to find at *a major international organization* and in particular at that legislative body that ultimately held the key to our long-running case against the Italian state. There was a noisy silence until the Avvocato Malerba now saw fit, as an outsider, he said, with a particular perspective to offer, to intervene, and having begun by saying that he himself thought it might be unwise of us to discuss these matters over dinner, rather than in more formal circumstances, he proceeded to analyse the legal weapons that the Community, as he insisted on calling it, as if there were but one community in the whole world, laid at our disposal. Like children admitted to the adults' table for the first time,

the students sat paying serious attention to the Avvocato
Malerba of lean neck, dusty features and ponderous manners,
as he took us through the niceties of that clause in the Treaty
of Rome which forbids discrimination against citizens of
other member states and posed the question how best *such
discrimination could be made to emerge* for the kind of people we
would find ourselves presenting our case to. The students sat
listening, Plottie on my left and Nicoletta to my right, and
then dozens of sensible and silly and pretty and plain girls
under the dim *stube* light, faces concentrated, even devoted, as
if any of what the Avvocato Malerba was saying could
remotely matter to them, while Colin on the other hand,
half-way down on the left-hand side, Colin to whom this
matter matters enormously, since Colin has neither the inclination nor perhaps the capacity to engage in any serious work
and counts greatly on his gravy train and his adequate supply
of fresh tottie, is rolling up small balls of baguette and flicking
them insolently at the various girls he is interested in, who
smile and look pained. And *she* of course has pulled out a pen
and is taking notes. Upon which it occurs to me that *she*
and the Avvocato Malerba are the only two people who
have dressed up for this dinner. The only two people who have
made that kind of effort. For beside his sober suit and tie,
which I now realize has on its blue background that circle of
yellow stars which symbolizes our European solidarity, twelve
identical yellow nebulae encircling a void, *she* is wearing the
tight black chiffon dress with black beading down into a pro-
nounced cleavage which she liked to wear the two or three
times we went to the theatre together, or the opera once, and
beneath which I know she invariably has her black suspender
gear with red trimmings that so excites her when she sees
herself, ice-cold Martini in hand, in the full-length mirror of
a hotel wardrobe, just as it excites her, she always said, to have
her thick dark hair pulled up tight, as it is now pulled up very

tight, with a great wooden pin through it that keeps the tension on her scalp all day, and as her slightly undersized bra, she said, kept her slightly oversized breasts forever in a state of slight tension, at once *uncomfortable and exciting*. And precisely as the Avvocato Malerba, pressed by Dimitra, explains that his point is that any presentation must approach the problem from two angles: on the one hand *a genuine feeling of injustice*, this for those Euro MPs who are not experts in the field but will respond emotively, and on the other *a meticulously technical presentation* of the legal nitty-gritty, for those on the Petitions Committee who would be only too ready to find the kind of flaw in our case that would save them from having to consider it seriously – precisely at this moment, when the Avvocato Malerba is trying to establish the strategy our representative must adopt and hence, by inference, the qualities he, or she, must have, I am seized, seeing that low-cut dress I know so well, by such a vision of love-making, such an immediate and overwhelming impression of skin and hair and perfume, such a *meticulously technical* sense of the adherence of underclothes to slightly heated flesh, the give of a bra unclipped, flattened nipples plumping, and then the glassy pornographic reflection of all this in the mirror of the fake, or no, perhaps genuine, antique wardrobe on the fourth floor of the Hôtel Racine, so inflamed by the smell of skin and sex, that I have to grab my glass and down, in one gulp, a very considerable quantity of very poor quality house wine, a gesture that has Nicoletta turning to me in concern, while Dimitra predictably interrupts the Avvocato Malerba to say that all things considered she is not convinced that Vikram Griffiths is really the best person for either of these modes of presentation. Plottie bangs me on the back when the dregs go down the wrong way, then bangs again, harder, upon which it comes to me, coughing fiercely over remembered rapture, a comic, ludicrous figure with cheap wine in his windpipe, a girl thumping on his back, it comes to me that the presumptuous, judgemental Nietzsche went mad at forty-five. Didn't he? Wasn't it forty-five? Or at least in his forty-fifth year, I can't remember. I must check. Assuming there is still time.

CHAPTER EIGHT

She was proud of being French, she said, because the French Revolution lay at the heart of modern Europe. The principles of *liberté, fraternité, égalité* had transcended national borders and become the rights of every man, and finally the principles upon which the whole of Europe was built. In the great release of energy which came with the separation from her husband and her daughter's first attendance at nursery school, she bought quantities of books and suggested we read them together and discuss them together. It would be exciting, she said, to have a fresh and intellectual relationship with some-one after the years of tedium and near-moronic materialism with her picture-frame-entrepreneur husband. Plus it would be good for me, she said. It would be important for my sense of self-esteem, my sense of *being someone going somewhere.* So we read Chateaubriand and Benjamin Constant and the Duchesse d'Abrantès and Michelet, which had been her special area of study, and we read Xenophon and Thucydides and Plato and Aristophanes, which had been my area of study, and we discussed them together, usually after making love, in the afternoon in the *pensione* she stayed in when she taught consecutive days in Milan. We lay on the narrow bed, still clasping, still hot and damp, and we discussed, after perhaps hours of mutual adoration and oral sex and never without a bottle of Martini, for she was addicted to ice-cold white Martini, Plato's notion of a realm of ideal forms, and we would try to relate that to the way the Revolution had, as it were, discarded men to champion an idea of man, an ideal man, since surely, or at least this was my feeling, it was this shift that lay behind the notion of *égalité* and of a single civil code for all the world. Man should be an incarnation of an idea rather than himself. Man should be *a European*. Or we would discover that Plutarch's picture of Sparta was not unlike stories of Stalinist Russia, not unlike, in other ways, The Reign of Terror, or Nazi Germany – a European speciality, it seemed – and apropos of police states various we came across that other line of Benjamin Constant where he says: There is no limit to the tyranny that strives to extort the symptoms of consensus. Then discussing all these things quite seriously – orthodoxy and state terror and media hype – while drinking Martini and smoking the Gauloises Blondes she smokes, we would fall to making love again, remembering how all the great men we were talking about had loved women passionately, Talleyrand to start with, and more coyly Chateaubriand, not to mention Alcibiades, and how the great women we were talking about had loved men likewise, and likewise passionately, Ariadne and the Duchesse d'Abrantès, Madame de Staël and Medea, and how Napoleon had certainly been lying to Madame de Staël when he said the best women were the women who bore most children, that was Sparta talk, since the best women, it was obvious I said, coming up for a moment's air from the taste of my triumph, the best women were the women who turned you on most and fucked you best. And fucking then, after those long and learned conversations, perhaps in the soft warmth of an autumn afternoon with the shriek of the trams clanging through the open window from the streets of an ever-industrious Lombardy, we felt so sensual, and so intelligent, and intelligence seemed part of sensuality and sensuality part of intelligence and both together at once sacred and revelatory, though revelatory quite of what it would have been hard to say. Of their sacredness perhaps.

But how infantile! I think now, sitting up suddenly in another narrow bed and feeling the chill on my shoulders, a flash of yellow light crossing my face. How utterly infantile! And how extraordinary, I tell myself, sitting bolt upright on this narrow bed and shivering in this miserable hotel room, how infantile that you should ever have engaged in such conversations! How humiliating to think that you were not aware of the merest vanity in all this, the spurious stimulation of imagining yourself wise and communing with someone wise, discussing the world of pure form, or the noble savage, or the social contract, etc., when the only thing really speaking between the cheap sheets of that cheap *pensione* with the supermarket Madonna over the bedstead and the daguerreotype of the Duomo by the door was the sly old complicity of cock and cunt. What else? And remembering how, after my not incomprehensible choking fit at the farcical *stube* supper, I had retired to the loo to piss, to get a grip on myself, and seen a certain graffito there and thought certain thoughts, until I shouted out loud (over a urinal produced by Ideal Standard), How little philosophy helps! it comes to me now, in the soft slide of passing headlights, that the reason philosophy helps me so little is because the kind of philosophizing we traded on that narrow bed in the Navigli, the grand thoughts and acute perceptions we whispered back and forth, the parallels across thousands of years and the flattering identifications of ourselves with the great figures of Western history and mythology, was no more than another tool of mutual seduction, like the smell and smoothness of skin, like the tone and accent of her foreign voice, her French laugh, like the diving cleavage of that beaded black chiffon and the delirious awareness of her tottie-tackle (Colinism) beneath. *Thought itself is an erotic memory for you*, that is the truth, I am bound to admit now, sitting up in my narrow bed in this Strasbourg hotel which might be any of a whole series of hotels we once stayed in. Yes, the headiness of thinking, and I mean the sort of thinking that approaches mystery and sacredness, *the sort of thinking that makes life exciting*, is the same headiness of bur-rowing into her twat on soft Milanese afternoons with the clang of the trams ringing in the air and a low honey sunlight stealing across the wall. Thought, like hotel rooms, reminds me of *her*. And perhaps this explains why I simply stopped reading, from one day to the next, after the Napoleonic dé-bâcle. For two years, I tell myself, you read intensely, insatiably, with immense pleasure and with a deeply gratifying sense of power and self-esteem, because reading was to do with *her*, and to do with conversations you had with her, to do with what she wanted to make of you and what you wanted to be for her, until, from one day to the next, *you could not read any more*. And not only were you unable to read any more, but the meaning of everything you had read to date was suddenly and frighteningly shifted, was even inverted, from self-esteem to self-loathing, from a belief in your own intuition to a convic-tion of your own blindness, a conviction born from the irony that you had read in so many places of the experience you were now going through, to wit the experience of betrayal, of being cut off, abandoned by the gods, of intensity enjoyed and intensity lost – and, quite apart from reading about it, you had even inflicted that same experience on your wife – but still without ever believing that one day this might happen to you, just as one never truly believes, perhaps, in the sense of savouring fully and accepting completely, that one is going to die. From one day to the next you stopped reading entirely. *Black Spells Magic* is perhaps the first book you have seriously tried to read in a year and a half. Does this explain your inappropriate anger with your daughter? That she should have invited you to start reading again with this ridiculous tale of the magical and politically correct powers of sexual passion! And how bewildering, I tell myself, sinking back on my pillows, how ominous, that once again today, this very evening in fact, on the coach returning from the *stube* supper, you should have sat by *her* side, her in her black chiffon dress with full French tottie-tackle beneath, and once again heard her say, *vis-à-vis* the founding brief of the Petitions Committee of the European Parliament − its function, that is, as a body for *righting all wrongs* − that the principles of *liberté, fraternité* and *égalité* lie at the heart of modern Europe.

Still choking with wine over the *stube tisch*, I escaped Plottie's strong hand to recover in the lavatory. And it was here, relieving myself before returning, that my eyes unerringly picked out one of a score of graffiti above the urinal I had chosen, or that had chosen me: *Elène*, someone had scribbled − *amour fugitif di quelques minutes, dont je me souviendrai pour toute la vie!* My immediate response to this, splashing on to Ideal Standard in the semi-basement lavatory of a German restaurant on dubiously French territory, was to laugh, to laugh out loud, too loud, to tell myself, in the words of the man who went mad at forty-five, that *There are no facts, but only interpretations.* This biro scribble between smutty porcelain and barred window giving on to a courtyard of bins and sodden boxes has no more to do with you, I told myself, than the number 45 printed on a plastic oval and sunk into the synthetic plush of a luxury coach seat. Freud was right, I thought, to laugh at those who feared conspiracy in the contingent world. And if he suffered from the same problem himself and feared he might die at sixty-two because of the number's frequent appearance right around his sixty-second birthday, then he had all the more reason for laughing at it, for laughing at himself. *You can never go wrong when you laugh at yourself,* I thought, and I told myself that what I must do was to take control of my mental processes, to repossess myself, as Freud no doubt had repossessed himself, I must stop functioning as a Black Hole dragging down all around me into a solipsistic world of unbearable density. No facts, I told myself, re-reading that graffito, only interpretations.

But how little philosophy helps! Tucking my cock in my pants, I was reminded for some unfathomable reason of the Eleusinian mysteries. My special study it was to be, at last light thrown on that most obscure of Athenian traditions, the twelve-mile dance down the Sacred Way to Eleusis, the group hysteria under pure light of midsummer: sex, ecstasy, possession. I read everything I could find about the subject and discussed it at length with *her* in Pensione Porta Genova, and once I remember her hugging me tight and gesturing to the room and saying this was our Sacred Way, these embraces our Mysteries, she had tears in her eyes, but I never mentioned to her then what now seems the only sensible comment I ever found on the subject, or rather somebody else did, because it was quoted in the kind of scholarly work I once dreamed of writing myself. What were the mysteries, asks Aristophanes? The saying of many ridiculous and many serious things. *Elène, amour fugitif.* Thank God *her* name was not Elène.

How infantile! I sink back on my bed. But will there come a moment, I ask myself, when your disgust now will seem as infantile as your vanity then? Will there? One can only hope so. One can only hope that self-loathing will one day seem as foolish as self-esteem. Certainly there will never be a point of rest, I tell myself, never an *equilibrio interiore*, the mind anchored to a world of pure form or in reposeful contemplation

142

of the Dantesque divine. Not even if forty-five does prove fatal. I remember stopping in amazement once at those lines in Chateaubriand when he talks about the dusty thoughts of the dead, when he asks, musing in some revolutionary cemetery: Who knows the passions, the pleasures, the embraces of these dry bones? More than once it has occurred to me that there is already something posthumous about my present existence.

Returning to my meal from *Hommes et Elène*, it was to find my colleagues in the middle of an amicable show of hands. While I peed and philosophized, Vikram Griffiths had already been voted out. His minority culture credentials, his friendship for animals, his generosity with other people's money, his considerable charm, had not been enough. And it occurred to me, as I sat down at the *stube tisch*, how appropriate it was of my colleagues not to have waited for me. I had said nothing during the discussion. I had said nothing on the coach trip from hotel to town during which Barnaby Hilson, experimental novelist of middle-class Protestant Dublin family and bland good looks, had played traditional Irish tunes on his traditional Irish tin whistle and Indian Welsh Griffiths and English Colin danced an unsuitable highland fling in the aisle while I was forced by powers beyond me to analyse every back and forth of the ill-judged telephone conversation with my daughter. So much for your decision to be extrovert, I told myself. So much, I thought, returning to my seat from the lavatory, for all your decisions. Then sitting down I was just in time to cast the vote that deprived Dimitra of a majority. I raised my hand as the count was being taken and I thought, apropos of absolutely nothing: *Dimitra is the spy.* Dimitra announced the shock-horror of Professor Ermani's having a list of those who had voted for the trip to Europe precisely because, having given him the list herself and having agreed to keep him informed, as *a matter of courtesy* (after all she had voted against the trip), she felt it wise to invent the spy story so that nobody would ever imagine it could be her, Dimitra, who had told Ermani what everybody would be surprised he knew, assuming that knowledge should ever come out. And at once I felt fascinated, appalled, by how devious people can be; then, reflecting that I had no grounds for believing what I had just supposed, I felt even more appalled by how devious I could imagine people being. As if in a world where nothing can be said (to my daughter for example), where the truth can only bring offence (to my wife for example), there were nothing for people to do but be endlessly, infinitely devious, though always behind a smoke-screen of the noblest values. So you betrayed your wife for years, I thought, telling yourself all the while that it was precisely the outlet this betrayal afforded, the pleasure and emotional release you derived from it, which would allow you *to keep the family together*, telling yourself, ludicrously, that betrayal was *a form of faithfulness*, as if love, obsession, whatever, were things that could be managed and manipulated and made to serve an overall strategy rather than simply things that happen to you and that you will never never understand, like being born or dying.

I sat down, somewhat flushed still with the wine and my choking fit and my inflammatory memories, to find, on the table before me, pork and dumplings abandoned in a stagnant pool of thin broth, and immediately, without mental mediation, I cast the vote that tipped the balance five to four against Dimitra, the spy, whose fiercely powdered glare upon my raising my arm cheered me up, galvanized me, to the point where I was actually paying attention. And the person I paid attention to, of course, was *her*. Because this must be the moment, I thought, that *she* had been waiting for. Unfrocking Griffiths, I thought, with all he had drunk and the way he was behaving, winking at all the girls and putting arms round shoulders and talking about going on the razzle afterwards, trying to translate the notion of razzle for those who didn't understand, and using the sleeve of his tatty blue sweater to wipe the dumpling soup from his chin, had not, for all his apparent political astuteness, been too difficult. And the students understood in the end, despite their groans, despite their no doubt *vraie sympathie* for someone who not only was not quite white but was giving them a cheap meal into the bargain. They were all from wholesome middle-class families in the end. They understood that Vikram Griffiths' kind of revolutionary behaviour would not impress a major international institution of the variety they themselves would one day like to work for. Why else were they studying for a degree in languages if not to work one day for *a major international institution*? So it is, I thought, sitting down at the table to discover from Plottie that Vikram Griffiths had already been voted out, six to two, in my absence, so it is that while one's sympathies lie in one direction one ends up choosing another, or accepting another, out of a sense of realism, by which of course we mean a sense of fear, a sense of obedience to laws we imagine greater than ourselves. As for example morality, or society, or history. So it is, I told myself, forking a dumpling into my mouth, that one stomachs more or less any mess one's nose is pushed into, in the name of history and common-sense and realism, until the day comes when something inside simply compels us to behave in the least realistic manner imaginable, compels us to fly in the face of all prudence, as when I said on that same narrow bed in Pensione Porta Genova: *I want to leave my wife for you*, or later still when, quite gratuitously, after years of caution and realism, but definitely operating under the strongest of compulsions, I told my wife everything that had happened and destroyed her world for her.

Getting rid of Vikram Griffiths had been easy. Then the

hostility Dimitra aroused by speaking against the Indian Welshman, Dimitra of the brick-orange lipstick and solid Teutonic nose under Macedonian black eyes, had been sufficient to prevent her from being elected either. We had elected Dimitra as president of the union on two or three occasions now because on each of those occasions no one else would contemplate doing the job, except Vikram, who again was unacceptable since he would have proposed an indefinite strike more or less every time we had an assembly, and this was something that the German contingent in particular just could not deal with. But when it came to representing us to the powerful institutions of the European Community there were more than two candidates. For this was a brief appointment, and perhaps interesting, perhaps useful. So now it must be time, I imagined, for *her* to put herself forward. As she had no doubt always planned. Or for someone to do that for her.

Amidst the general chatter, having returned to my seat and cast my vote and filled my mouth with German dumpling, I watched her. She was looking across the table at Georg. And I thought, She is still in complicity with Georg. They only made love once or twice, she said. Out of friendliness (this around the time I said, I want to leave my wife for you). Yet she is still in complicity with him, in a way she could never be with me. And quite probably, I told myself, their names were indeed together on that list you so hastily and unwisely signed in the drab offices of the *Istituto di Anglistica* that morning of three weeks ago. Their names were together, above and below each other no doubt, and written no doubt, for all I cannot rightly recall it, with the same pen. As far as this trip is concerned, they were already and always *in complicity*. As two people who have briefly been lovers then use that intimacy as a bond, an alliance, a secret society, for all future mutual convenience. And one can't help wondering at the maturity, as *she* would say, of this, the good sense, the fact that

146

there are people who know how to enjoy themselves without coming to grief, without intensity, those lovers who see each other occasionally, when convenience permits, and fuck each other *cordially*, perhaps with a little healthy back-massage to boot, and then are perfectly content if the opportunity doesn't present itself for weeks and even months. And one can't help wondering why you came on this trip, I tell myself now, if their names were together on that list, if they were already in complicity. Why did you come? Why did you insist on this mistake, when you had the perfect alibi of your daughter's eighteenth birthday party, now to take place in your much-censured absence? And the only idea that springs to mind is that you came on this trip, having seen their names together on that list, *to savour defeat once again*, to rediscover intensity. The defeat and intensity, for example, of finding that this trip is precisely one of those convenient occasions when *she* and Georg can get together and, *cordially*, fuck. Now, in this very hotel perhaps. At one in the morning. A few rooms down from your own. Who knows? As yellow headlights pass over some reproduced masturbatory ecstasy by Gustav Klimt. And I am reminded of the time she told me that she had bought an ammonia spray and was keeping it in her handbag. We were speaking on the phone, and she said, So don't say I didn't warn you, but then immediately began talking about the possibility of another night together. It was me who hung up.

Then Georg had indeed just begun to raise his even, *pacato* voice above the chatter, no doubt to propose *her* as our representative, this being part of a pre-arranged plan, when Barnaby Hilson, he of the experimental novels and traditional tin whistle, cut in. And this is what Barnaby said in his rather Irish Italian: that the important thing was for us *to remain united*. He fiddled with his cutlery as he spoke. That there must be no hostility between the representative and other key members of our union. He looked down at his fingers,

disarmingly embarrassed. That we must work together to wi
our rights, with no suspicion that the person doing the repre
senting was in any way acting in his personal interests. H
looked up and smiled with impeccable mildness and clean
shaven good nature. He himself could be such a person, h
admitted. He had never shown any ambition for power in th
union, he said, and indeed was thinking of leaving th
University in another year or two, as this was not, as most o
us knew, his principal career, he remarked. His tone wa
apologetic, since the embarrassment, the endearing embarrass
ment, of superior beings upon their declaring their differenc
from the rest of us is only another way of foregrounding tha
superiority, of course. Also, he said – and now his shy wrynes
was illuminated with a youthful smile – also, an Irish perso
would never put the backs up the powers-that-be in th
Community the way a German, a French, or above all
British representative might. Because Ireland, he said, stil
speaking in this amiable tone, was a weak member of th
Community and a willing member and clearly represented th
oppressed rather than the oppressor on *the international worl
stage*, which was an important advantage, he said, again lower-
ing his eyes to fiddling hands. Thus in the present circumstances, Barnaby Hilson said – and I noticed what exceedingly
long and blond eyelashes he had – he was willing, though
only too aware of his limitations, to put himself forward as *a
compromise candidate in what was rapidly becoming a delicate
situation.*

Barnaby Hilson's modest self-candidature was immediately
seconded by Doris Rohr, who had clearly enjoyed their
animated *Dead Poets* conversation, and again by Heike the
Dike, who perhaps finds those long eyelashes attractively
effeminate, and again by Luìs, who, coming as he does from
the Basque country, perhaps has a sentimental affinity for the
evocative if limited music of dead if not decently buried

minority cultures. A vote was thus proposed over what remained of the dumplings in broth and the ten jugs of very poor quality house wine, and there was a definite look of concern on *her* face now at seeing herself about to be pipped at the public post by this charming, experimental and above all Irish novelist, about to lose this role that she had no doubt hoped would lead her to important contacts with figures, pre-eminently male, in important institutional positions, men with whom she could perhaps profitably have discussed her essay on *A Future Constitution for a United Europe.* The vote was thus about to be taken, doubtless in favour of our charming philosopher-king Irishman, who I do honestly believe would have made a presentable and conscientious representative, when, out of the complete silence I had maintained through-out, indeed had imposed on myself ever since putting the phone down on my daughter and hearing that the Avvocato Malerba preferred Spinoza to Nietzsche, I suddenly and for no reason I could imagine found myself quoting, in Italian, the same Benjamin Constant I had once read with such plea-sure, between fucking and fellatio perhaps, in Pensione Porta Genova: *The mania of almost all men,* I said, leaning across the scrubbed *stube tisch* where two or three of Colin's tottie-directed baguette pellets had fallen into a pool of spilt wine and broth, while another stuck to the fur of Dafydd ap Gwilym, now furiously attacking his hind parts on the seat beside Heike the Dike, *is to appear greater than they are; the mania of all writers, Barnaby, is to appear as men of state.* Benjamin Constant, I added, feeling dazed as one who has blundered into stage lights, or a fly compelled to halogen, *De l'esprit de conquête et de l'usurpation.*

Immediately I had finished speaking, Vikram roared with laughter. For Vikram Griffiths of course, despite his show of general bonhomie, despite his apparent couldn't-give-a-toss attitude to losing his representative role on a trip which is entirely his own inspiration, loathes Barnaby Hilson. Vikram Griffiths loathes Barnaby Hilson in part because Hilson usurps his, Vikram's, role of *charismatic figure from much-loved ethnic-minority culture* and in part because Hilson has a serious project in life and gets on with it, working hard in the mornings and pursuing an entirely stable and sensible private life with his rather older English wife, who is commendably jovial and practical, and their two small, doubtless delightful children, boy and girl. Vikram Griffiths, understandably, loathes Hilson, and now, quite probably in a fragile emotional state after having been voted out by his colleagues on this trip which was absolutely his own invention, and with a child-custody battle going on back in Italy with his first wife, a woman frequently obliged to seek psychiatric help, not to mention financial claims the second wife is making in their protracted and apparently extremely acrimonious separation proceedings, involving, amongst other things, the ownership of their ugly mongrel dog, he roared loudly with laughter, perhaps drunken laughter, and said, *Compagni!* I propose our English Jeremiah as a candidate! At least he can always quote the bastards someone they've never heard of! Upon which, immediately, without any mental mediation whatsoever, but rather as even a suicide might instinctively grasp at a rope thrown to him in swirling waters, I said okay, I would do it, if people wanted to vote for me. But I would need, I said — and how quickly one thinks when one doesn't try, when one is *possessed* by one's thoughts, rather than possessing — I would need somebody to advise me on what exactly I would have to say. I would need advice and help. From somebody who knew something about Europe. Surprisingly, Dimitra at once and enthusiastically seconded Vikram Griffiths' proposal, remarking that my Italian had a more official flavour to it than Barnaby's, plus I was quite a lot older, which might be useful, she said, in allaying the unfortunately widespread impression that foreign language lectors were, as in some other countries, or should be, mere graduate student teachers on a brief stage away from home. Then, after a moment's hesitation (the Avvocato Malerba being unexpectedly deep in conversation with the tiny southern girl beside him), *she* spoke out to accept what had so obviously, I felt, been my invitation to her. *She* would advise me, she said. She had done a lot of research on the European issue, she said, speaking not to me, oddly enough, but across the table, to Georg perhaps, perhaps to Dimitra, as if to say, This is an okay solution, we can go with this. Then she was writing an essay, she said, on *A Possible Constitution for a United Europe*, and as far as our own case was concerned, she said, she knew all the pertinent decisions of the European Court of Justice and its exact area of competence. She would assist me in talking directly to people, if I liked. And I was voted in. Eight votes for and only one abstention. My own.

On the square outside the cathedral, the students danced. I can see them again now if I shut my eyes. This is the square where Michelet tells how Saint-Just chained Eulogius Schneider, ex-monk turned revolutionary, to the guillotine for having forced a girl to marry him, pain of death to her whole family. The coach was late. The rain had stopped. Laughing together, the girls began to sing on the wet flagstones in a flapping breeze with the great façade of the cathedral rigorously floodlit behind, and then to dance. They sang the same song the radio had played three or four times during the journey, *Sei un mito* – You're a myth – and they danced in damp anoraks. The dog was sniffing against wet walls. And gazing at the façade as these girls swayed and danced, full of enviable high spirits and with that lightness young women have when they move to music, gazing at the cathedral, as Colin joined in, beside Monica, and Doris Rohr in maroon trousers studied the cosmetics advertisements in luxury shop windows, I reflected, leaning against a post forbidding parking, that every major monument in Europe is now cleaned and floodlit. Everything ancient and medieval, I thought, as the girls danced, some beautifully – and *she* was deep in conversation with Georg, by a window full of pipe tobaccos – has been appropriately sandblasted, cleaned and illuminated. It is impossible, I thought, hugging myself in the cheap coat with which I recently replaced the leather jacket *she* bought three years ago, even to imagine these stony martyrs being in the gloom now, impossible to imagine these angels and gargoyles in a dark wind or under moonlight. I should never have told my wife, I thought, as the dog cocked a leg. Impossible to see them as part of our lives, our nightmares, potent in the gloom, sacred in darkness or starlight. I should never have opened my mouth like that and destroyed her life. Why did this thought come to me now? These monuments have been *neutralized by the light*, I thought, by the light and by carefully researched detergents. They have been made part of the modern city. They have been subtracted from us and made possible for us. I should never never have told my wife that the only person I had ever been truly happy with was *her*. Why on earth did I do that? Squares where people hanged and lynched and guillotined each other and, in general, committed all sorts of irremediable crimes, are now attractive areas of *floodlit public art*, I thought, emptied of their potency precisely by the zeal with which we have focused on them, cared for them, illuminated them, absorbed them into the on-off neon of our intermittent modern night, our world of time-switches and default settings and above all discrete units of measure – I should never have told my wife that even the smell of her body repulsed me – where nothing is absolute, I thought, nothing is safe from division and subtraction and quantification, where no one sacred façade, or person, or vision looms supreme in the consciousness, singular or collective, but cars

pass endlessly, lights stretch out endlessly, and above all at regular intervals, where you count your lovers, all *égales*, all *libres*,
at regular intervals, each a discrete and equal unit, clasping
and unclasping in endless reproduction under intermittent
light, this world where Colin says, Orgasm achieved, all tottie
is old tottie. How could I tell my wife that the only sex that
mattered to me had been with *her*? I should never have done
that. I should never have beaten *her* across the face.
Napoleonic débâcle or no. It was the end when you hit her, I
told myself outside the floodlit cathedral, when you saw the
blood at the corner of her mouth. New pastures, Colin says
over the billiards table, new treasures in tottie-town. Onward.
The girls are singing, *Sei un mito*. The dog shivers at the end
of his pee. They are even holding hands in a circle, wonderful
twenty-year-old Italian girls under yellow French street-light,
the willowy Nicoletta, the pouty Veronica, the breathy, breath-
taking Monica, all swaying together, all apparently unaware of
one of the great cathedrals of Europe hugely floodlit behind
them on a square where the guillotine once stood. Why on
earth did I take that line on the phone with my daughter, as
if her choice of reading material could possibly matter?
Except that occasionally a girl stops and exclaims, *Che bello!
Che bella piazza!* And now they want to draw their teachers
in. Now they want to dance together as a group, with their
professori, whose jobs they've come to save, as young women
are always eager to save something or someone far beyond
their power to save, singing a song together, something they
have heard on the radio, to do with solidarity, *as a group*,
and already Vikram Griffiths is clowning with them, a cigarette between his lips, and now *she* has joined them, with
Luìs, so pleased about the collapse of the Lira because he
means to change all his savings in Barcelona into lire to buy
a flat in out-of-town Milan. And watching these people dance,
together, as a group, in this Cathedral square in the centre of

Europe, in many ways a beautiful scene, in many ways a touching scene, I ask myself if I will ever be able to sandblast and floodlight *her* image in such a way as to turn it, like this cathedral, into an attractive decorative landmark in my mental landscape. Will my wife ever be able to do the same with me, with the man who so completely and carelessly destroyed her? The rain falls again. The Avvocato Malerba skips under an umbrella plucked by the wind. The girls are giggling. The dog barks at their heels. Will I ever be able to dance careless of the rain in front of her neutralized floodlit image, having accepted it as a central but perfectly manageable interior monument from a past one may as well remember for the good as the bad, the kind of once sacred place one might choose to visit occasionally, on high holidays perhaps, just to get a feel for how it was, how *I* was, but without any sense of obligation or compulsion? Will I ever be able to do that? Will I ever be able to read a book again? Will I ever be able to talk like old friends with my wife? Until it occurred to me, leaning against a post in suddenly heavy drizzle in the central square in Strasbourg staring at the white light over white sandblasted Gothic figures, as young Plaster-cast-tottie, unable to dance, hobbled up and stood beside me and – after the bold hand on the knee under the *stube tisch* just a few minutes ago – now took my arm and actually leaned against me, as if in need of support – it occurred to me, smelling a perfume so sweet as to be sickly, that perhaps the time has come to start using *her* name. Perhaps I came on this trip to start using her name. Perhaps I got myself elected union representative to the European Petitions Committee to put myself in a position of inevitable attrition, to be obliged to speak with her, to work with her, to start the sandblasting.

The great Mister Jeremiah Marlowe, said Georg approaching. Georg wears a trilby out of doors, though he is not balding as I am. The coming political man, he said, drawing us under the awning of a bar. I said Vikram had taken it well, being voted out, and Plaster-cast-tottie, detaching herself a little, but not entirely, said how sorry she was for Vikram because he was such a comic and 'simpatic' person, and you could see he cared, she said, but hadn't wanted to show it. Georg shrugged his shoulders. Griffiths is a maverick, he said. Then he began to ask if I genuinely felt I was up to making the presentation of our case, because if not, there was a written speech which he and *she* and Dimitra had prepared for whoever had to make the presentation, detailing the exact nature of our grievance and in particular the legal justification for our claim both to permanent contracts of employment and to salaries equivalent to that of an associate professor, albeit at the most junior level, i.e. two-and-a-half million lire a month after tax. The whole thing was a question, Georg said – and this was absolutely crucial – of *comparison within the relevant framework*. And while he began to explain then, very seriously, that the point was that all comparisons had to be made within *the reality that was Italy*, rather than allowing myself to be drawn, should there be any open discussion, perhaps with the press, into comparison with legal systems outside Italy, which tended to be less favourable to employees in general and University employees in particular (since European law stated that we should have equal rights *within the system of the country we lived in*, rather than generally across the Community) – while he explained all this carefully and usefully, I found myself recalling, as Plottie gave my hand a squeeze, for the coach had arrived now and people were trooping towards it, I found myself remembering how *she* had once made a comparison which was supposed to be favourable to myself. In response to my continued anguish at her betrayal, she remarked that he, and she meant Georg (though she has never to this day admitted it was Georg), had not been *alla sua altezza a letto*, not *at her level in bed*, as I on

155

the contrary was. She laughed, she was naked, we had made love. She said – no, she sighed – He wasn't really at my level in bed, you know. The way you are. This was perhaps a week or two after the phone-call when she talked about the ammonia spray. She sighed again: In the end, we only made love two or three times, she said. And the fascinating thing here was how she imagined this comparison would cheer me up, offering as it did, as she doubtless saw it, a convincing reason for her decision to come back to me, particularly after I had done the honest thing now and left my wife, she said. Whereas what struck me was the subtext that, had Georg proved to be *at her level in bed*, then perhaps she would have stayed with him. Love does not, or should not fall within the realm of comparison, I thought, walking through blown rain across the central square in Strasbourg towards our big modern coach with the pally Plottie to one side and sensible Georg to the other, the latter properly concerned about the source of income that allows him to support the chronically sick mother of his child. Love should lie outside the world of analogical procedure, of comparisons within the relevant framework and discrete units of measure, I thought, climbing on to the coach in a press of girls giggling and singing and with the distinct feeling that Plottie was seeking to appropriate me and was being remarkably straightforward about it. Though of course, I thought, climbing the steps, looked at from another point of view, one is always seeking comfort in comparison. One is always saying to oneself, At least you're not so badly off as so and so, at least you haven't had such an empty life as so and so, or suffered so much as so and so, this person you read about and that person you knew. Or one even catches oneself comparing the bodies of casual lovers with *her* body and saying, This arse is better and younger and fresher than *hers*, this skin is smoother and softer and sweeter than *hers*. One believes, I tell myself here in the hotel room gazing at those clasping Picasso lovers, who would perhaps have looked well against the anodyne façade of a floodlit cathedral, one believes one desires uniqueness, yet one seeks comfort in comparison. One constantly, obsessively, compares one's own story with everybody else's, until, not finding quite the like, one realizes that one's banality lies precisely in uniqueness.

In the crush of the coach, *she* called, Sit here a moment, Jerry, so we can go over tomorrow.

There were Dimitra and Luìs in the seat in front, Vikram Griffiths with Heike the Dike behind and the wet dog wagging his wet tail in the passageway. At which it flashed across my brain, quite inappropriately, undecided whether I should sit with *her* or not, that I dislike dogs intensely. And particularly wet dogs. I dislike the easy affection people have for dogs, which costs nothing and can never be betrayed. The animal was frantic for some reason, leaping up to paw Vikram and slapping its wet tail in the passageway. I hesitated. People thrust their dogs upon you, I thought in the crush of the coach, undecided whether to sit next to her or not, expecting you to show affection for the creatures, merely because they are dogs, when the truth is you feel no affection for them at all, only a profound sense of irritation, expecting you to respect themselves, the owners, for the relationship they have with their pets, the sacrifices they make on behalf of these representatives of a now vanquished Nature, when you feel nothing of the kind, only dismay that people should find such relationships necessary. All the girls were laughing as the dog pranced. Hey up, Vikram called. He rubbed the creature's nose against his own, so stuffed with catarrh. And suddenly I was aware of a great loathing for dogs, as if they and all they stood for were entirely responsible for my inability to decide whether to sit myself down beside my ex-mistress or not. I was furious. We should go over what you have to say

157

tomorrow, she said. The creature slapped its wet tail repeatedly against my leg. There are some important political decisions. Plottie came back along the corridor and tugged at my sleeve. Her smile was warm. Clearly the girl believes she has established some kind of intimacy or complicity with me, I thought, whereas Nicoletta, towards whom I thought I might have felt something, has disappeared. Where was Nicoletta? I should sit next to Nicoletta. And somehow that decided me and I sat down next to *her*, without so much as exchanging a glance with Plottie, entirely spurning the girl and her generously open advance.

Ah, the polis! I said facetiously as I sat down, and immediately I was trying to jog *her* memory again, as I had tried and failed to jog her memory with Benjamin Constant, tried and failed to jog her memory earlier in the day with Thucydides. A protagonist in the polis at last, I repeated. Thinking of Aristotle. Thinking of *her*. The dog barked. Of the Pensione Porta Genova. But from in front, her face poking between two head-rests, Dimitra said, The police? Where? She seemed anxious. I would have laughed, but nobody else had seen the joke. For everybody had begun to advise me. I was sitting on the fourth or fifth seat from the front on the left-hand side of a powerful modern coach negotiating the ancient centre of floodlit Strasbourg and I was being advised by five or six people at once: the Petitions Committee at eleven o'clock, the lunch with the London *Times*, the meeting of Euro MPs, the different approaches required for each, the importance of getting and keeping all the students there to show we had support, the importance of seeming seriously professional. The wet Dafydd now on his lap, Vikram said, With the Italian Euro-MPs you have to stress there's no way out for the bastards in the *Ministero della Pubblica Istruzione*. The legal point we should stress, the Avvocato Malerba said, a little breathless from his exertions, is that the only employees in the Italian state education system who do not have permanent contracts are yourselves, foreigners. This is clearly a case of discrimination. *She* said: The purpose of the Petitions Committee is to set in motion the necessary machinery to right all wrongs presented to it within the Community. That was fair enough. But when she went on to say that as such – and since the president of the commission was French I might usefully remark on this – as such the organization was inevitably founded on the same principles that had guided the French Revolution, and indeed the whole formation of Europe over the last two centuries, to wit, *liberté, égalité, fraternité* – when she said this, my mind froze. You are sitting, I told myself, next to the woman who took you to the furthest extremes of erotic pleasure, the woman with whom you imagined you were sharing serious philosophical conversations in a *pensione* in the Navigli where trams screeched on soft spring afternoons, the woman whom you described, criminally, to your wife, as the only woman to have made you truly happy. You are seated next to her and she is wearing her black chiffon dress, short above black-stockinged knees, which she often wore in those days, to please you, and she is repeating, in your presence, perhaps hoping to impress the Avvocato Malerba, who does not seem immune to female charms, the same banal reflections she has forgotten she once expressed to you on the second floor of the Pensione Porta Genova, and again quite probably on the fourth floor of the Hôtel Racine in Rheims, where we did everything and promised everything in an intensity never to be recovered or repeated. *Fraternité*, she was repeating now from three years before, is just an older formulation of the modern ideal of *solidarité*. This is the woman you are sitting next to, I told myself. And I thought how fortunate it was that I was surrounded now by six or seven other colleagues and that Dimitra was once again discussing the question of the *spy* (convinced now that it must

159

be someone from the ever-diffident German department), and in short how lucky I was that there was no danger at all of my suddenly trying to beat some sense into life, to recover some meaning by pounding her chiffon dress with my fists. This is the part she acts, I thought, as she went on to say that a proper presentation of our case within a historical perspective could only help. She acts a part. With everybody. How she laughed when I told her Plato wanted people who acted parts to be banned from his Republic. Georg wasn't at her level in bed, she said. She only did it two or three times, out of *vraie sympathie*. I should never have told my wife, never never have said such terrible, destructive words to a woman I had lived with eighteen years. The last piece in a mosaic of friendship, she said. Because he phoned so much and sent flowers. Above all I should never have said I found the smell of her body repulsive. However true it is. And then the business with *the mother of his child*. The mother of his child was so ill, poor thing, and he so heroic to stay with her. How could I care so much *about a fuck or two*, she said. How infantile of me! There was a way in which the English were still barbarians, she said. Why do I care what books my daughter has been reading? No wonder they had trouble with Europe. They lacked the subtlety Catholic cultures had. They lacked the flexibility. Unless Suzanne really is *her* lover? The spirit of compromise, she said. Of *negotiable identity*. It was an expression she had found in a book on psychoanalysis in the period when she was convinced an analyst could save me. People still talk about salvation. Though not my wife. My wife knew from the moment I opened my mouth that there was nothing to salvage. She who had spent all her life pretending old things were new. Your eyes are glazing, I told myself in the coach, speeding out to the suburbs. You are losing your grip. You are no longer following the excellent arguments being deployed by your excellent colleagues with a view to protecting the excellent job you cannot bear. Analysis could save you, she said. It could save *us*! My wife never talked about saving anything. Give her that credit. This was in the days *she* implored me to go back to her, the days she seemed happy to be slapped about, if it helped me to get over it, she said. I should see an analyst. But my wife knew when something had been blown to smithereens. And once *she* said very earnestly: They weren't just *mots sur l'oreiller*, Jerry, the things I said to you, not just *frasi di letto*, pillow talk. I really meant them. But I was appalled, and I was appalled again now in the coach, eighteen months on, to think that there was, there existed, a set and accepted expression in French – *mots sur l'oreiller* – and again a similar expression in Italian – *frasi di letto* – and that she knew these expressions and used them, and that she distinguished, so readily, between the times she meant the things she said in bed and the times she did not mean them. This was Catholic subtlety. They weren't just *frasi di letto* Jerry, she said, and doing so she managed to transform everything she had ever said to me into a *frase di letto*, and I hit her. Perhaps that was the night I finally hit her too hard. The night of the second trip to a second hospital. You are losing your grip, I told myself, sitting in the fourth seat from the front on the left-hand side of this powerful coach now shuddering over at a suburban traffic-light, all the panels trembling. The night of the story about the bicycle accident. The last night. How could you have lain in your bed and told your wife everything? Everything we did. Has *she* used her *frasi di letto* with your daughter? Has your daughter replied with expressions from *Black Spells Magic*? Your eyes are filling with tears, I told myself. You are on the edge of making a major spectacle of yourself. Lick me inside out, baby, the lead singer says to the record producer's wife. You have not a single sound cell in your brain. Just one more moment of this, I thought. One imagines a dog's tongue. Just one more moment. Then Colin leaned over to me from across the aisle, Don't know about yours, he whispered, but my evening's soubriquet is Tittie-tottie. Keeps letting me take a dekko down the Grand Canyon. He meant Monica. And four seats further back Barnaby struck up on his tin whistle. *Whisky in the Jar*. Daffy-dog licking his chin, Vikram began to sing: the Kilkenny Mountains; Captain Farrel; *mushereen m'doran da'*. And he shouted: Who's for the nearest bar as soon as we're back? The girls roared. Barnaby played his tin whistle, *But the devil's in the women, sure they never can be easy, mushereen m'doran da'*. To everybody's delight the dog yowled. Get a grip, I told myself. People were shaking with laughter. No facts, I told myself, only interpretations. The dog yowled again. As if he understood, Vikram clapped. And in the hubbub *she* leaned over and said, with *vraie sympathie*, whispering in my ear, Are you okay, Jerry? I said yes. I laughed. Just feeling my age, I said. Forty-three isn't the end of the world, she told me.

CHAPTER NINE

The outrage of obstructed energy. Impulse without fulfilment. Can any Petitions Committee ever right this wrong? Very deliberately, on my narrow bed in this nondescript hotel room where at one-thirty or -forty the apparently staid Avvocato Malerba still hasn't returned to his bed, I start to masturbate over Plaster-cast-tottie. I start to masturbate, after my normal fashion. But to do this I have to remember what she looks like. What does she look like? And all I can remember is the unconcealed disappointment in her bright glassy eyes when, rather than remaining behind in the hotel lounge on our return from the *stube* supper, I elected to follow Vikram Griffiths and others out into the night in search of a bar, leaving her and her hobbling plaster-cast behind. I elected to go on this alcohol hunt, I reflect now, because *she* had elected not to go on it, just as I elected to come on this coach trip because *she* had elected to come on it. Whether I choose to be where she is, or where she isn't, it is always she who governs the choice.

Vikram Griffiths exchanged some words with the sour proprietor, who apparently gave directions as to where we might find a bar open. But Vikram spoke no French and the proprietor did not seem eager that we find this bar. Perhaps he imagined that a fruitless walk in the suburban rain would bring us back respectably sobered. My mind buzzing with the thought that *she did not even remember my age*, which is somehow forgivable between a father and his children, or even between man and wife, but not between the lovers we were, I pushed through the glass door with other students to be pulled aside then by Colin, who confided that he could hardly shag in his room with Saint Barnaby there, could he? The experimental Irish novelist had already twice phoned his wife about a baby with a sore throat. Because our affair was about being a certain age, I told myself. So he would have to go to Tittie-tottie's room, Colin said, where gentlemanly courtesy might just oblige him to shag Tittie-tottie's tottie-mate as well, he laughed. Our affair had to do with age, I was suddenly thinking, as Colin marvelled at the alliteration of Tittie-tottie's tottie-mate. Though she was more the kind of party who was likely to go down well at a charity ball for the blind, Colin laughed. Go down, damn you, he laughed. He gestured with an imaginary cue. How could she miscalculate, I thought, knowing so well, as she must, the exact difference in ages? Charity ball! Colin laughed. Colin brays rather than laughs. Get it? He sneers rather than brays. Tottie-mate would be an excellent title for a centre spread, he said. But there is no evil in Colin, I thought now, reflecting that he too was exactly ten years younger than me. You never feel Colin could harm anybody. Never broach the breach unsheathed, he laughs. And I thought, looked at in a certain way, age was the only truly important factor in our relationship. We would never have had an affair *like that* at a different age, *at different ages*. How could she have thought I was forty-three?

People milled under an awning outside the hotel where wind was sweeping the thin drizzle against carelessly parked

cars. Beyond a low hedge lay the road that now sends intermittent light flitting about my room. Vikram Griffiths came
out singing *Whisky in the Jar* again, then explaining that he
never put his dog on a leash. Never. He laughed, scratching a
sideburn, and apparently he had quite forgotten about the
question of our representation at the European Parliament,
the precariousness of our jobs, his acrimonious court cases
back in Italy. With a *studentessa* under each arm of his loose
open mac he shouted, Follow me! and made a dash through a
gaggle of girls into the phosphor-lit rain. And, still obsessed
by the notion that we had loved each other only and exclusively because we were a certain age, I found myself admiring
Vikram Griffiths for this, this drunken cavalier carefreeness,
and I envied him. I envied Vikram Griffiths for the way he
turns his energy outward to *whatever is available*, whatever
woman, whatever amusement, and appears to be satisfied with
it, willy-nilly. While I implode. You eat your heart out, I told
myself, watching Vikram with a girl under each arm heading
towards the glare of oncoming traffic, singing about Captain
Farrel and his treacherous Jenny. You eat your heart out and
vomit it up, and eat it out all over again. Why have you suddenly become obsessed with this question of age? And I
experienced then, so soon after sitting in the coach and hearing *her* talking about the principles of the French Revolution,
as if she had never said these things to me before, indeed as if
nothing had ever passed between us, as if the earthquake that
completely altered my mental landscape had not even been
registered on any of the scales properly established for
measuring these things, I experienced such a sense of desperation and self-loathing and absurdity that I turned back, on
impulse, towards the hotel with the intention, hardly creditable, of venting my rage on Plottie, of simply grabbing the
Plottie girl and dragging her, plaster-cast and all, to some
secluded corner of the hotel to be thoroughly shagged, as in

165

the past, I suppose, I have vented my rage on Psycho-tottie and Photo-tottie and Dimple-tottie and others more memorable for their soubriquets than their sentiments. One says one's rage was vented, but the truth is it never was, it was always intact after orgasm, if not magnified, with the added curiosity that these women never felt that any rage had been vented upon them, never imagined anything but affection on my part, even passion, they mistook rage for passion, and so were happy as a rule and spoke eagerly of a next time, as witness Opera-tottie and her generous phone message. One hadn't even been cruel! And this makes matters worse: I mean when every woman is the wrong woman but reminds you of the right woman, when venting is not venting, but reminds one of venting, or of how things were before the notion of venting had even occurred, the time when it was impossible to imagine not having an outlet for the person one had become through being with *her*. And lying in my narrow bed, recalling that moment in the wind-swept carpark when I envied Vikram Griffiths for the ease with which he turns his energy outward to whatever's available, and, as a gut reaction, turned back to vent my forty-five-year-old rage on Plottie, it occurs to me now, here in my hotel room, casting about for an image to masturbate over, that what Picasso's lovers are really seeking in this flat reproduction of their intermittently lit clasping, this miserable simulacrum of a great modern masterpiece that I have been staring at now for upwards of an hour, is themselves again. *They are seeking themselves as they were when they made each other themselves.* Yes, this is something I understand now, as one understands so many things no sooner than it's too late. And I had just turned round to go back to the lighted porch, to go back to the Plottie girl – and through wet sheet glass I could see the Avvocato Malerba deep in conversation with Georg, no doubt discussing the finer points of the legal case I shall tomorrow, incredibly, be presenting to the Petitions Committee of the European Parliament – when an umbrella burst open in front of me and Nicoletta said, Don't go back. Share my umbrella. And immediately I was elated.

Here then is another bizarre thing: the fact that you were elated when Nicoletta, entirely absent from your thoughts for at least the previous half-hour, now opened her yellow umbrella and invited you under it, immediately slipping her arm into yours, as she had done earlier on in the day climbing the concrete stairs of the Chambersee Service Station. You were elated, over the moon no less, the mental volatility of the perfect lunatic.

Unable to masturbate over Plottie's glassy disappointment, I find myself sitting up in bed again. I'm sitting up shivering in my bed. First you set off, I tell myself, on the trip to the bar because of *her*, then you turn back from the trip to the bar because of Plottie, and finally you set off on the trip to the bar once again because of Nicoletta. You are no more than a ball in a bagatelle, shot for one brief second over the moon. Nicoletta opened her umbrella and invited you under and slipped her arm in yours and immediately you were over the moon. Immediately a voice sang out: You're on here, Jerry! And it sang, There must be something about you today! First Plaster-cast-tottie and now this. Sneaky Niki. Spoilt for choice I am! Thus your own mental rhetoric. In the space of one split second, I tell myself, you went from the most total misery (over *her* extraordinary miscalculation of your age) to the most gushing exhilaration and optimism. You thought, Love is a movable feast, Jerry, go for it. Thus your criminal naïvety. You thought, why should I *cry over split milk*, and you thought, there is no reason at all why I shouldn't fall in love all over again with this young and beautiful if somewhat flat-chested girl. Thus your asinine presumption. At which juncture, sitting here rigid and shivering on my narrow hotel bed, it has to be said that there can be no hope for a person as absurd as I am, no hope for someone capable of such extraordinary vanity. Though quite what one might mean by hope, I'm not sure; I suppose what *she* meant when she spoke of an analyst being able to save me; or perhaps what Plottie meant when she spoke of some improbable *equilibrio interiore*.

I was under Nicoletta's umbrella. We were striking off on a walkway beside a dual carriageway. Vikram Griffiths was trying to teach his two girls *The Green Green Grass*, explaining in between whiles that before coming to Italy he had never been south of Eastbourne. Nor north of Clwyd if it came to that. Then came a long gaggle of students and lectors under umbrellas and rain-hoods beside a muddy verge with no sign anywhere of any sort of building that might house a bar, though a huge billboard above chasing cars announced *La ville veste les femmes nues*, and at the rear there was myself and Nicoletta, with me wondering, as she spoke of difficulties at home since her father's cancer, whether this was one of those occasions where one would ask for a kiss or simply try to snatch one. Her mother, Nicoletta said, speaking to someone she had only met that morning, a man any woman should have seen had designs on her, had become terribly morose and withdrawn after her father's death and hardly talked, but at the same time she, the mother, tended to get upset if she, Nicoletta, or her twin brother or older sister, went out of an evening, as if they were somehow deserting her. *Yes, they'll all come to greet me*, came Vikram's voice. Then a peal of laughter. *The green green grass*. And while I began to appreciate, not without a prick of resentment, that the kind of complicity Nicoletta had imagined, on inviting me under her yellow umbrella, was one of *friendship*, and far from the variety that might require for completion the cordial placement of my cock-piece in its mosaic centre, I nevertheless, resentful prick though I am, became extremely helpful and began to talk persuasively to this tall-necked young girl with her over-sweet perfume and delightful red hair-tie on the blackest, raven, almost blue hair (which I would be so willing to bury my face in and adore) – began to talk about modern theories of grieving and about her mother's inevitable jealousy that her children had their lives entirely before them (a feeling I have all too often experienced with my own daughter) whereas her life (the mother's), at least as she was probably seeing it at present, was behind her, had ended, and badly at that, or at least unluckily, with her husband's death. Vikram Griffiths started into *Men of Harlech*. And the only thing to do, I suggested with the sort of wisdom that comes from knowing absolutely nothing about a situation, was to be patient: her mother would no doubt come out of this with time, life would force her to.

We were talking under the girl's yellow umbrella while I resentfully tried to come to terms with the idea that her invitation to walk along under its dripping rim had had nothing to do with any plans to seduce me, let alone shag me rotten before the evening was out. Perhaps your mother will even take another husband, I announced thoughtfully. I had as much chance of sleeping with Nicoletta, I thought, as of taking the Madonna from behind. It was as easy and as difficult as that. But Nicoletta said that that was impossible, her mother could never love anybody else. She could never love anybody after her father. With whom she had been very much in love. To the exclusion of all others, she added, unprompted. I asked her her mother's age, and she said forty-five. Then, responding rather well I think to the nth recurrence of this number, almost as if it were an old ailment I had finally learnt to put up with, I laughed out loud, even good-heartedly. I laughed and said, Perhaps I would marry Nicoletta's mother myself, *we were the same age, after all*, and instinctively the two of us, man and girl, squeezed each other's arms a little harder

169

and exchanged entirely friendly smiles in the street-lit gloom of the umbrella as Vikram Griffiths now stopped the group at a crossroads surveying blocks of flats to the right and, across a soaking urban highway, low industrial buildings to the left, and admitted he had no idea where he was. My mother would like you very much, Nicoletta laughed, I think, and I laughed – call me Niki, she said, everybody else does – and Vikram Griffiths said we would have to turn back. That miserable bastard at the hotel with his miserable directions! Dafydd! he shouted, then slowly sang for the girls who were learning, With the foe towards you leaping, You your valiant stance are keeping. Dafydd! And lying here now on this narrowest of divan beds, not even waiting for sleep, not even trying to masturbate, not even wondering about the Avvocato Malerba's delayed return, I am struck by the amusing fact, this very early morning of the fourth of the fifth in my forty-fifth year, that not only did a young woman offer me *her friendship* this evening, rather than her body, *her affection*, rather than her sex, but what's more that I amazingly walked along beside this young woman for almost an hour in the sifting rain, and condescended to her, discussing fashionable grief-theories and other psychoanalytical simplifications of everyday calamities, some of which I vaguely remember allusions to in the atrocious *Black Spells Magic*, not to mention the execrable *Dead Poets Society*, and even began to pretend to myself, like the infantile and *incorrigible* romantic I am, that perhaps this gesture of friendship, of affection (complete with jesting *vis-à-vis* a possible relationship with her mother!), was somehow better or more appropriate than the gesture of straightforward sexual complicity offered by the Plottie girl (young enough to be my daughter), as if, apart from the easy good conscience that comes from talking sympathetically to another human being about their insoluble troubles, there could possibly be any use to me in the mere affection of a no more than moderately intelligent twenty-one-year-old.

Why haven't I given the girl her tottie-tag as yet? What is wrong with me? Or am I simply hoping that chaste friendship first will eventually lead to more serious sex later? Will lead to Rheims?

Quite suddenly I'm furious with myself. Furious. How could I possibly have imagined that the caress under the table, the blunt message of the hand on the knee, the leaning against me in the drizzle by the floodlit anodyne cathedral, was not infinitely preferable to earnest talk under umbrellas about the nature of grief? Grief. I was offered sex with no frills, for Christ's sake, and turned it down for a discussion of everyday misery, playing kind Uncle Jerry, wise Uncle Jerry, disinterested Uncle Jerry, who might at most amount to a sensible last resort for Mummy. It would have been less absurd, I tell myself, to have joined in with the choral expression of Welsh nationalism led by a man whose features and skin-colour suggested the subcontinent. An Englishman, I tell myself, in France singing a Welsh nationalist song, led by a man whose mother came not from Bangor but Bangalore, would have been less absurd! And if I cannot masturbate over Plottie, I decide, and I can't, because I can't imagine her, then I shall masturbate over someone else. My mind wrenches viciously to Opera-tottie. I rehearse our first meeting at an evening course I gave for high-school teachers: *Echoes of the Greek Classics in Modern English Literature*. A tall, solid woman, handsome legs boldly crossed in the front row. I recall the first smiles of obvious complicity. I remember the difficulty of approaching her at after-course drinkypoos in a busy bar in Via Fatebenesorelle with one particular pain-in-the-butt who just would not go away. Somehow I appreciate that despite a kind of sadness that hangs about her – no, it's *because of that sadness* – she goes. She's *porca*, I tell myself, drinking too much after my mediocre lesson. She wears stockings, not tights, I tell myself. And all the while, as I become outrageously unpleasant with this pain-in-the-butt who just will not leave us alone, who will not understand that I want to make a pass at this woman, here in the bar, now, I'm thinking that the amused awareness of her smile across the table definitely promises *porcheria*, promises filth. As likewise the blonde-brown hair that keeps falling across her face. A lined face, carefully made up, with exactly that bold poignancy of recently lost youth, exactly that shrewdness that recognizes a red carpet when it's rolled out before her. Then her postcard, then my phone-call, then the dinner, the ritual swapping of our sad stories, somewhat tedious, but at least safe in the knowledge that it was definitely *on* – one can listen for a long time to someone's failure to become anything more than an amateur opera singer when the brushing of knees under the table reassures you that some pretty high notes will be struck later on. Then at last the undressing, the slightly thick, softening body squeezed tight in tight underwear, the particularly high waistline of fancy pants, and then my tongue under the flop of the breasts. But no sooner have I started to fist myself seriously over this stuff than I get a very strong image of myself masturbating over her breasts, myself coming over her breasts, and she taking the sperm on her finger and rubbing it on her lips and drawing me down to kiss me. And the reason I get this image is perhaps because this is exactly what we did, only last night to be precise, only about twenty-eight hours ago. Incredibly. Though I haven't thought of it so much as once since then. And the reason I masturbated over her breasts, which is also perhaps the reason why it hasn't so much as crossed my mind since, is that I set up the whole evening, clinically you might say, with the specific intention of doing just that, the specific intention, that is, of repeating what had been done before on one quite mythical occasion with *her*, in her husband's second house in the mountains, if

I remember rightly, when for the first time in my life I masturbated in front of a woman. So that immediately *her* image is now superimposed over Opera-tottie's, though Opera-tottie's expression sticks, a haunting mixture, on a rather pudgy face, of lust and compassion, as if aware that she is acting out a part for me, doing me a service, perhaps, who knows, in order to save me, such missions being something that so often seems to get mixed up with female gratification. This superimposition upsets me. I become conscious of the words I am muttering to myself as I masturbate, the same words that so excited Opera-tottie: I want to smother you in sperm, I want to come on your breasts, in your face, in your mouth, in your hair, I want to drown you in sperm and then fuck you and fuck you and fuck you, etc. And I become conscious, but I was always conscious, it was never out of my mind, that these are words I first spoke with *her*, since before her I had never experienced the liberation of saying such words to any woman. The first time I came on her breasts, in her face, the first time she flicked her tongue in my anus, the first time I flicked my tongue in hers, the first time she finger-fucked my arse while blowing me, and all the words we spoke as we did it all, the wild wild words we spoke, in Italian, in French, in English, and the book we found that claimed that the whole elaborate structure of Greek rhetoric and philosophical dialogue had been built around the art of seduction. How excited that made us. The Athenian obsession, this rather unorthodox book said, that the beloved should concede her or his graces *willingly*, rather than being forced, *had been the driving force behind all dialectic.* What important discoveries we imagined we were making! Behind all persuasion lay the libido. Lay our sex talk. Our shag chat. How superior we were, what initiates, and how we despised a crass world that had forgotten how to love, as the Athenians despised the mental sloth of the Spartans, whose women were merely obliged to submit. And for the first time, here in this Strasbourg hotel room, in the heart of Europe, it comes to me, perhaps prompted by that ridiculous conversation about Nicoletta's grieving mother, that masturbation will always be an expression of bereavement for me. Every sexual fantasy I ever had was fulfilled with her. And so, in a sense, stolen from me. The day seized and lost. There is as much chance, I tell myself, of my concentrating on Opera-tottie or Plaster-cast-tottie as of seeing the moon beside the sun. Over the moon indeed! I cannot masturbate, that is the truth. I cannot masturbate, in the same way I cannot read, in the same way I cannot think, in the same way I cannot talk. Because all of these things are intimately connected with *her*. Yet, I have to masturbate, I have to read, I have to think and above all I have to talk, inside my head and out. I have to be with *her*.

With mindless urgency, in the small hours of the fourth of the fifth, perhaps fatal, not long after my forty-fifth birthday, I catch myself stumbling out of bed and into my trousers. My shirt I left inside my sweater and I pull them on together. I have no idea what I shall do, only that it must bring some resolution. There is still soft chatter from along the corridor, the occasional giggle. Closing my door I'm aware I haven't put my shoes on, my hair is uncombed. I stride with empty determination on a coarse synthetic carpet. And two exquisitely disconnected thoughts cross my mind: that I am the University of Milan's lectors' representative to the Petitions Committee of the European Parliament, instituted to set all wrongs to right, and that Nicoletta's tottie-tag will be Not-So-Sneaky. Or no, Sneaky, for irony. Sneaky-tottie. My mind is in pieces. Each door I pass could be *hers*.

The lobby-cum-lounge opens up at the end of the corridor: armless armchairs scattered about low tables, cut-glass ashtrays under concealed fluorescent light, great windows polished black behind lace curtains. A low ceiling is supported by thin, square white pillars. Wass the difference, girls, comes a voice from the far side, Wass the difference between fear and horror? Tell me that. There are still ten of them perhaps, sprawled over chairs and carpet round a table full of bottles glasses empty packets of eats and fags the far side of a tropical tree that must be fake. Titter and giggles. Under the table, the dog is again licking his genitals. With loving absorption. Fear, Colin begins, fear is . . . Lurching round the tree I see that Plottie is sitting on the Avvocato Malerba's knee. . . . the first time you don't make it the second time. Georg is not there. *She* is not there. While horror is . . . *They* are not there. Immediately, I must know who Georg's room-mate is. Who *her* room-mate is. I couldn't give a damn what Plottie's up to. Are they around or are they in their rooms? I couldn't even masturbate over Plottie. The quiet rhythm of the dog's licking makes a mockery of your attempts to masturbate, I reflect. Are they together, or are they not? Horror is . . . Oh I don't think I can tell 'em this, Colin laughs, perched on the edge of a chair with Tittie-tottie's decidedly grand canyon beside him, and either they have shagged already or have missed out on shagging, perhaps due to difficulties with the experimental Barnaby and the charity-ball party. Jerry, you know this joke. Do you think I can really tell 'em what horror is? *Who are they sharing with?* Why didn't I make a mental note when the rooms were being allotted? Why wasn't it obvious that the Avvocato Malerba came on this trip solely and exclusively to tottie, came because Vikram Griffiths coined that expression The Shag Wagon? No, it was Georg coined that expression. Georg. I am suddenly overwhelmed by the need to know if they are fucking *now*. A matter of absolutely no importance to me. It's vital. I must find out, I must resolve something. All these years and I haven't resolved anything! I am still exactly where I was when I first hit her so long ago. Vikram Griffiths, with his arms round Heike the Dike of all people, is splashing whisky on to the dregs of something else. Wine? Grappa? Jerry, where did you fuck off to? He offers the glass to me. Full. And now I need a cigarette too. Better late than never, he grunts, sucking in catarrh. Or is this the first of the breakfast crowd? He prods his dog with his toe. If I could lick my cock like that I'd never go out of the house. He laughs. You can even hear it, he laughs. *Per favore*, one of the girls says, *per carità*. But suddenly I need a cigarette. Who'll give me a cigarette? The shameless old shagger, Vikram grins, scratching in a sideburn. If fear, Colin repeats – Colin always has that facetiously patronizing tone to his voice, why do they put up with him? Why don't they hit him? – is the first time you don't make it the second time, what do you think horror can be? Heike says she hasn't the slightest idea what he's talking about. Somebody grabs the ashtray just before it falls, but sending stubs flying all the same, while I can already see myself going down the corridor and listening at every door. *I must know.* It's an entirely vivid picture. There are only, what, forty rooms. Fifty. And myself with my ear pressed to the brown-pink-painted door of every one, listening for sighs and squeaks. Listening for her *Mais oui, mais oui!* It's the blatancy of people like the Avvocato Malerba that amazes me. *Mon Dieu! Mon Dieu!* Not unlike the blatancy of a dog who licks his genitals in public. And of course like every awful, inappropriate and above all humiliating action, this image of myself eavesdropping all along the corridor, listening for her *mots sur l'oreiller* at every door, is immediately immensely seductive. The blatancy of a respectable professor on the point of retirement stroking a girl's thigh as she sits on his knee in a hotel lounge. But why not for heaven's sake! Why not? As when I prowled about outside her Verona flat for hours, chain-smoking tipped Gauloises because they reminded me of her. I must have a cigarette. To catch them at it. To know. To confront. *Georg's car was there.* To achieve some resolution. To

176

suffer. I'm sure it was Georg's. And Plottie, first with her hand on my knee, then her arse on his. Why not? Why didn't I take the licence plate to compare it later? Statistics have proved, Vikram is claiming, that people of mixed race shag more and better than their pure-bred counterparts. His laughter is raucous. I cadge a cigarette, having imagined, during what I now see as that masterpiece of self-deception which was my 'recovery', that I had stopped smoking. Do we expect the likes of Plottie to be faithful? What for? I hate cadging cigarettes. Especially from someone you've never spoken to before. A student with red hair. If you have a bad idea, I tell myself, be sure you'll act on it. How could I ever have imagined I'd stopped smoking? *Per l'amore di Dio* tell us! says Tittie-tottie. Tell us what horror is. Red-hair lights my cigarette. Cadging a cigarette, it occurs to me, becomes an image of one's humiliation, of everything one's been reduced to. She's called Serena. But then how could I ever have imagined I'd recovered? Horror, says Vikram Griffiths – would I beat on the door if I found them? Would I be able to restrain myself, would I be able to stop myself from becoming *totally violent*, from seeking to resolve the situation *once and for all*? – horror is a wet afternoon in Swansea with no booze and your girl-friend with the Red Army in. He laughs loud, squeezing an arm round Heike the Dike's shoulders. But it's forced. I suddenly see that now. Vikram Griffiths is morose from hours of drinking. I'm suddenly aware of that. Then I ask myself, could it be that *her* room-mate is Heike and Georg's Vikram? Could it be that these two, Vikram and Heike, are only here in the lounge so late to give the others some time in bed, their own jokey arm-in-armness a sort of comic reflection of the others' embrace? Perhaps they wish they'd gone to sleep hours ago. They're only staying up to do the others a favour. Horror is English Three, says Plottie, when Ermani sets the dictation. Incredibly, I've managed to sit down, rather than set off along the corridor. Incredibly, somebody actually giggled at Plottie's unimaginative remark. How could I ever have wanted to sleep with her? Tubby, dull, silly. The Avvocato Malerba is playing with the beads of her blue necklace. I'm on the floor. She's pushing her fringe back. I've got the whisky in my hand and I'm on the carpet with my first cigarette in weeks between a certain Valeria, small and peppy, tousled black hair, boyish body, and the belligerent Maura, who sat beside Nicoletta, sorry Sneaky-tottie, on the coach, saving her very occasional remarks to further the cause of the moderate Left. Nah, nah, Colin says. I can't tell them. Too adult. Three of the girls are pulling at his clothes and pinching him to get him to finish his joke. You can't just leave a joke hanging in the air! But I've seen him do this trick once before. In a bar in Sesto San Giovanni. No, I can't be responsible for corrupting a group of nice young women, Colin protests. He smoothes his moustache in a pantomime of serious reflection. It was the first night I slept with Psycho-tottie. Which resolved nothing. He finds a Queen's English: You are acquainted with my moral values, I'm sure. Plottie watches from Malerba's knee, though somehow they're not quite together. The truth is I admire their blatancy. My vocation, says Colin, for the preservation of innocence. Comes a shout: *I'll strip off my top if you don't tell us inside one minute!* It's the peppy Valeria. Exactly one minute, she shouts. That'll show him who's innocent! Peals of laughter. Go on then! One minute, she shouts. And counting. Now where were me reading glasses, Vikram Griffiths says. 'orror . . . Colin begins again, again pauses. Sorry, *horror.* Where are your aitches? Mum always used to say. He has a huge teasing grin on his face. Then he whispers something to Tittie-tottie. Laughter. You don't believe me? Valeria stands up. I'm counting. *Cinquantuno, cinquanta,* you don't believe me but I'm going to take my top off, *quarantanove.* Whoo-oo-oo-ooh! Vikram

Griffiths shouts on a rising note. But still obviously morose. Nobody, I suddenly tell myself, sitting on the floor observing the Indian Welshman, pretends to enjoy themselves more than the sullen, the morose, the defeated. Our respective ages were definitely the crucial factor in our affair. I see that now. *Quarantasei*. The girl untucks herself. Clearly tipsy. *Quarantacinque*. Age was the colour of our affair, you might say. *Quarantatre*. Nobody, I tell myself, throws themselves into life more determinedly than the terminally ill. Clearly drunk. How on earth could I have been so blind as to envy Vikram taking two girls under his mac and then singing *Men of Harlech* of all things? *Men of Harlech!* With those ridiculous sideburns. To end up the evening in a drunken embrace with a woman renowned only for her many economically advantageous affairs with women older than herself, and most notably with the appalling Professoressa Bertelli, who gave her her job. A man obliged to keep a dog in order to have someone or something around who will not betray him. *Trentacinque*. Perhaps age is the key to everything, I tell myself, drinking my whisky. The Avvocato Malerba shifts Plottie on his knees to get a better view around the tropical tree. Sixty if he's a day. *Trentadue*. From the carpet below I'm looking up at a solid young butt in jeans and at bitten fingers beginning on bottom blouse buttons. Perhaps none of us are truly ourselves, it occurs to me, but only ourselves at a certain age. Whoo-oo-oo-ooh! shouts Vikram. The dog looks up from his genitalia. We have no identity apart from our age. And now it occurs to me that all day Vikram Griffiths has never been anything but morose. That all day what I took for cheerfulness, for high spirits, was just a vain attempt to defend himself from his melancholy. I see this now. A depression perhaps even greater than my own. Otherwise why would he trail around with a shaggy dog, with a whisky flask? Am I going to listen at the doors or not? They must be fucking. *Ventinove*. Heike the

Dike shakes her head. *Pessimo gusto*, she says, with her heavy German accent, but watching. You imagine somebody is happy, I tell myself, and instead they are choking with despair. You imagine somebody wants to seduce you and instead they want to tell you about their father's cancer. You imagine somebody finds complete fulfilment in you and instead they're completing a mosaic of friendship with someone else. *Ventiquattro*. This kind of thing doesn't happen with dogs, I reflect. *Ventidue*. For example, it would not be beyond *her*, it comes to me (how fertile my mind is when everything is going wrong), first to fuck Georg, now, cordially as ever, in the room with the Modigliani reproduction, and then (*venti*) to fuck Heike, if fuck is the appropriate word, equally cordially, in the room with the Gustav Klimt reproduction. And why not? Why shouldn't people do these things? Why shouldn't my daughter do just whatever she wants? It's her eighteenth birthday tomorrow. Today. Why shouldn't she read trash? And why couldn't I just have gone to sleep without thinking about all this? *Quindici*. Or just got drunk without thinking about all this? *Tredici*. Georg's woman, after all, is crippled with muscular dystrophy. *Undici*. It's quite reasonable for him to want to shag around. Not much point if you've got a bra on, Plottie says, wriggling on the knees of a sixty-year-old who prefers Spinoza to Nietzsche. The mother of his child, as he always describes her. Horror is Berlusconi becoming president for life, says Committed-moderate-left-tottie. Why do I hate the word *committed*? But the peppy Valeria is making that beautiful gesture women have of arching their backs to enable their hands to get up to the bra fastener, so that their tits, and I remember remarking on this to *her* and getting her to do it over and over in front of the mirror of some hotel or other, so that their tits are pushed forward and upward, foregrounded a modern grammarian might say, at precisely the moment nakedness is promised, the sudden give when the fastener is released more dramatic and more exciting than if you had undone it for her. *Nove, otto.* She raises the tone of her voice. The accent is Roman. All this abundance of beauty, I tell myself, watching Peppy-tottie pull her bra out through a sleeve, is somehow more present to me now than it ever was, and more unavailable. *Sei, cinque.* Nothing could better convince me, Colin gloats at the now bra-less girl, that what fragments of innocence remain to this fallen child must be preserved at all costs. I'm afraid I really cannot reveal the end of this joke. Plottie has started to croon strip music. What a prick you are, Heike says in her Austrian accent. I'd never forgive myself, Colin gloats. And will somebody please get that disgusting beast out of here! Tittie-tottie tries to cover his eyes. A skirmish. Though her own must be altogether more impressive. *Quattro, tre.* Peppy has a curious grin on her face, there's a gleam in her eyes. As if removing her shirt were an act of terrorism. I'll do it, she shrieks. You don't believe me, but I will do it. Whoo-oo-OO-*OH!* Thus Vikram Griffiths. Morose. Promptly echoed by his lyric hound.

Then just as she arrives at *uno*, I announce: *Fear is the first time you can't come the second time. Horror is the second time you can't come the first time.* That, ladies and gentlemen, is the joke. So called.

Peppy stops. For Christ's sake! Colin says. Spoil-sport! You miserable bastard, Jerry! Thus Vikram. Peppy waits. What did you say? she asks. Because the girls don't understand. Haven't understood. WHAT! There's a chorus. They're too young to understand. *WHAT!!!* And the same goes, it occurs to me, for my encounter with Sneaky-tottie earlier on. Didn't understand. I drain my whisky as Peppy-tottie hesitates, holding on to the one last button of her blouse. And what I am thinking, as everybody shouts and groans and hisses at me, is that this joke says nothing other than that horror is gasping after lost intensity, that horror is a terrible awareness that the best is past. Too soon. Picasso's lovers are gasping after lost intensity. That much is obvious. The whole Western world, I tell myself, as the room is in uproar, is obsessed with remaining young – thus my immediate thoughts, as Peppy-tottie sits down, groaning, the joke having now been laboriously explained, by Heike the Dike! The whole Western world has attached its identity to falling in love over and over again, marrying over and over again, coming over and over again. Men! Heike shakes her head. As if we were immortal! We are driving ourselves mad – thus my reflections as Colin hurls an empty pack of fags at me, as Vikram Griffiths roars, Let's see the tits anyway! – with our love-making and ogling and orgasms, first, second and third. We are driving ourselves *insane*. Any girl who wants a good result in her exams, roars Vikram Griffiths, shows her tits now! The Avvocato Malerba is going crazy, I reflect, pouring more whisky. Vikram Griffiths is going crazy. I am going *completely* crazy. This coach trip, how could one conclude otherwise, this Shag Wagon, is entirely emblematic of a phenomenon general all over the Western world, I tell myself. We are behaving *entirely inappropriately*. Peppy-tottie hesitates. At least dogs are spared this, I reflect. I'll do it if someone else does, she says. Perhaps this is the difference between animals and ourselves. And while everybody is yelling, Yes!, and Plottie gets up on her plaster-cast pulling off her sweater, gyrating, awkwardly, on her plaster-cast – and her breasts are big – it occurs to me, draining for the second time what is a whole glass of whisky, that the bother of coming a second time is unimaginable now. Who would I ever make that effort with now? To come a second time! Who could I care that much about now, once I had vented or failed to vent my rage? Once I had defined my trap again. Dogs just fuck once, I reflect, then retire replete to the hearthrug. Plottie has got the old hands up her back. She's smiling at me. She's swaying her hips over the plaster-cast. I would never be able to come a second time with her, I tell myself. But I will cadge a second fag, though. At forty-five surely, thus the thoughts crossing my mind as the noise level rises, as Plottie's breasts spring loose in a tight T-shirt, one should have reached the point where one is free from anxieties about coming once or twice. Or three times. Or four. At least at forty-five one might achieve a dog's serenity over such matters. She extracts her bra from a sleeve. The dark hair of unshaved armpits. That's always a wonderful gesture. Unless it's precisely at forty-five, even at forty-three . . . Then I remember that *Georg is forty-three* . . . I'm on my feet. Of course. Georg. Georg is coming a second time. Now. At forty-three. He said he was forty-three. Not the end of the world. *She* was thinking of Georg. Just as Peppy releases the last button, I'm on my feet. In the roaring, the whoops, the shouts of More! of Nice! of *Belle!* of *Brava!* I'm heading for the corridor. I'm already listening at the first door. Georg is forty-three. Why wasn't that obvious? Can't hear anything for the shouts of, Everybody, come on, everybody take your tops off. But how could she mix me up with Georg? Colin goading Tittie-tottie to join in. He wasn't at my level, she said, as if that was supposed to be reassuring. Can't hear anything at the second door. Nothing. Nor at the third. Do I want to hear anything? Then the French proprietor rounding the bottom of the stairs. Furious. Slippers slapping. I turn to him. In his dressing-gown. *Que faites-vous? Silence! On veut dormir!* His shout is a whisper, pushing past me along the corridor to crush the rowdiness. Then a door closing. Turn back. To find, suddenly, here's Georg striding along the corridor with his black executive's weekend bag. Georg, from nowhere, in the corridor. Hurrying, hurriedly dressed, unkempt. Georg! Crisis at home. Thus his explanation. Urgent phone-call. None of his normal *pacato*. Got to rush. Thus his muttered words.

Drowned in a dog's bark. Serious. Crisis. The proprietor and Vikram shouting. Georg shouting. The dog. None of his normal cool. Got to call a taxi. Got to get to the station, to the airport. To Milan. The mother of his child! Which leaves me at two-thirty a.m. the fourth of the fifth stranded along the corridor of a cheap hotel in the heart of Europe, inappropriately dressed, inappropriately occupied. Drunk. Sick. This is faithfulness, I tell myself. Rushing off at two-thirty in the morning, interrupting second orgasm because the mother of your child has phoned, or her mother, *this is faithfulness*. Thus my immediate thoughts. Nothing to do with sex, I tell myself. Could I have stayed with my wife? Shagged around and stayed with my wife? Georg is more faithful than I am! How I envy his caring enough to rush off. But which room did he come out of? Wait to see if *she* emerges? Thus my reaction. My unforgivable reaction. Which room did he come out of? If only I hadn't been distracted by the French proprietor, now hissing and raving at Griffiths. The dog baring his teeth. Wait? The dog growling. The others dispersing to bed. Defending his master. The others escaping the French proprietor, and Vikram Griffiths starting *Men of Harlech*, mockingly. *How you bravely live for glory*. Then fiddling for my key, the sound of a door opening further back. Almost manage not to turn. But . . . out slips a figure. *As they brave the arrow's shower*. Woman's figure. Girl's pretty figure. Pretty white night-dress, pretty brown hair. *Though your men are sick and dying*, Vikram sings. Pouty lips. Veronica. The one he was angling for in the coach. *And your loved ones sad and crying*. But did he really come out of that door? Thus my uncertainty, my envy. *Freedom in the flag is flying*. Giggling at her door. Gazing back along the corridor to the lobby. Final show-down with the proprietor, the dispersal. Calling to Plottie. The girl is. Giggles. Vikram Griffiths still humming, *All the nation with you weeping*. Pulling her in. Plottie allowing the others to shag? Freedom will not die!

The Indian Welshman slams his door. And in my own room the lights flit less often across the great modern masterpiece, across the lovers stranded in their nostalgia for intensity. That's why it's on the beach, of course, with the sea now behind them. I see that now. Such a calm, flat sea. A dead sea. What good fun, says the Avvocato Malerba coming in, closing the door behind him. What a great evening. Terrible news about Georg, says the Avvocato Malerba, shaking his head. Is he the spy? He collects information to discredit us, to tell them Vikram Griffiths offered good exam results for any girl who'd show her tits. Aren't young women such fun, announces the Avvocato Malerba, finally loosening his pompous tie. Blue background, little rings of yellow stars. Europe. Tomorrow. The Petitions Committee. In the bathroom I shake out six tablets of bromazepam and fill the plastic toothglass with tap water.

Part Three

And I sometimes wonder if I ever came
back, from that voyage. For if I see
myself putting to sea, and the long hours
without landfall, I do not see the return,
the tossing on the breakers, and I do not
hear the frail keel grating on the shore.

Samuel Beckett, *Molloy*

CHAPTER TEN

Plato did not believe in the realm of pure forms. That much is clear from any reading of *The Republic*. Nobody saw more plainly than he that the world was a place of change and betrayal, and if he chose to deny that place any ultimate reality and spoke insistently of an ideal, more real realm beyond, it was perhaps his way of expressing his outrage, expressing a mental space, a place of yearning that is in all of us. For things to be still. Like my wife, like the foreign lectors at the University of Milan, like the visionary architects of our United Europe, he longed for the world to declare its final form and be still, or at least for all motion to be neutralized in repetition, in ritual, as the rigidly ordered world of his philosopher-kings must reflect the eternal harmony of the cosmos. He longed for each man to assume his definitive station, forever, each role to be exactly defined and assigned, forever, authority imposed, balance achieved, justice done. Thus Europe. Thus our final home. Our permanent job. The end of conflict. The end of poverty. The end of history. The shape of an apple, defined. The ingredients of an ice-cream, defined. Pure form. Ultimate solidarity in a world where perfected technique will remove all suffering. All wrongs righted. By the effective agency of the Petitions Committee . . .

The entrance to the European Parliament in Strasbourg presents a row of flags commanding a large area of green below and offering a tangent to the curve of a concrete structure behind, which, despite its imposing scale and the monumentality conferred by wide expanses of paving and long flights of shallow steps, might well have drawn its inspiration from a study of the Chambersee Service Station. There is a flaunting of technical know-how in such a building, of mechanical *savoir faire*. A fan of radiating external buttresses supports the whole. Tall panels of glass reveal curves and floors within, ramps and stairs, and, more in general, that combination of polished wood, stone and stuccoed mural which expresses at once power and luxury and ideals. For the themes are those of fraternity, of peace among all men, and the building is circular, of course, so that no nation should feel they have been pushed into a corner, so that the parliamentary hall itself should not display the harsh geometry of the rectangle with its symbolic freight of opposites, its hints, as the Italians like to say, of *muro contro muro*.

The students milled on the grey esplanade taking photographs of each other and of the flags twitched by a damp breeze. It had stopped raining but clouds were constantly forming and breaking in a liquid sky and the light was shattered everywhere by steaming puddles and gleams and sudden sunshine stabbing in the shadows of concrete and glass. The Parliament is isolated from the rest of the town, as well it might be, set apart on an artificial mound in its own abstract space, and the flags, I noticed, through a haze of bromazepam, as the students photographed each other, joking and laughing and standing on one leg, embracing and pulling faces, were studiously arranged in the random abstraction of alphabetical order, this to avoid, one presumes, any offence of hierarchy.

And staring at their bright colours – the Belgian flag, the Danish flag, the German flag (Deutschland), the Irish flag (Eire), the Greek flag (Ellas), the Spanish flag (España), the French flag, the Dutch flag (Holland), the Italian flag, the Luxembourg (ish?) flag, the Portuguese flag, the Union Jack (UK) – it occurred to me how notoriously difficult it is to arrange objects in space without generating meaning. Without causing offence. Since all meaning, so-called, causes offence to somebody, I reflected. As my wife always objected to my objecting to her keeping all the wedding photos so prominently displayed along the piano-top. As I threw a tantrum when I saw *she* had inserted *The Age of the Courtesan* alongside all the books we had read together: Chateaubriand and Sophocles and the *Satyricon* of Petronius. The arrangement of the flags outside this Parliament building must be *entirely meaningless*, I told myself. Otherwise it would give offence. Or rather, any meaning here expressed must lie in the absence of meaning, in the absence of any hierarchy in the relation of these flags the one to the other. Here arrangement must point away from arrangement, I thought through a fog of bromazepam, must point to that ideal of perfect indistinction and equality which can only come, perhaps, in the absence of any real relationship, only exist for people, countries, thousands of miles apart. Or with death, I told myself. The indistinction of death. The cemetery is the only level playing-field, I told myself. Where Chateaubriand and Robespierre and Eulogius Schneider are equal at last. And I recall now, sitting as I am at present in this not unattractive space which forms the *Meditation Room*, so-called, of the European Parliament, that it was looking at the flags, or rather the arrangement of the flags, with the Avvocato Malerba getting himself photographed, by Plottie, in double-breasted suit and European tie, then returning the compliment (close enough to get all the signatures on her plaster-cast braced against a flagpole), and with a general atmosphere amongst students and lectors alike of self-congratulation, and also of awe, as of pilgrims newly arrived at a shrine, it was milling about the esplanade in the damp breeze as we waited for entry passes to be made up so that we could penetrate this shrine, this sanctum, as supplicants, and present our petition to those appointed to set right whatever wrongs had been done to us, that I observed that there was no Welsh flag, for of course Wales does not constitute a nation-state, and I set off to find Vikram Griffiths and to mention this fact to him, in jest. That there was no Welsh flag. That he wasn't properly represented, didn't even turn up, as the Scottish and Irish did, as decorative elements, trophies really, within the British flag, the Union Jack, which anyway Europeans notoriously refer to as English. How could he sing, Freedom in the flag is flying, when there wasn't one? Not to mention the absence of Empire. I looked for Vikram, thinking this was the kind of provocative if banal reflection that might elicit some wit and sparks from a man who claimed to have been the first, perhaps the only, non-white to have been a card-carrying member of Plaid Cymru. Might cheer him up. In the way that old enmities can be heartening, galvanizing, as I myself in my bromazepam haze had felt galvanized earlier this morning seeing the numbers 4/5 on the cheap flap-down calendar in the hotel reception, galvanized (so far as the bromazepam would allow) and somewhat ridiculous for having ever given any importance to something that could hardly be more significant than the arrangement of the flags outside the European Parliament, or indeed any mere arrangement of numbers and letters. But I couldn't find Vikram Griffiths.

The passes appeared. We were shuffled into a long queue in an antechamber with the group in front of us on wheelchairs, paraplegic, and before them a crocodile of schoolchildren come to observe the workings of the Parliament, which today would be debating, a slip of paper said, the standardization of *religious education* across the Community, and above all the vexed question of treatment of *minority religious groupings*, especially where these coincided with *marked ethnic distinctions*. Unless an emergency debate were to be tabled on the total collapse of the Italian Lira (not to mention the Greek Drachma) following the decision of the German Bundesbank, apparently a sovereign institution and thus outside the jurisdiction of the Community and even the German government, so they say, not to lower its interest rates. Or equally an emergency debate might be tabled on the conflict over Community Policy towards Yugoslavia, ex-Yugoslavia, in conflict, in chaos. In particular, huge numbers of children were being killed there. Our queue shuffled behind jerking wheelchairs where disabled people of different, perhaps differing, nationalities kept each other company in pidgin English and in front of them four French teachers tried, but not very hard, to stop twenty ten-year-olds from shrieking. Where was Vikram? I wondered. And what was I going to say in my speech, which according to my watch was only twenty minutes away now? I had prepared nothing. I had thought of nothing. Then in the crush between security doors where only four people could go at once (closing one door before another could be opened), Sneaky-tottie took my arm, as she had done the day before while climbing the stairs of the Chambersee Service Station, or when offering me the refuge of her umbrella under blowing rain, took it, that is, with remarkable confidence and intimacy, as if we had been great friends for years, and remarked with a flush on her face (as though after sex almost), that it really was exhilarating to feel oneself *at the heart of Europe* and to see that Europe wasn't just an idea but a concrete entity. My first reaction to this, between the two security doors, and apart from some quip to reverse the positive connotations of 'concrete', might normally have been to reflect that the existence of this parliamentary building on French soil, doubling up as it does for a similar parliamentary building on Belgian soil (so that once every month twelve articulated lorries, meeting Community Requirements of course, have to set out from Brussels to Strasbourg bringing with them heaps of documents and archives which then have to be trucked back only a week later when the Parliament returns from Strasbourg to Brussels, while at the same time five-hundred-plus rooms, of a certain standard and quality, have to be kept available in both cities for five-hundred-plus MEPs, so-called, not to mention their secretaries and interpreters, and of course two staffs of menials have to be kept in permanent and generous public employ to service these structures, so reminiscent, though on an infinitely larger scale, of the Chambersee Service Station, this in order to enhance the prestige of one *founder member*, France, a favour granted once upon a time in return for the concession to another *founder member*, Germany, of a greater number of Parliamentary seats than might otherwise have been allotted) – the existence, I might normally have said, in response to the innocent and ingenuous Sneaky-tottie, of this parliamentary building hardly inspired enthusiasm in the European ideal. Yet I did not react like this, but merely squeezed the young girl's arm benignly and sexlessly. Her cheeks were so full of colour and excitement. Just as I did not react as I might have reacted when finding, a few moments later in a glossily marbled area where we had been told to assemble around the secretary of a Welsh MEP beneath an announcement in more languages than one would care to count, that *she* was explaining to Doris Rohr and Heike the Dike and Luìs and a small group of students that in the formation of a constitution for a United Europe, such as the one she was drawing up in the hope of a year's scholarship in Brussels (and it crossed my mind that she was saying this because of the presence of the

Welsh MEP's rather attractive blonde secretary, who might prove a useful contact), the key issue was the establishment of those mechanisms which would regulate a genuinely pooled sovereignty. The expression *pooled sovereignty* immediately reminded me of that other execrable but intimately related expression she had once favoured, *negotiable identity*, and then of the time when, on noticing a considerable puddle on the bed of a fourth-floor room in Pensione Porta Genova after an afternoon's epic exertions, I remarked, laughing and embracing her, that that was the only sort of pooled sovereignty that meant anything to me. I was reminded of these things, as I say, on entering the foyer of the European Parliament, and I was irritated, as always, by the shallowness of it all, by her criminal forgetfulness of those moments that had been intense, by the fact that the world had not chosen to stand still at what had appeared to me to be its only moment of true harmony, of *equilibrio interiore*. I was scandalized, I suppose, like Plato, like my wife, by how much and how callously the world could change. *Waterwords*, I suddenly thought, in a haze of bromazepam, in the impressive foyer of the European Parliament, remembering a poem from somewhere. Kallimachos, perhaps. Meleager. I couldn't remember. '*Oaths such as these, waterwords.*' Thus some ancient poet, jilted; thus my extraordinary memory, despite the bromazepam. So that it occurred to me, for example, that I might well remark that on the matter of pooled sovereignty the last word had been spoken some two thousand five hundred years ago by Thucydides in his description of the Athenian alliance. Again that memory, as if all drawn to the surface, pus-like, by a single sore, everything I have ever known brought to focus by a single rancour. Yes, *The weaker states* – I might quote Thucydides on the subject of pooled sovereignty – *because of the general desire to make profits, were content to tolerate being governed by the stronger, while those who won superior power by acquiring capital resources brought the smaller cities under their control.* I might have quoted that, and not inappropriately it seemed to me on a morning when the currency markets are still *in turmoil*, as the radio would have it, over the sovereign decisions of the German Bundesbank, a morning when for some dealers the Italian Lira has to all intents and purposes *ceased to exist.* But I did not. And the reason, I'm aware now, sitting here in the Meditation Room, so-called, hunched forward in what to a casual observer might be supposed to be an attitude of prayer (and what is prayer if not an attitude?), the reason that I did not quote Thucydides, or Meleager, or anybody else, in the foyer of the European Parliament, nor object in any way to *her* reflections on how a new constitution must contribute towards the construction of a European identity, was perhaps partly because I did not believe she would recognize such a quotation, recognize I mean that it had passed between us before, in the days when she always agreed with me, when I always agreed with her, and perhaps partly because, in the daze, the haze, not entirely unpleasant, of last night's bromazepam, still happily smothering any responsible anxiety I might otherwise feel relative to my total impreparation for the two speeches I was supposed to give, one in only twenty minutes' time, I now found that I couldn't care less. I could not care less what *she* or Sneaky-tottie or anybody else said about *Europe.* Whether true or false. And for a moment it even occurred to me that *I might join in.* Why not? That I might myself remark on the need to use a constitution to reinforce those characteristics we Europeans, north south east west, do doubtless have in common, to wit our belief in reason, our belief in progress, our belief in technique as the tool of reason for the promotion of progress, not to mention our post-Christian obsession with charity, with self-sacrificial love (showing solidarity to a man the mother of whose child was in hospital with an incurable disease), our respect for animals, ancient poets and dying languages, our undoubted vocation to solve the problems of the entire world, the planet, the cosmos (substituting ourselves for the loving God we have lost), our unslakeable thirst for the imagined gratitude of those nations (and animals) we shall save – all these creditable characteristics might usefully be reinforced, I could have said, perhaps interrupting Doris Rohr, who was now airing that stale piety about Germans feeling safer from themselves in a United Europe, by a constitution of *immense sophistication* that took into account at every point the need to make decisions collectively, across nations, across religions, across classes, across economic categories, industries, regions, and then across those even deeper divides that separate the old and the young, the sick and the well, that make the old incomprehensible to the young and vice versa, the sick incomprehensible to the well and vice versa, right down to that deepest divide of all that keeps men and their women, women and their men, in a state of *total and mutual and irretrievable incomprehension.* Collective decision-making was the key, I might have said announced proclaimed in the foyer of the European Parliament, and I was suddenly amused to think that should I choose to, I myself, Jeremiah Jerry, as people have frequently called me, could make the bold proposal to use a new European constitution to engage every element of society across the entire continent, wherever its borders might eventually be established, in *the decision-making process* and thus simultaneously and necessarily to render, which is surely the European ideal *par excellence*, every aspect of life *political*, and hence, with patient planning and negotiation, *soluble*, from cross-border immigration to the size of a condom and the quality of a mushroom and the strength of a perfume. As problems in a relationship could also always be solved, dissolved, *she* said, if only two people were *sincere* and thus had all the facts before them to manipulate. But I insisted, on that particular evening, that there had been no problem before she had decided to be sincere. Before she so gratuitously told me of her infidelity. The problem *was her sincerity* — why on earth had she told me? (why had I told my wife?) — her gratuitous sincerity relative to the generosity, so-called, of her friendship towards a man who sent her flowers and phoned insistently, the mother of whose child was dying, slowly, of muscular dystrophy. Her sincerity was mere bragging, I told her that evening. And again this was a time when I hit her, no, when *she asked me to hit her*. Bragging about her sexual escapades, bragging about her sensitivity towards this sufferer, bragging about her confessional vocation. If it makes you feel better, go ahead and hit me, she said. She was naked. Go on, she insisted. She screamed. Hit me! She said it in French. *Frappe-moi!* And when I hit her it was always across the face, the façade. Her generosity! No, when I hit her it was across the mouth, the mouthpiece. How was this kind of sincerity going to help us solve anything? I shouted. I hit her where the words came. The waterwords. I felt desperately ugly, desperately stupid. And breathing deeply, there in the impressive foyer of the European Parliament, breathing out long and slow as if one could simply exhale one's angst with a lungful of air, I almost choked out laughing to think that I was perhaps about to make this bold political statement, in favour of the most comprehensive constitution the world has ever seen. Was I going to make it? After all, and this came home to me with some force, gazing around the smooth surfaces of wood and marble and brushed metal laminates, after all, *You have nothing against Europe*. So you told yourself, with some surprise. You have nothing at all against Europe. It was a surprise for me to realize that. Or such projects in general. You have nothing against the fantasy utopias of *Black Spells Magic*, or the ecology movement, or happy monogamous marriages, or even the United Colours of Benetton. You just happen not to believe in them.

Not to be able to believe in them. It's a detail! A joke. It wouldn't get in anybody else's way. And for a moment I allowed myself to imagine how I might say what I had just thought of saying and how *she* might feel grateful to me for making such a contribution, for applying my intellect, such as it is, to the not inconsiderable problem of *a constitution for a United Europe*, and how she might say, with a bright, intelligent smile, that if I didn't mind she would rather like to introduce my central concept of, what shall we call it? *permanent pan-factional compromise*, into her *preamble*, the preamble to the constitution she hoped would win her the prize of a year's scholarship in Brussels. This she would say loudly in the presence of the Welsh MEP's secretary, who might be useful, if only in bringing her to the attention of the Welsh MEP, who was Vice-president of the influential Petitions Committee. She might even, I told myself, should I actually say what I had thought of saying, and should she then be in a position to get a word in edgeways – the Avvocato Malerba having this minute taken it upon himself to hold forth to all the young students, only two of whom were boys, on the principles that had inspired the original architects of the Community (of whom not the least important, he insisted, was the Italian Alcide De Gasperi) and namely, above all, the desire to eliminate *forever* the threat of armed conflict between our nations, of violence between one European and another, he claimed, which would always be civil war, the Avvocato Malerba said, family violence, he insisted, fratricide, as in Bosnia at this very moment, while the Welsh MEP's secretary (herself from Yorkshire it seemed, a county not without a certain vocation for civil war) was now suggesting that we might follow her towards the *left hemisphere* of the building – yes, had *she* been able to get a word in edgeways in all this group confusion and the general fervour of solidarity that had invaded our coach party upon entering the indubitably impressive, not to say lush, atmosphere of the European Parliament (and if anybody was capable of getting a word in edgeways it was her), she might have wanted to *thank me*, I mean for my idealistic formulation, had I formulated it, and bestowed a smile on me, one of her quick French pouty smiles, a smile which would doubtless have reminded me of so much. But I didn't say it, I did not propose the notion of permanent pan-factional compromise, just as I didn't quote Thucydides. And more than anything else perhaps, my reason for remaining silent, as all the girls now chattered about Europe and we proceeded up a gracefully curved staircase, was that I was looking for Vikram Griffiths. Not because I wanted to remark to him on the absence of the Welsh flag, which in fact I had now forgotten, but simply because I was suddenly intrigued, surprised, disconcerted by his absence, and perhaps because I had begun to nurse a vague fantasy that at the very moment I was to stand up to address the Petitions Committee of the European Parliament I might, with nothing in my head, feign some kind of illness, or even collapse, mental or physical, and, perhaps gasping for breath, choking, invite my colleague Dr Griffiths, doubtless better prepared than myself, to speak in my place.

Where's Vikram? I asked as the actually extremely pleasant Yorkshire blonde secretary of the Welsh MEP was telling Colin that one referred to the European Parliament building, designed as it was, in terms of its *right hemisphere* and its *left hemisphere*. Oh, just like the old brain, Colin says, the old noddle, and he started to make jokes about the left hemisphere controlling what the right side of Europe was doing and the right the left, and then quipping, as he put an arm round Tittie-tottie's waist (and now we were straggling along a curving third-floor corridor padded with green and plastered with posters announcing worthy concerns and complex directives) about this perhaps being why his left hand never knew what his right was up to. Or where it was up. Ho, ho. Biblical, he added, wiping the smile off his face. How's that for a range of reference?

Where's Vikram? I repeated.

Not quite, MEP-secretary-tottie said.

What?

The blonde secretary glanced at Colin with that wry humour of the woman, the quietly beautiful woman, who knows all men are pigs, but is somehow resigned to charming them anyway. It was when giving alms that the right was supposed not to know what the left was doing.

I wasn't doing anyone no 'arm, Colin laughed, pinching Tittie-tottie, who jumped and giggled.

Then when I asked once again, Where was Vikram, perhaps a little louder this time, Barnaby remarked that most probably he had gone on ahead to the office of the Welsh MEP with whom he had been in correspondence about this trip for some months and who had been instrumental in setting up our crucial encounter with the Petitions Committee, upon which, far more than on the meetings with the London *Times* and the Italian Euro MPs, it seemed our future careers must hang. I asked the experimental Irish novelist how his child's throat was and he said, Better thanks, when he'd phoned his wife this morning the antibiotics had begun to take effect, the fever had come down. Had anybody phoned to find out if Georg had got back, I asked then, had he taken the plane or the train or what, but at the same time Dimitra was saying that this was just typical of Griffiths, he'd been voted out as representative but all the same couldn't stop himself from meddling in the affair, sneaking off like this before anybody else to get a first word in with this Welsh MEP who was Vice-president of the Committee and of course in league with Griffiths because they both came from Wales. It was against the spirit, Dimitra said, and she quickened her pace along the padded corridor, of yesterday evening's democratic vote.

But Vikram was not in the Welsh MEP's office. Only the Welsh MEP was in his office, a small, lean, wiry figure with oversize head who did not immediately appreciate who we were. Professionally affable, he sprang to his feet and shook three or four hands vigorously over the polished desk, earnestly demonstrating his goodwill, but perplexed, not knowing who we were, his big head nodding eagerly. Until: Ah, but where's our young man, he demanded, suddenly realizing. What's his name, Griffith, Griffiths. Vic Griffiths. The representative? Who wrote in Welsh. There are one or two things still to clear up.

Vic Griffiths!

The leading members of the group were annoyed. Dimitra was annoyed. *She* was annoyed. Heike was annoyed. By Vikram's absence, by the notion of his presence elsewhere. By our apparent inability to speak to the Welsh MEP without him. What had been discussed in this correspondence? Did anybody know? In Welsh! But I was thinking of that change of name. How it spoke worlds. Of subtlety and insecurity. Of subtlety bred of insecurity. Unless he had merely been staging a surprise. There was a senseless milling on the office carpet. Vikram loved such surprises. The shock of his foreignness. Why wasn't he here? There was a loss of direction. Questions flew. Had any of the students seen Dr Griffiths? Or his dog. On the coach? Outside the building? Yes, he would have been savouring the moment when he introduced himself to the Welsh MEP, I thought. Savouring the disbelief. An Indian who spoke Welsh. People turned away from the MEP to talk. In Italian. They had not seen him. Or his dog. Unless he was afraid, it suddenly occurred to me. He had suddenly lost his nerve. Luìs went to the door to look down the corridor. Afraid the colour of his skin might ruin things. The lectors

huddled together. Might upset this influential man who imagined him pure-bred Welsh. They were nervous. Could he have
gone to talk to some other member of the Committee,
Dimitra wondered, or some member of the press, and all at
once Doris Rohr and Dimitra and even Luìs and Barnaby
Hilson and above all *she* became immensely concerned that
Vikram might in some way be *queering our pitch*, might be off
speaking to others. Vikram who had dreamed up this whole
mad trip himself, researched it, organized it, believed in it, in
an attempt to defend the job, call it that, that paid the rent,
paid the lawyers who represented him in various private
actions, not least the custody case for his seven-year-old
son, Vikram was now suspected of ruining the whole thing,
with his over-enthusiasm, his lack of restraint, his love of
conspiracy. Whereas I wondered if there were any telling,
with our charismatic leader, whether pride in his hybrid destiny, or fear, was uppermost. Was he subject to sudden losses
of nerve? Had anybody noticed if Dr Griffiths was drunk
this morning? someone asked. Had anybody spoken to Dr
Griffiths at all? He was ruining everything. First the shouting
match, Heike said, with the hotel proprietor, in the early
hours, and now this. Doris said, Because he was voted out, no
doubt. Immediately there was a hum of indignation with the
lectors standing at the front, crowded about the Honourable
Owen Rhys's desk, and the students behind spilling out into
the curved corridor of the outer left hemisphere of the
European Parliament, in Strasbourg, France, all asking each
other when they had last seen Vikram Griffiths.

But this was hardly important, Dimitra now suggested to
MEP Rhys in her execrable Greek English. Surely the important thing now was to be on time for our appointment with
the no doubt busy Petitions Committee, and get our case
across to them. This with the implication: Before Vikram has
time to do *untold damage*; though it was clear from the

Honourable Rhys's polite confusion that he had been rather looking forward to meeting his fellow-Welshman. He still hadn't registered the name Vikram. Unless, Colin laughed, there's a young lady missing likewise! Know what I mean? But I was suddenly struck, at that moment, by my sense of distance from it all. Not that he wanted to suggest that Vic Griffiths, he grinned, was notorious, nudge, nudge, but such an eventuality would offer a hint of an explanation, would it not? A *soupçon*, Colin laughed. Why do you feel so distant sometimes, I asked myself, even at moments of drama, and I heard Heike whisper to Luìs that Vikram had made a pass at at least half the women in the group yesterday evening, her lesbian self included. Especially at moments of drama. I was a million miles away. In vain! she laughed. He went to bed with his tail between his legs. Like his dog.

The situation, as students and lectors, having only just arrived in this decidedly executive office, began counting each other to see if one of their number could be imagined to be having sex with another, must have been disconcerting for the Welsh MEP. Marooned behind two metres of polished vice-presidential wood, he must now be aware that the person he had been corresponding with, in Welsh, and to whom he had granted the favour of an audience with the powerful Petitions Committee of the European Community, was actually considered a liability, a drunk and a rake by many of his fellow-petitioners. So that I became distinctly aware, even from the immense distance from which I suddenly found myself obliged to observe events, that the matter should be taken in hand, at once, and that I, as official representative, should immediately step forward to introduce myself to the Welsh MEP as Jeremy Marlowe, the recently elected spokesman of the University of Milan's Foreign Lectors' delegation, and on shaking hands vigorously should engage the man, who was doing his best to be pleasant, though no doubt he had matters more pressing on his plate, in some discussion as to the desirable length of the speech I should give and the desirable tone to adopt with the Committee of which he was so fortunately, for ourselves, and no doubt deservedly, Vice-president. But I did not step forward. Just as previously I hadn't spoken out either for or against the Euro-chat in the foyer. And the reason I didn't was perhaps the bromazepam again and perhaps an intense bewilderment, partially due to the immense sense of distance I was experiencing (so reminiscent of the distance I felt between myself and my wife in recent years), but above all to the fact that at this very moment I heard Doris Rohr suggest that perhaps in the end *it had been Vikram who was the spy*. Perhaps Vikram had always been in league with the authorities to make us look ridiculous. We would claim too much, we would be seen to be greedy, the Petitions Committee would turn down an appeal which the University and Vikram already knew to be legally inadmissible, and they would fire us all. Thus Doris Rohr, muttering, to no one in particular, at just the moment when I should have stepped forward and spoken sensibly to the Honourable, the Right Honourable, is that how they call them here? Owen Rhys. Pure-bred Welsh. Two girls began to shout that Valeria was missing. Valeria being last night's Peppy-tottie. They couldn't find her. Where was she? Colin began to laugh. Didn't want to say I told you so. Perhaps Vikram was the spy, Doris Rohr repeated rather louder. Valeria, who'd flashed her tits. Nothing new under the bum, Colin laughed. But how could Vikram be the spy? I thought. How could anyone even imagine Vikram was the spy? The Welsh MEP had at last been engaged by the Avvocato Malerba in a discussion as to the exact executive powers of the Petitions Committee and in particular the relative areas of jurisdiction of national and Community law. All the same, he must have been aware of a general tittering and muttering *vis-à-vis* the absence of Vic Griffiths and now

Peppy-tottie. He shot a nervous glance at his secretary, who was examining her watch with studied unconcern. You are the official representative, you should take the situation in hand, I told myself, but vaguely, distantly, through a haze of bromazepam. It was irresponsible of you to take so much bromazepam, I told myself. And then to get up at six in the morning and take so much again. It was one thing taking bromazepam at two-thirty a.m., I told myself, to get to sleep, but quite another to get up at six in the morning and take so much again. The secretary pointed at her watch. Totally irresponsible, I told myself. It would have been better not to have slept at all. Or at least not to have slept after six. Doris Rohr was saying something to Barnaby Hilson and Luìs, along the lines of her having always *thought him schizophrenic.* Presumably Vikram. These people, I told myself, though aware that really I should be taking the situation in hand, that really I was behaving irresponsibly, these people, who only yesterday evening were laughing and drinking and joking with Vikram Griffiths, and even following his rolling gait and his dog through the rain in search of a place to get drunk, many of them showing, despite the problems *vis-à-vis* his electability as our official representative, a genuine affection for him, even joining in his singing of *The Green Green Grass of Home* and *Men of Harlech*, these people are now suspecting him of every possible villainy and betrayal. And mental illness. This was irritating. And yet Vikram's behaviour was irritating too. I began to suspect him myself. Could it be that he had proposed me, knowing I would be hopeless and that he would disappear at the last moment leaving all of us to the fate we had amply deserved when we had voted him out? There *was* something schizophrenic about him. My colleagues were right. Even if his Indian Welshness gave every excuse. Betrayal is the norm, I told myself. None of us had the guts to get stuck in politically like Vikram Griffiths did. But perhaps he had lapses. Mental illness is the norm. Not even *she* had the guts, so-called. Vikram Griffiths, I thought, was perhaps the only one who was willing to expose himself, to throw himself into things, *heart and soul*. Because crazy. But likewise equally capable, again because crazy, of stabbing us in the back. Or perhaps because not *so* crazy. He'd called himself Vic Griffiths, after all. And while I did nothing, said nothing, the Welsh MEP was clearly embarrassed by the fact that he knew less about Community law than the Avvocato Malerba did. Much less. The Avvocato Malerba, in dapper suit and Euro-flag tie, was leaning across the desk now speaking in the most extraordinarily clipped and intimidating Italian tones, explaining the complications of Italian labour law in the public sector. If there is one thing Italians love, I thought, it is complications. Could the Petitions Committee, the Avvocato Malerba asked, really be expected to appreciate these nuances? He preferred Spinoza to Nietzsche, I thought. It explained so much. And perhaps Plaster-cast-tottie to both. The blonde secretary explained to some students where the bathrooms were. Colin pulled out a packet of cigarettes, then realized he would have to put them away again. Quite a girl, he was laughing. I take my hat and scarf off. And still nothing clear had been said about my speech, due to take place now in five minutes' time. Our whole expedition, I thought, is foundering on this animosity between Vikram Griffiths and the others, this disorientation brought about by his absence, the absence of the person who arranged everything, the absence of the only appropriate, despite the shock of his colour, interlocutor for the Honourable Owen Rhys, MEP and Vice-president of the powerful Petitions Committee. Or perhaps it's just that he hasn't been able to enter the Parliament building because of his dog, I thought. I suddenly thought. For of course he would be looking forward to the moment when the Honourable Owen Rhys saw the colour of his skin as he greeted the man in Welsh. What warmth and handshaking! Ridiculous to imagine him afraid. As official representative, I thought, you are unfortunately too full of bromazepam to take matters in hand. The whole thing was going to pieces because of a dog. A mongrel. A man's excessive concern for his dog. And although I had never cared even minimally about saving our jobs, and indeed on more than one occasion had expressed the ardent desire to be fired, to have the decision, that is, whether to stay or to go taken peremptorily out of my hands, I now experienced – perhaps it was the bromazepam fading, perhaps that was the problem – a sense of impending disaster, even disgrace, at the thought that everything was going to go wrong and that this would be my, together with the dog's, fault. But perhaps this was inevitable really, I thought, on the fourth of the fifth for a forty-five-year-old man who lived at 45 Porta Ticinese and whose ex-girl-friend's ex-phone number began with 045. I began to look for the numbers in the room, in the Vice-president's office. Certainly everything had gone wrong during that disastrous conversation with my daughter yesterday. Whose birthday it is, I now remembered. Today. I must phone her. But there were no numbers in the Welsh MEP's office, aside from a list of dates indicating when the canteen would be closed for renovation. Not the fourth of the fifth, as it happened. I must phone her as soon as I have a free moment, I thought. Above all, everything had gone wrong *inside my head* from the first moment I set foot on that coach. It was a terrible mistake, I told myself, for you to come on this trip. You knew that. And yet more than ever now, wondering when I would be able to phone my daughter, and what on earth I would say to the Committee, and again whether anything at all of any seriousness was going to pass between *her* and myself, whether anything would be *allowed to happen*, that is, as Barnaby Hilson had so curiously put it, on this farcical trip, I was aware that this was a mistake I was born to make. This was me. This is the kind of thing you do, I told myself. You come on a farcical trip that you don't for one moment believe in, you get yourself voted into a position of power for all the wrong reasons, and then you let everybody down quite miserably. Very nice. I thought: If only Georg were here. Yes, I remember now, sitting head bowed in the Meditation Room of the European Parliament, this obvious and anodyne surrogate for a chapel, embarrassing reminder of our old yearning for some kind of metaphysic, but amorphous, shapeless, to avoid the old contentions, no altar, no cross – I remember very clearly that I began to wish Georg was here. My rival. Georg would have taken matters in hand. Georg has an immense composure, I thought, which he has earned somehow, probably through the business with the mother of his child, her sad illness. In fact, it would be wonderful if Georg could be here now in the Meditation Room with me. It would be a great comfort. There is a strange decency about Georg, I suddenly thought. Despite *The Age of the Courtesan*. I feel ludicrously close to Georg now, here in the Meditation Room, there in the Welsh MEP's office, as I felt ludicrously close to Vikram Griffiths when we stood together at the front of the coach and I told him, he told me, that he didn't give a tinker's shite for Europe if they didn't give him what he wanted. Vikram Griffiths was honest. He had no fine words. Or rather, he had them, of course he did, when he needed them, but recognized them for exactly what they were: words. He recognized that he manipulated words. That he charmed and seduced people. Whereas *she* was now saying to Dimitra how typical this was. As soon as he lost his leading role, he lost interest. What a prima donna! He didn't give a damn about the group, just stayed at the hotel to sleep with whichever scrubber would sleep with him. She said this in Italian, otherwise how would she have communicated with the Greek Dimitra, her French Italian with its overaccented 'r's and underaccented 'l's, but I remember it in English, as I remember everything in English in the end, films, books, horror stories, in that great dubbing process my mind must be. And I remember thinking: These two women are so indignant that they are even forgetting to ingratiate themselves with the Welsh MEP, Owen Rhys, upon whose goodwill so much depends. Unless now they were here they were suddenly nervous. Maybe you should go forward, Barnaby Hilson whispered in my ear, and introduce yourself. Don't you think? You're the official representative. But already the Yorkshire secretary, the demure, amused and I'm beginning to find extremely attractive blonde MEP secretary, was herding us out of the office, to meet our tight schedule. Nice tits, Colin was laughing. Not in your league though. This to Tittie-tottie. Incredible nobody missed them on the coach, I thought.

Halfway back around the left hemisphere, though on the second floor now, Sneaky-tottie again took my arm and this time began to marvel at my not being at all nervous. Are you going to quote them somebody? she asked seriously. Despite her youth, the strong chin gives an impression of strength. I just can't believe Vikram letting us down like this, I told her. The bromazepam was fading. He's the only one has all the facts in the end. He would have been useful.

It then appeared that on the podium there would be the Avvocato Malerba, Dimitra, the Honourable, perhaps Right Honourable, Owen Rhys, and then beside him myself with *her* on my other side. She was to prompt me if I ran into trouble. The bromazepam was more or less gone. In the audience there would be the Petitions Committee and the other lectors and the students.

We filed into an auditorium, a rather large auditorium with rising banks of blue upholstered seats, semicircular in three segments, shelving down to where the polished wood floor emerged like a last stretch of bright sand before the monstrous battleship of an apparently ebony conference table bristling with microphones. The Petitions Committee was late. We filed in and sat down, fussing with the arrangement of the places, each appropriately provided with notepad and pen, mineral-water bottle and sparkling glass upturned on white napkin. The Petitions Committee had got involved in another meeting. An emergency meeting apparently. Looking up as I crossed the polished floor I saw that one upper wall of the amphitheatre was a glass panel with desks behind and head-phoned figures, mostly female, looking down at us. The interpreters, Owen Rhys told me. The nodding of the big head was clearly a default setting. Wonderfully skilled people, he nodded enthusiastically, and I thought: Your speech, which you haven't planned or prepared at all, is to be translated instantly into seven or eight or nine languages for the benefit of the several and single members of the Petitions Committee, who quite rightly cannot be expected to be as proficient in English as in their native tongues. This was per-fectly reasonable. But all at once, waiting for *her* to return from whatever she had suddenly gone to say to the blonde secretary at the back of the auditorium, I became extremely anxious at the thought of this sophisticated and expensive infrastructure being called upon to disseminate a speech which I knew would be worth absolutely nothing in any language. The world is full of fantastic infrastructures, I thought, quite inappropriately, full of extraordinary machinery – telephones faxes E-mail automatic translation radio TV satellites fibre-optic cables – all dedicated to transmitting propagating broadcasting speeches messages that are worth absolutely nothing. What will Philadelphia have to say to New York? I remembered someone having once said when some technological milestone was passed. The sort of quote you read in an encyclopaedia. Vikram Griffiths himself produced one of the most fatuous speeches, I thought, on a luxury coach equipped with an admirable PA system which made it perfectly possible for me, slightly right of centre on the back seat as we sped towards the heart of Europe, to hear every mispronounced, mistakenly inflected, hypocritical word of it. We are overwhelmed by the sophistication of the machinery that propagates our hypocrisy, I thought. Just as our ancient buildings are neutralized, nullified, by the sophisticated technology we have used to clean and illuminate them. The machinery encourages the hypocrisy, I thought. The drivel. Surely Vikram Griffiths would never have spoken such drivel if not into a microphone. Surely the people who speak on our radios and TVs would never utter the idiocies they do if they were not on the radio or TV, if they faced the funeral crowd Pericles faced when he said the last word that ever need be said about democracy and about those who have died in a just cause. What drivel was I myself about to produce, I wondered, into the microphone before me, to have dubbed and transformed into seven or eight or nine languages for the several and sundry members of the Petitions Committee, who still hadn't arrived almost thirty minutes after the appointed time? Amazingly, both the Honourable Rhys and the Avvocato Malerba were showing great interest in Dimitra sandwiched between them, her Greek face a picture of bright cosmetic truculence as she explained to the Honourable Owen about the business of the spy. *The spy!* Then *she* arrived on the other side of me and whispered in my ear, It's to do with Bosnia.

What?

She sat down and I was shocked as always by the numbing effect of her presence, her perfume. Looking away to avoid eye contact, I caught sight of Peppy-tottie among the chattering students. What on earth was I going to say?

Their emergency meeting is to do with Bosnia, she said.

Could Vikram be back? I wondered, determinedly looking away. To save me. Clearly they weren't shagging if Peppy-tottie was around. My eyes scanned the auditorium. Faking a collapse would be no problem at all, I thought. With her beside me it would be no problem at all to appear to be struck down by some kind of stroke or seizure. On the contrary. Then call on Dr Griffiths. Let him do the speech. No, the notion, I suddenly realized, overwhelmed by the effect of her presence, of your calmly asking her for a little guidance, a little help with the opening words of your address, is perfectly crazy. You're not even able to talk to her, to sit next to her. So why on earth did you set up this situation where she was to prompt you, to answer your questions? The only question you will ever be able to ask her, I told myself, is Why? Why? And if she asks you, Why what? God knows what damage you may do. Not a trace of the bromazepam left, I thought. Perhaps that was the problem. If she asks you, Why what? God knows what may happen. You should have taken more bromazepam, I thought. Trembling, I turned my glass over and filled it with water.

So it's fair enough their being late, she was saying. Then she actually leaned across the table and made an announcement into her microphone. The Petitions Committee were late because they were hearing somebody addressing them on Bosnia. Our sufferings could hardly be compared with those of the children of Bosnia, she said into the microphone to the chattering students on the Euro-blue seats of the auditorium. So we were perfectly happy to wait. Looking all around, I was aware that the Honourable Rhys didn't even lift his head as *she* made this announcement, so busy was he with Dimitra's spy. Clearly the emergency meeting was not something he had felt duty-bound to attend. And if Vikram Griffiths wasn't shagging Peppy-tottie, where was he? I wondered. Outside with his dog? The hotel proprietor wouldn't have the creature.

The coach driver likewise. Certainly there was no trace of him here. But now *she* was saying to me that sometimes she felt ashamed.

What?

All the suffering going on there, she was saying. She had a slim black dress on that turned her cleavage to cream. It's so outrageous we haven't done anything to stop it. The perfume was L'Air du Temps. It makes me feel ashamed, she said. Ashamed of my material wealth. My comforts, my easy life. You know. Her ear-rings were the golden scorpions of her birth-sign. Ashamed of being European. You know what I mean? For some reason she was proud of her birth-sign. As she was proud of being French. People are dying, she said, and we're worried about the conditions of our contract. The golden creatures had ruby eyes. People are dying, she insisted, and we're sitting here worrying about our terms of employment. Thus the woman, I thought, determinedly looking away, but still picking up a familiar rattle of bracelets as she pushed back her hair, with whom you had the most intense relationship of all your life. People are suffering, she was saying. It makes you wonder how many of us really have a proper perspective on life. And she said this, it occurs to me now, sitting here in the Meditation Room, so-called, perhaps twenty-four hours afterwards, my body assuming that attitude frequently referred to as an attitude of prayer, though this is not *a place of worship*, head bowed, hands clasped together, though I am not *a believer* – she said this as if I myself, as official representative of the lectors' union, had been somehow responsible for stirring the inappropriate rancours of the threatened but always comfortable lectors, as if she were the only person in the world with the sensibility to appreciate that our suffering, or perhaps she meant my own suffering, was as nothing to that of the *unfortunate children of Bosnia*.

Really we live pretty well. She wears pink lipstick when she dresses in black. I mean in comparison with those kids being slaughtered and starved every day. You know. And she never fails, which is something I love, to have the finger-nails match. I love that. While our institutions – I love that feminine attention to detail, to their own sense of them-selves as objects of beauty – are doing nothing but cast about for a fig-leaf to drape over the shame of their selfish non-intervention. It's outrageous. We go into the Gulf when it's a question of keeping our cars running. But do we bother about the children of Sarajevo? Not at all. It makes me so ashamed.

Thus *her* speech, and probably there was more of it, in French no doubt, though recalled now, by myself, here in the Meditation Room, after all that has happened, in English, following a process not unlike that which my own speech was about to undergo at the hands of seven or eight or nine inter-preters. And I recalled that during the Gulf War we drove out into the hills above Como once and made love in her husband's BMW Series 7.

Maybe you should make some statement to that effect, at the beginning, she said. I mean, to make it clear that we're aware that our own sufferings are nowhere near on the same level. You know. And then it would set the right tone. Because we mustn't come across as shrill or . . .

I had turned to look straight at her. I had turned against my will. I was looking into her eyes. I said how pointless it was to make comparisons.

What?

You can't compare suffering with suffering, I said. Then I realized I was back in the territory of the phone-call to my daughter. Philosophical niceties. It was dangerous to be look-ing in her eyes. To cover my tracks, I casually remarked that Vikram Griffiths, for example, was totally obsessed by the fear of losing his job and being unable to meet his commitments, to maintain his child. He was desperately afraid of losing this key card in the custody case with his manic-depressive first wife. His superior ability to support the child. Vikram could think of nothing else, I said. Vikram was a haunted soul. I had seen that clearly enough yesterday evening. All his high spirits were just so much desperation. To tear his mind away.

But surely you can't . . .

Il faut cultiver notre jardin, I said.

But when I see those children on television, she began, and think how we . . .

I reached under the table, gripped her leg at mid-thigh and dug the nails in fiercely. Her cry was immediate, but immediately stifled. The others were chattering about the spy. Our eyes met. I said there was no discrete unit of measure as far as suffering was concerned.

You're sick, she said.

I hate you.

She laughed her French laugh, of old, tossed her hair. Oh come on, I was only talking about Bosnia.

Precisely, I said. Only.

What do you mean, precisely? Only?

Work it out.

You're shaking, she said.

Then she said I must swallow my pride and go and see someone. She put her hand over mine still on her thigh. And what she meant was an analyst. You've got to make this speech any moment now, she said. For Christ's sake think about that. Think about other people instead of yourself for a change. Our jobs are at stake. Jerry, please. Grow up!

Things should never be compared, I said. It wasn't me had started talking about Bosnia. One lost all sense of things when one compared them, I said. They had to be savoured one by one. And you could only really savour the things that were yours, not other people's. You had to savour them for what they were. Who's looking after Stephanie while you're away? I asked.

If you cultivated your own garden at all, she said, you'd know that she was going to Suzanne after school and then sleeping with her grandparents. Suzanne's so wonderful, she added. You're so lucky to have such a lovely daughter. I can't understand why you don't see each other more often.

Thus the woman for whom I left my wife.

I see her more often than you do, she said.

It's her birthday today, I said. I was totally in love with *her* again. Jealous beyond all comparison.

I know, she said, I gave her a present. Then I asked her what she had given and discovered she had given my daughter underwear. All girls of that age love nice underwear, she said. They love to fantasize themselves. You know? But all I knew was that *she* was wearing stockings and suspender belt. Her tottie-gear. I'd felt them. She said: Suzanne's got such a stunning body. She asked, What did you give her?

I leafed through the three typed pages of the notes she and Georg and Dimitra had put together for the speech I was about to deliver. Then my hand clasped her thigh again. The finger-nails cut right through the silk. They sank into the skin. This time she didn't cry out. The door swung and the Petitions Committee filed in. She gasped, Jerry! And thinking about this now, sitting here in the Meditation Room, when really I should be thinking of other things, and most particularly when I should be asking myself whether there wasn't something I might have done to prevent what was perhaps already happening, it occurs to me how completely she had freed herself from me. To the extent that she could allow herself to play with my violence, my ineptitude. Though at least I hadn't asked her whether there was anything between her and Suzanne. To the extent that later that day she would even be able to suggest we spend one more night together, for old time's sake. When I withdrew my hand, she held on to a finger for a moment.

The Committee filed in. People in their fifties and sixties, men in suits and spectacles, one with a limp, then a token woman of sober elegance. Talking amongst themselves in fragments of various Indo-European languages, they ambled to their seats on the front row, where one took a light-hearted swipe at a fly. Perhaps with a sheaf of papers from Bosnia. The tall man limping was intent on a plastic cup which steamed. Thus the Petitions Committee. Thus my perception of the Petitions Committee, brimming with unpleasant emotions, deprived of all bromazepam, still casting about for Vikram Griffiths, hoping for a saviour.

The Vice-president, who hadn't seen fit, or hadn't been able (because of us?) to attend the emergency meeting on Bosnia, now stood up and introduced us. We were foreign-language lectors from the University of Milan. We were representing both the European lectors at our own university and those at universities all over Italy. It was our contention, the Honourable Owen Rhys said blandly, head nodding with ritual conviction, that, contrary to articles 7 and 48 of the Treaty of Rome, we were being treated differently from Italian citizens. Unfairly, that is. Our case would be presented briefly by Dr Jeremy Marlowe, a British lector who had taught English at the University for over twelve years. After which we would be submitting an official and thoroughly documented petition signed by more than four hundred lectors presently working in various regions of Italy.

It was at this point that it occurred to me that I hadn't seen the petition itself. Not since I signed it. Who has the petition? I whispered to *her* as I stood up to speak. The look on her face, her French face, her razzled face Vikram Griffiths had said, but handsome, was one of alarm. And she actually said,

218

Oo la la! As when once she imagined she heard her husband's car arriving while we were making love in his second or third or fourth house up in the mountains. Above Selva di Val Gardena. But it was only the technician come to prepare the swimming-pool for summer. Now things were far more serious. She closed her eyes theatrically, as one receiving appalling news. From Sarajevo perhaps. From Bihac. Vikram has it, she said. Vikram had the petition itself, the papers and signatures. Then, as I pulled and pushed at my microphone, she was walking round behind me to whisper to Dimitra, who swiftly vacated her seat, so that as I began to speak the Greek woman was already striding swiftly, unpleasantly somehow, up the aisle between two banks of seats with chattering students.

Ladies and gentlemen, I said. Members of the Committee. I spoke softly, shakily, wondering what I would say, but the microphone carried my voice right around the auditorium, magnifying its tremors and nerves, while three or four of those in the front row adjusted their headsets the better to pick up their translations. From the back, on her feet, Heike the Dike smiled with great warmth, great encouragement. Likewise Sneaky-tottie. The door banged and Dimitra had gone. In search of our petition.

Ladies and gentlemen, you have just left a meeting where you have discussed the grave and worsening situation in Bosnia. I coughed. I looked down and looked up. We can hardly claim that our poor problems today can in any way compare with those.

Beneath the desk, I felt a hand lightly caress my thigh as *she* returned to her seat. I breathed deeply, waiting for the words.

No, it would be ridiculous to draw comparisons, I said, between ourselves and that war-torn population. On the other hand, one can hardly ignore the fact that the situation that I shall now briefly describe to you is nothing other than an infinitely milder form of the same thing: the desire by one group, one majority ethnic group, language group, to deny full rights and privileges of citizenship, European citizenship, to another group.

Thus the drivel the microphone drew from me, the interpreters above were interpreting for me. There were knitted brows on the bowed head of the token woman member of the European Petitions Committee as one hand pressed an earpiece of her headset and the other scribbled on a slip of headed paper. Barnaby Hilson nodded approval. And sitting here in the Meditation Room it is perfectly clear to me now that one need only open one's mouth in a public situation and the words will come. You will do what is asked of you. Bromazepam or no bromazepam. Orthodoxy is in the air. That is the truth. In the patterns of speech. The inertia of what you hear around you every day will take you through. Will write your speeches and your books. Will even explain to your wife why you're leaving her. Why hadn't I understood this before? Why had I worried so much about everything I said? Why had I fought so hard, stupidly criticizing the book my daughter gave me (swim with the tide, she had told me), stubbornly refusing to accept that *her* gesture of friendship to Georg was indeed a gesture of human friendship? After all, she did come back to me. Why hadn't I simply said what was required of me? The words that are in the air. The water-words. Some comment on us all belonging to the human race. Under the table *she* touched my leg again.

Then one says, I went on, more confidently now, seeing sombre faces nodding in agreement, one says, 'an infinitely milder form', but the truth is that discrimination, however apparently mild in comparison, is always discrimination, and always ugly, especially when perpetrated along ethnic lines. One population keeping another out. One population denying another the equal right to a job. The loss of one's livelihood, I said to the sombre faces of the Petitions

Committee, the loss of one's vocation – for this is what I am here to talk about – can cause immense suffering, mental and physical, even in situations of apparent well-being, even when the victims do not risk hunger and violence. The woman in particular, I noticed, was taking notes. One of our members, for example, I said, had to return urgently to Milan in the early hours of this morning because the mother of his child had suffered another disabling crisis in her ongoing muscular dystrophy. You can see, I said, how the loss of financial security in such a case could prove disastrous. Not to mention the humiliation, I said, for a man in his forties who loses his ability to care for those close to him. The Committee listened. Another member confessed to me this morning, I invented, that he had not slept for weeks because he was anxious about losing his job, a job he has held and faithfully performed for more than ten years. The only job he really wished to do, he told me. Perversely, I was beginning to enjoy this. The only job he honestly felt he was suitable for, I insisted. I was beginning to feel powerful. His concern being, that since he was living in a foreign country, supporting a family in that country, a family made up of Italians it must be said, it would be far more difficult for him than for a local national to find another form of employment. If not impossible. I paused. I'm referring to one of our group who should have been presenting our case here now, in my place, to the person indeed who organized our petition to the European Parliament, but who in the end felt too nervous even to be present, so much is at stake.

The job of the Committee is to hear about people suffering, I thought. One must impress upon the Petitions Committee that people are suffering. And then identify a guilty perpetrator of that suffering. This was what was in the air, I thought. Not unlike *Black Spells Magic*.

Let us go on to consider, then, I proceeded, marvelling at how easy it all was, the simple though sly injustice that is being perpetrated at our expense, the subtle discrimination that the Italian state is operating to the benefit of Italian citizens and the detriment of those from other areas of the Community, a Community that the Italian government is always and so hypocritically the first to uphold, as it is likewise always and so destructively the first to flout.

There was silence in the audience now, and, I could sense, genuine admiration, not only on the faces of Sneaky and Plottie, but likewise on those of Luìs, whose Spanish pesetas were worth more lire with every moment that passed, and Barnaby Hilson too, and Doris Rohr, who had probably never been more convinced than now that she was a victim of racism. And I remember, here, now, in the Meditation Room, how, as I went on to describe the way we were subject to rules relative to the termination of our employment which no Italian in the state sector was subject to, singled out, that is, for an entirely different and harsher treatment than any other state employee, I remember being overtaken by a sort of exhilaration, a sort of restrained hilarity, as if drunk and dazzled by the facility, the credibility, the power of these words that, though true, in the sense of factually accurate, I nevertheless did not believe in at all, could not believe in, and would never have sunk to speaking save into a microphone and on behalf of my feckless colleagues. Drunk too, and spurred on by *her* frequent, light touches of my leg. Her approbation. Her encouragement. Was it all about to start again? Was it? I was so excited. Then I had just reached the whole delicate question of salary, entirely convinced that I would have no problem at all in making it appear that we lived a life of extreme poverty, and even toying, at the back of my mind, with the idea that I might conclude by quoting, if only to satisfy Sneaky-tottie, Pericles when he says: *As for poverty, no one need be ashamed to admit it: the real shame is in not taking practical measures to escape from it.* Yes, I was seriously considering winding up with this remark, however ludicrously inappropriate, in order to explain, to justify, as it were, our extraordinary and dramatic decision to come to Strasbourg, to present our grievance to the highest authority, insisting, I suddenly realized I might then add, on those principles of *liberté, égalité* and *fraternité* which more than any other lay at the heart of Europe – and certainly everybody was going to say, for I could feel this, what a talented public speaker I was and why had I never offered to be representative in the past? – I was just about to launch into this preposterous conclusion when Dimitra came rushing back into the auditorium.

Dimitra banged through the double doors, almost knocking over the Welsh MEP's secretary. Distraught and tight-lipped, she raced down the shallow steps of banked seats, skipping and stumbling, until finally she threw herself against the battleship table at the front.

Ine foverò, she screamed, her voice only half amplified in the directional mikes. *Aftoktònisse. O trelos! Aftoktònisse, O theotrelos!*

Sobbing for breath, her big breasts pressed and heaving against the desk, Dimitra shouted these words, and others, two or three or four times, apparently not understanding why we didn't understand, until the tall, lean member of the Petitions Committee in the front row hurriedly pulled off his headset and in a heavily accented English demanded, Who has hanged himself? Where?

CHAPTER ELEVEN

Vikram Griffiths lived alone in a dilapidated third-floor apartment in Via Pastrengo. But roomy. Thus I describe to myself my colleague, my acquaintance, sitting here with my bag beside me in the Meditation Room of the European Parliament. He did not die with the lectors' petition pinned to his tweed jacket as this morning's *European* claimed. Nor was the petition signed by more than a thousand names. Pastrengo was a battle, as I recall. Another Napoleonic triumph. Unless that was Marengo. Or both. When I phoned his wife – I think both – she asked was this what the British called a practical joke?

But to say he lived alone is to give the wrong impression. Everybody on the coach returning from Parliament to hotel was eager to rehearse, in lower voices than before, though the driver had not forgotten to turn the radio on, their memories of Vikram Griffiths. And for most these focused around the time they had rejected, or in one or two cases accepted, a pass from him. For the men it was a question of recalling times they'd got blind drunk and he had told his life-story before they fell asleep on his floor. Only two men said Vikram made passes at men as well as women. It is inexplicable, I thought, travelling back to the hotel on the coach, how strong my desire for Georg is. How much I wish that he were here. He made a pass at me last night, *she* said. Most of the women remembered he went quite brutally for the hand up the skirt. And they laughed about it, as if it were a minor and indeed endearing misdemeanour. He'd had a couple of drinks, one student explained. But when had he not had a couple of drinks? And *she* said, If only I had accepted, last night, perhaps none of this would have happened. She had tears in her eyes, speaking to four or five people, and her accent was more French than ever. The 'r's, the 'l's. Why on earth didn't I accept? she said. Because you were fucking Georg, most probably, I thought, before he was called away to the mother of his child. A cordial fuck, I thought. How can I wish so hard that he were here? But I do. I like Georg, it occurs to me now. We were good friends after all, she was saying. What difference would it have made? I should have gone to bed with him, she said, apparently with real remorse at a generous deed undone. Then she said we must make a collection for Vikram's widow and his orphaned child. We must make a collection. Though the two were not connected. She wanted to find a hat or something there and then and make a collection, in the coach on the way back from the Parliament only a couple of hours after the body had been found. It would be important for her to see she had our solidarity, she said, even though they were engaged in acrimonious separation proceedings, even though the second wife had apparently testified on behalf of the first in their bitter child-custody battle. And she actually began collecting money, holding out a small plastic bag of the variety they put cheese and sliced meats in at the supermarket. She began to go up and down the aisle of the coach as it drove around the Strasbourg ring road to our remote and cheap hotel with its cheap reproductions of modern masterpieces. Goya's *Executions* perhaps. You could see into her cleavage when she bent over. *Guernica* even. She knew it. Her black dress was quite short above her slim knees. The poor woman will be frantic, she said. Her heels dug the purple carpet of the aisle. It's the least we can do, she said, bending over Colin with her plastic bag. Everybody was eager to give, as befits people who have lost a friend and leader. But nobody had any currency. What with the collapse of the Lira, the decisions of the Bundesbank. Better to wait till we're back at the University, Barnaby Hilson said. A student asked where the dog was. We should start *a fund*, the Irish novelist said. Certainly the creature wasn't in the coach. Doris Rohr promised to give generously, though she was apparently the only female lector Vikram Griffiths had never made a pass at. He seemed so full of fun last night, Plaster-cast-tottie said. Sitting beside her, the Avvocato Malerba said there were special rules for setting up funds of this kind and he would be glad to sort out the legal side.

No, to say that he lived alone, I reflect, sitting in the tiny Meditation Room of the European Parliament with its thick blue carpet, its disturbing plexiglass mural backlit with neon, its odd white lectern – to say that he lived alone would be as misleading as to say that his first wife was a psychopath. Though he himself liked to use these words. I live alone, he would say, my first wife is a psychopath. He liked their drama. Vikram Griffiths was addicted to drama, I reflect, as he was addicted to drink. And to public meetings. He was addicted, perhaps, to the nervous coercive fervour of drink-inspired drama. His second wife was a witch, he said. And I reflect that it wasn't so much a good decision, on my part, not to return to Milan on the coach with the others, as a *necessary* decision. An *imperative*. You could not have returned on the coach to Milan with the others, I tell myself. It was impossible. You simply could not have climbed up the steps of that modern

226

coach and worked your way down the purple aisle between the blood-red seats to the back. You would have vomited. Barnaby Hilson playing Irish laments on his tin whistle. Or *Men of Harlech* perhaps. Colin recalling what an extraordinary tottie-man Vikram was. At some point you would have vomited. But then by the same token, I reflect, you could not have not come on this trip in the first place. That too was impossible. To climb on the coach and set out for Strasbourg was an imperative, I reflect, just as now *not* to climb on the coach for the return to Milan is an imperative. So there was no merit in my obeying this more recent imperative, I tell myself, in my deciding that I would die, that something inside me would die, if I stepped on that coach for the return journey to Milan, to the University, to the Vikram Griffiths Memorial Fund, if I had to listen to Barnaby Hilson's Irish laments, on a variety of tin whistles, and perhaps some sad cross-reference to the narrative astuteness of the suicide in *Dead Poets Society*. Or to a further discussion of the spy. The spy! Vikram Griffiths didn't live alone, I thought, there on the coach driving back to the hotel for another night with Picasso's lovers. And he certainly didn't kill himself because Robin Williams had urged him to *carpe diem* but his parents wouldn't let him go to drama school. I should never have made that ridiculous speech, I thought. I made a perfectly ridiculous, sublimely hypocritical speech to the Petitions Committee of the European Parliament, a speech worthy of the very best drama school, and I even felt proud of myself, I remembered, and powerful, and *on for it*, and this precisely as Vikram Griffiths was knotting two ties round his thick neck. Beneath his stubborn chin. Vikram Griffiths *carped* the *diem* every day, I thought. He didn't live alone. Almost every day he brought someone back to his dilapidated, unheated apartment rented to him by the husband of an ex-mistress (in her late fifties) who couldn't afford to renovate. Quite apart from the parentheses of his marriages, the safer company of his dog. It was, it is, a beautiful apartment. It has ancient oak beams and the remnants of frescoes, but at the last stage of dilapidation, as only apartments in Milan can be. The only time I visited him there, I remember, after the first wife, before the second, we were drinking beer on sofa cushions and after about half-an-hour a tiny girl he had made no mention of emerged from the bathroom in a robe too long for her. A tiny girlie. Plus the grandmother he boasted paid him to shag her. Money helps you get it up, he boasted, when he'd had a lot to drink. But when had he not had a lot to drink? Though on every issue bar women he was political correctness itself. He was the *révolution permanente* in person, Vikram Griffiths. He would have agreed with *her* about the children of Bosnia, I thought. And here in the Meditation Room beside my packed bag it occurs to me that his decision to kill himself wasn't a decision, perhaps, but, like mine, an imperative. For some reason he had to kill himself, as for some reason I knew that I could not step on that coach and face the journey back to Italy, beside Doris Rohr, or Sneaky-tottie, or beside Colin saying perhaps that Vikram Griffiths should be remembered not just as a tottie-man but as a *tottie-master*. There is no merit in choosing to do something, if the decision is imposed upon you, I tell myself. No merit at all. But on the other hand it is ridiculous at the point I'm at to be worrying about merit. To be constantly judging what I do. Why on earth should I care about accruing merit? After making a speech like that. But now I recall that *she* also said, She couldn't help herself. He phoned so often, she said, and sent so many flowers, how could I refuse? She also claimed the excuse of the imperative. Perhaps there is merit, then, it occurs to me, in the kind of imperatives we impose upon ourselves. But it is ridiculous to hear yourself talking about merit after abandoning your wife and daughter, I tell myself. The Greeks, I reflect, understood

228

these things better than us. Only the gods can be causes. Thus Priam to Helen at the Scaean Gate as Troy fell. Only the gods. Unless it's a question of health, perhaps. Your decision not to go back on the coach, I tell myself, should perhaps be seen as a more *healthy* decision than *hers* to sleep with a man just because he insisted so much, than Helen's to run off with Paris, than Vikram Griffiths' decision to knot two ties around his thick neck beneath his theatrical sideburns. A more healthy imperative. But how can someone who lives in your state of mind talk about health! Someone whose head is a constant fizz of contradictions. It's laughable. You promised not to make comparisons, I remind myself. Comparisons are pernicious, you said. Helen of Troy and Vikram Griffiths! As the coach pulled into the parking-lot of the hotel, I asked Doris Rohr how old exactly Vikram was. She didn't know, but Dimitra in the seat behind said, Forty-five.

Vikram Griffiths didn't live alone. And the numbers were not for me, I thought. Four five. I saw the numbers, but they were for him. Omens were ever deceitful, I thought. The oracles were always a mockery. He told me his life-story one August Bank Holiday, I mean the Italian holiday, Ferragosto, when he came to dinner. That I can use the expression 'came to dinner' indicates that this was the period when I was still with my wife. He brought his little boy, apparently abandoned earlier on in the day in the entrance to his dilapidated *palazzo* by his, as he put it, psychopathic ex-wife, always plunged into the most extreme of depressions by the hot August weather. The boy was about four and disturbingly silent, hugging a fluffy puppy-dog. Perhaps I could at least go to dinner with my wife when I return to Milan, I reflect. The wife was furious about the dog, it seemed, a birthday gift from Vikram. He chuckled. But perhaps I won't return. We spoke on the phone for some reason and he said his present wife was with relatives, he had nothing in the fridge and all the restaurants closed for Ferragosto. Fucking Italy. Fucking hot, he said. We laughed. For a bloke brought up in Merthyr Tydfil. It annoyed him his wife felt she had to visit her parents, he said. I invited him to dinner. He said his mother had died only hours after childbirth and he had always felt guilty. This was in Coventry, where his father had gone to work. She called him Vikram, after her brother, then haemorrhaged and died. Father took him back to Wales. He knew he wasn't guilty, but he had always felt he was. That was a strange state of mind. He felt he bore the mark of Cain, he said, he laughed, and this had to be explained to my wife and to Suzanne, who, being good Catholics, know nothing of the Bible. My wife was visibly embarrassed. He meant his colour, of course. She served the meal she always served when we had guests, an excellent *risotto ai funghi*, and she wouldn't let him smoke. Martino, the son, kept getting up to look on the balcony where my wife had banished the puppy, to stop him dirtying. But that meant closing the big french window. The creature rubbed its nose against the glass. The heat was suffocating. It had been his evangelical aunt, Vikram said, told him he bore the mark of Cain. Always with that nervous tic of clearing his throat, drawing in catarrh. His sainted aunt, he laughed. Suzanne gave Martino a Magicube to play with. That is to say, his father's younger sister. My wife said people could join the dog on the balcony if they wanted to smoke. Dilys still lived with her parents, his grandparents, and it was she who brought him up, Welsh as Welsh, they spoke Welsh, always telling him he bore the mark of Cain. A miserable, plain woman, Vikram laughed. He had thick brown forearms on the table. She was terrified that no one would marry her, he said, she was always in church. And the turning-point in his life had been, he said, when in his early teens Dilys raped him. My wife almost choked up her risotto, appalled of course for what Suzanne was hearing. She makes no attempt to check up on the lesbian literature she reads, I reflect, three or four years on, but she was appalled then at Vikram's confession of a coercive incestuous relationship practised by a woman upon a man. Vikram was by now deep into the second of the four bottles of wine he had brought and he admitted he had only realized this, brought it to consciousness that is, with the help of analysis. Only with the help of analysis, he said, had it dawned on him that his problems began in his incestuous relationship with his religious aunt who always used to say he bore the mark of Cain. Martino took his Magicube to the balcony door to gaze at the dog, but by now Suzanne was totally concentrated on Vikram's story. At this point then Vikram felt guilty not only for his mother's death but likewise for what had happened with his aunt. Since she claimed he had seduced her. For a while she came to his bed every night. This when he was thirteen or fourteen. As he talked on, I also became embarrassed. Like my wife. She cried and made love, he said. I was wishing I had never invited him. How can you respond, I asked myself, to people who start telling you this sort of thing in front of your then fifteen-year-old daughter, your propriety-obsessed wife and a four-year-old boy who may or may not understand everything? Certainly the child was muttering things under his breath through the glass to the dog. But then it was Ferragosto, in Milan, and the weather suffocating. She was good at making love, he said. The dog whined and scratched. The heat was unbearable. Vikram wore a loose T-shirt, the neck open on a froth of black chest hair, cotton shorts above thick knees. I found it impossible, I remember, to meet his eyes. I kept looking down at my risotto, wishing I hadn't invited him. Even if one did feel sorry for him, I thought, it was surely wrong of him to start telling us these things. But then embarrassed as I was, I was also amused by my wife's embarrassment, by her over-protectiveness towards my daughter, who must be exposed to the world, I thought, like the rest of us. Thus my *laisser-faire* attitude, before I began imagining lesbian relationships with *her*. Before analysis, Vikram Griffiths said – we protect people from what we're scared of ourselves, I reflect – before analysis he had always imagined that the most important conditioning factor in his life had been the death of his fiancée in his first postgrad year at Cardiff. It was at this point that I remembered I was supposed to call *her* at eight-thirty. I was supposed to make a phone-call. He had been climbing with his fiancée in the north. Above Dolgellau. The days when one had fiancées, he laughed. His throaty laugh. Such a romantic word. The days when one climbed mountains in mist and rain. How could I leave the room to make that call? I thought. It was almost nine already. The days of Plaid Cymru. And what if *she* called when I didn't? If she called here? He was the only card-carrying member of 'coloured extraction', as they used to say. He shook his head. How could I answer in the sitting room with all the others right there in the kitchen? Anyway she had fallen, Vikram said, and smashed her skull. Suzanne let out a little cry. When he had got down to the rocks her brains were all over the shop. Literally. My wife fussed with some tiramisu. But then the autopsy said there had been signs of a struggle before her falling. Opening the third bottle, Vikram Griffiths was earnest and very nervous. Later I learnt he tells everybody this story as soon as he gets the chance. The autopsy said there were signs she had been pushed, he said. Clearly he was suffering. It was a hard story for him to tell. Clearly he was enjoying his performance. I couldn't look at him. I couldn't meet his eye. He dominated the table entirely. If I didn't call her we wouldn't be able to establish where to meet in Rheims, since she departed early tomorrow, and I was to join her two days later. They said I had killed her because she was pregnant, Vikram said. He spoke in Italian with his strong Welsh accent. Again my wife was appalled. How could anyone just come to dinner and tell us this? On Ferragosto of all days. A national holiday. Suzanne was fascinated. Martino concentrated on his puzzle now, as if the background were no more than television. It was almost nine and still no breath of air had come to relieve the August heat. The door to the balcony being closed against the dog. When I didn't even know she was pregnant, Vikram protested. Of course later, he smiled, I realized that the whole thing had to do with the political situation. You know. The nationalist years. He sucked in catarrh. We were supporting the boyos burning second homes. Suzanne asked him questions. An iron foundry was working to rule, he said, the authorities were out to discredit him, they had paid some doctor. My wife fanned herself vigorously with a table mat. All over the papers, he laughed bitterly, but they never actually charged me. The heat was suffocating. If there'd really been signs of a struggle they would have charged me, Vikram insisted. He personally had never burnt anything. I said I had to go to the toilet and, walking instead to the bedroom, risked calling from there, but her number was engaged. I tried twice. It was what the analyst called a confirming experience, Vikram Griffiths was telling Suzanne on my return, and it occurs to me now that Vikram would have shagged my daughter if he'd had half a chance. The girl in his apartment that day, the young girlie, could well have been a schoolgirl. They were fascinated by his foreignness. Then I realized my wife might have realized I hadn't flushed. Officially I'd been to the toilet, but there'd been no sound of flushing. In the sense, he explained, that it confirmed a paranoia he was unaware of having developed out of earlier traumas he had yet to come to terms with: his mother's death, Father's absence – back in England again – his aunt's saying he bore the mark of Cain, especially after the incest. It confirmed his unconscious belief that the world was against him. Thus Vikram Griffiths at dinner Ferragosto in my house, explaining himself most authoritatively (this, ultimately, was why he had left the UK, he said, plus his disillusionment with Plaid Cymru), while I worried away at a phone-call and an unflushed loo I hadn't pissed in. He felt hopelessly guilty, he said. He had tried to take his life on a number of occasions. Even after he realized it was all a set-up. Even though he knew he was not guilty and that people were merely getting at him because of his political involvement, and perhaps because of his colour. They let you become a member of the group because it was good for their image, their *credentials*, but they didn't really want you. Still, he was proud that his son had his same features, he said. Proud as hell. Vikram sat across the table from myself and Suzanne and poured his heart out, fragile with alcohol, tiramisu on his dark lips, while my wife cleared the dishes and his son beside him, who didn't resemble him at all, battled on with the Magicube, the dog forgotten. He had got all sides but two to come out. In response to Suzanne, Vikram was talking about guilt. He had loved the girl, his fiancée. She fell entirely by accident, he insisted. He was twenty-three. He didn't know she was pregnant, yet he felt terribly *responsible*, terribly *guilty*. He sat across the table staring at us triumphantly in thirty-five-degree heat and swallowed down another glass of something red. Wales had been crushed by the English, he said. It was nothing more than a holiday resort. But at that time, as I've said, I was at the height of my affair with *her*. I was reading the Greeks again. I was soon to depart for Rheims. I was euphoric, omnipotent, despite these minor problems with the phone. I knew I'd get through the next time I tried. And I knew there was no such thing as guilt or responsibility. I didn't feel the least bit guilty for betraying my wife. So I began to explain this vision to Vikram Griffiths, the Greek vision. That only the gods can be causes. Guilt was an invention, I said. Likewise political responsibility. Feelings of guilt were solipsistic, I insisted, quite harshly perhaps. It was arrogant, imagining you had more freedom of action than you had. Really you were in the hands of the gods. Thus my spiel, at that time, based on all that had been said and read in bed with *her*. Suzanne had never heard me talk like this. My wife seemed weary with the whole evening. She fanned herself with a table mat. It was all very well talking about the Greeks, Vikram said, but he had two thousand years of Christianity and English domination to deal with. And most of all he had to deal with his father, who had more or less abandoned him with his grandparents, and his aunt, who had raped him and then made him go to the Congregationalists to pray for forgiveness. He felt hellishly guilty, even when he knew he wasn't. He wasn't guilty for anything of all that had happened. But he felt he was. Suzanne agreed with him. She often felt guilty. No, he felt damned, he said. That was the point. Feeling guilty when you weren't was a way of being damned. In the end I just stood up and made my call directly from the sitting room, counting on my wife not to listen. She was so inattentive to everything I did. How could I ever have imagined she would notice I hadn't flushed? And sitting here in the Meditation Room now, remembering that dinner when Vikram Griffiths told his life-story, and above all remembering how he claimed he bore the mark of Cain, how he felt guilty for his mother's death, his aunt's incest, his pregnant fiancée's death, then his first wife's manic depressions, his present wife's abortions – remembering that evening, it occurs to me what an extraordinary intimacy there was between us at the table that night. And so much tension in the air. We really came together somehow that evening. It was extraordinarily intense: the silent young boy over his Magicube; the puppy scratching at the french window; my wife preparing the dinner she always prepared, generous but grim; Suzanne's eagerness as she rushed forward to meet life, lapping up

Griffiths' tragedies, like the students on the coach lapping up sad love-songs; myself euphoric, blind, stupidly philosophizing, stupidly quoting, wildly confident, as I made my phone-call, my tottie-call as Colin calls them, planned this week away at the very acme of our affair, the high point of my entire life. Go to the Hôtel Racine, she said. It's a five-minute cab-ride from the station. She said it in French, no doubt, though I remember it in English. All the drivers know it, she said. Yes, there was an extraordinary intimacy, I tell myself, between us all that evening. And an impossible distance. Just as on this coach trip to Strasbourg. Between lectors and students. Men and women. Myself and Sneaky. Vikram and Georg. People and dogs. We live in great intimacy, great closeness to each other, and we are worlds apart, I tell myself. She was worlds apart from me that evening she told me to go to the Hôtel Racine. The mosaic of friendship with Georg was already establishing its pattern, already circling in on the cock-piece. He phoned so often, she said. Perhaps it was Georg she was on the phone to when I called from the bedroom. Twice. I wish he were here now. The condition we live in is one of intimacy and distance, I tell myself. Intensity and incoherence. No wonder people believe in spies.

After dinner Suzanne sat at his feet with the puppy on the balcony while he proceeded with the sad story of his first marriage, then his second, already in difficulty, and my wife, perhaps having trouble following his Welsh accent, his mistakes, whether of stress or inflection, or both, in almost every Italian word he spoke, very kindly played by the now open french window with the silent Martino. She found an old Lego set of Suzanne's and they began to build a house together. It was one of those sets – and it's a surprise to me now that I recall this – with pink and primrose bricks and kitchen appliances and sunshades to set out on the terrace. White deck-chairs. Small figures to sit on them who never move, never change. Thinking of Rheims, I accepted a cigarette too. Vikram showed Suzanne a photo he kept of his first fiancée. The only photo he would ever keep of anyone, he said. He was on the whisky now and very near to being out of his head. The puppy buried its nose in Suzanne's jeans. He'd got it off a friend for Martino's birthday, he said, but the first wife refused to keep it. We've got to beat those bastards at the University, he told me. I was in the deck-chair opposite. They're determined to fire us. I laughed, euphoric, pulling on my cigarette, thinking of Rheims. It is from this collision of intimacy and distance, I reflect, that our collective dreams arise. Love affairs, families, Europe. We construct them in the dream of overcoming distances. We imagine we *have* overcome distances. Through these dreams. We *have* constructed something. An *equilibrio*. But she was already receiving flowers from him when she told me to meet her in the Hôtel Racine. The words were waterwords. *Frasi di letto.* The Lira has almost disappeared overnight. We've got to give them hell on every possible front, Vikram was saying. He had the dog on his own lap now and was ruffling its ears. Suzanne laughed and said Dad actually wanted to be fired. Oh, your father's a queer one, Vikram joked, ruffling the puppy's ears. He's a double agent, your father is. By this point almost all the conversation was between these two, while I smoked and watched my wife building a dream house with the young Martino, surprised to see how attractive she could be sometimes, and how kind, a big, kind body down on her knees with a little boy. Vikram was saying that he'd married his first wife because he felt he could help her get over her depressions, then his present wife because she had been pregnant, though she had then got an abortion immediately after they were married. And now again, last month. He couldn't understand why she had got an abortion. Nor why she insisted on visiting her parents every weekend and holiday. I'll have to keep the dog if Paola can't stand it, he said. I love dogs. Mart can see it at my place. Then in response to Suzanne, he said that apart from the fact that this pregnancy reminded him of his first fiancée, he was against abortion. It's called Dafydd, he laughed, turning the puppy upside down, after the Welsh poet Dafydd ap Gwilym. He'd always had a dog as a child. He cleared his throat. Though not an anti-abortionist, of course. He told these stories to everybody, I later discovered. Word for word. Not all of them were true. Now where shall we put the bathroom? I heard my wife saying very gently. Yes, beside the bedrooms, of course. Who said you hadn't got a tongue in your mouth, Martino? You're quite a chatterbox. Between the children's bedroom and the parents'? A very good idea. Her father is a newspaper editor, Vikram laughed. The first wife's. The puppy yowled when he pulled an ear too hard. You should never get pregnant by accident, Vikram Griffiths told my daughter very earnestly, you should always use contraceptives, he insisted. And remembering this now, I can't help but reflect on the remarkable intimacy that was developing between these two, Vikram Griffiths and my daughter, perhaps precisely because of the enormous distance between them. Do we love each other because of the distance between us, the foreignness? Of age and nationality? Of colour? Is it the combination of intimacy and distance that generates such intensity, such longing? Vikram Griffiths would have shagged my young daughter senseless if he'd got half the chance, I tell myself. She'd have been in a bathrobe in his dilapidated apartment, while he spoke on the phone to some other tottie, or to his analyst. Vikram talked a lot about anal sex and about having women piss on him, Colin once told me. In his mouth, apparently. On his pursed lips. He liked women to piss on his lips. Speckled that evening with tiramisu. Yesterday with spittle. Which reminds me of Opera-tottie, of the unanswered message on my answering machine, of Rheims hopelessly revisited. Where are the loving couples? I ask myself in the Meditation Room, so-called, of this important international institution. Where are the happily monogamous marriages, where the flourishing families, where Europe? To be invented, I tell myself. And I appreciate that I invented that speech because of *her*, to please her. I invented the unlikely image of a Jeremy Marlowe polemically engaged in the question of human rights. I was still imagining we might get together again somehow, over the lectors' crisis, over Europe. We would make love again. It's unforgivable the way I just can't leave be, I reflect. At one in the morning Vikram staggered to his feet and drove himself and his young child home. With the puppy-dog. In bed, my wife and I made love and laughed.

I invented the speech to please *her*. Encouraged by the touch of her hand on my leg. Perhaps if allowed to go on I would have introduced the concept of permanent pan-factional compromise. If allowed to go on speaking to the influential Petitions Committee of the European Parliament, and I was certainly planning to go on, I might have discovered some rhetoric to suggest that the whole process of European integration hung on the resolution of the lectors' crisis at the University of Milan, or on my relationship with her. A test case, I could have said. A test case in the application of the collective will to establish a new and more acceptable reality. Then Dimitra came. *O trelos aftoktònisse!* It never occurred to her she was speaking the wrong language. *Aftoktònisse!* Someone had to go and recognize the body. I volunteered. I was still in the buzz of my new authoritative role, my new success. *She* had always wanted me to realize my potential, to become the man she felt I had been born to be. Were we together again? We walked back around the left hemisphere, hurried along by an official in traditional dark suit, the Welsh MEP's Yorkshire blonde secretary quietly padding beside. On the first floor a small crowd had formed by one of the toilets. A doctor held *her* back. Only one, he said. It's upsetting. So she and Nicoletta and Luìs and Barnaby Hilson stood outside talking to journalists while I went in. And it occurs to me now how bizarre Vikram Griffiths' decision was. I would have imagined a man who enjoyed his suffering so much was proof against suicide, a man who had moulded his identity around an accident of birth that made him a minority of one, around his eloquent articulation of the world's endless conspiracy against him, who told his sad life-story with such relish, who discovered himself in his struggles, against the University, against his women, against the English, against God, luring everybody else into embattled complicity, for and against; a man who said, We've got to get the bastards, Jerry boyo, we've got to take our case to Europe. Full of energy, full of determination. In the Shag Wagon! A man safe in the knowledge of the just cause, and likewise of his insatiable appetite for trouble and for women. He should have been proof against suicide, I thought. Unless suicide was the ultimate *mise-en-scène* for his kind of theatre. Suicide was the one way he could become our representative again, and emblematically forever, centre-stage in the European Parliament.

They had taken him out of the cubicle and laid him out on the tiled floor. The face was almost black. The tongue stuck out of the thick lips covered in spittle. The ties he had used were one plain blue, the other striped. The petition was not pinned to his jacket. He wasn't wearing his jacket. But some sheets of paper were stuffed in the front pocket of his trousers, damp with urine. It was Vikram Griffiths, I said. The doctor pulled out the papers – they were damp – perhaps expecting a note. Instead I saw my signature. And *hers* and Georg's. Afraid I would vomit, I asked if that was enough and hurried out, to find *her* briefing the journalists. And what she was doing was repeating the exact words from my speech: that here was a man who hadn't slept for weeks because threatened with firing, his salary reduced, a problematic child-custody case to fight. In a foreign country. This was the person who had had the courage and vision to bring our case to Europe, she said. Our only hope must be that the death would not be in vain, that this suicide, in the heart of Europe, would finally draw attention to the urgency of our position. A fat man with long hair and indeterminate accent asked me for a statement, but I had gone to the phone. And it occurs to me here now, gripping my packed bag in the Meditation Room, that there is nothing worse than hearing someone else repeat one's words, exactly the same. One's waterwords. One's *frasi di letto*. Did I want to be together with her again? I was infatuated. It took me five minutes to get the number from directory enquiries. I remembered her surname was Cenci. I hope this isn't what you English call a practical joke, she said. I only had five francs to explain. There will have to be an autopsy. She wasn't sure if she would come. She hated him, she said. As the final pips went I heard a man's voice shouting in the background.

I explained I'd called his wife. *She* had come over to the booth. You're a fine man, Jerry, she said. Perhaps we are back together, I thought. Certainly she was deeply moved. She spoke emotionally. Her eyes had tears. But suddenly I was thinking how odd it was that we all had just the one child. You know, I told her. We all have one, just the one child, then something goes wrong. Vikram, Georg, you, me. Just one. Martino, Tilman, Stephanie, Suzanne. Then something goes wrong, I said. It seems impossible to have more than one child these days, I told her. I had never thought of this before. She attempted to embrace me, but we had to talk bureaucracy to the doctors and round up the students to get back to the hotel. I must phone my daughter, I thought.

CHAPTER TWELVE

The thing that most terrified the Greeks was that they would
be deceived by the gods. They would receive a message. A
dream, an oracle. Attack now, Agamemnon. Clearly it was a
message. Clearly it came from the gods. But it was the wrong
message. It led to defeat. Or they would be invaded by a
passion. Phaedra's for Hippolytus. Clearly it was an invasion.
Clearly it came from outside, from the gods. But it was the
wrong passion. It led to madness. To suicide. As whole nations
can be led to madness and suicide sometimes, on the back of
the wrong dream, the wrong passion. Thus Bosnia. Thus
Fascism. And sitting here in the Meditation Room, reflecting
on what happened in the aftermath of Vikram Griffiths' suicide, reflecting above all on what finally took place between
myself and *her* on our second night in the heart of Europe,
I'm overwhelmed by the conviction that my passion for her
was always and ever the *wrong* passion. For two-and-a-half
years I lived in a state of *total delusion*. My senses deceived me,
my emotions, my intellect. They deceived me. How can I
explain such a thing? Such an extraordinary mistake. It took
Descartes to deduce that God would not wish to deceive us.

The world must be as it appears to be, the Frenchman deduced, because a perfect God would never wish to deceive us. Nothing has been explicable since.

I came to the European Parliament again this morning to hand in the petition, now re-typed, though still with pages of urine-stained signatures. With nothing to do, I then stumbled across this Meditation Room, this pseudo-chapel, this distant echo of a dead if not quite buried religion whose corpse, like some petrified Atlas, still upholds the ideals on which Europe is built. Though it would be bad taste to mention the word Christianity, as it would be bad taste to have a platform that looked like an altar. One still finds chapels, or pseudo-chapels, in the most unlikely places, I thought, on realizing what the stylized sign must refer to – in conference centres, ships, air-ports – as one still finds oneself afraid in the dark. The Meditation Room is a small space with a blue carpet and soft cushioned benches along two walls. The neon-lit mural along one side resembles nothing more, I thought, entering the room and sitting down on a wall-bench, than some kind of bacterium enormously enlarged beneath a microscope. There are dark-coloured blotches and tangled threads. Some kind of virus. There are no windows in the Meditation Room. I have been here three hours. Ten minutes ago a young man in jeans came in and wiped down the mural, dusted the strange block of perspex and white plastic in the centre. I asked him how often the place was used, but he didn't understand my English and I couldn't be bothered to repeat the question in French. I find it very difficult to speak French these days. The only thing one can meditate on in this Meditation Room, I thought, watching the young man use a sponge on a stick to wipe down the neon-lit mural which shifts from blue to orange to yellow in webs and shadows above bars of neon behind, the only thing one might properly meditate on here, I vaguely thought, is the disappearance of religious art, or perhaps the pressing problem of standardizing religious instruction in schools across the continent. No, the only thing one can meditate on here, I thought, watching the young man flap his duster across the plastic surface – perhaps podium is the word – in the centre of the room, which I now notice has some electrical switches on it, is the disappearance of the cross, the crucifix, the disappearance of any image of the sacred that might genuinely focus the attention. The very amorphousness of this Meditation Room, I thought, this blue carpet, this atrocious neon-lit wall mural, somehow brings to mind the crucifix, *more than its presence.* We only savour something properly when it's gone, I thought. Rather vaguely. In the Meditation Room. Our love. Our religion. And I remembered reading a book once that said how the Australian aborigines didn't even appreciate that the land was sacred to them until it was taken away.

I did not tell the others why I had decided not to return to Milan on the coach. I said I would look after the red-tape to do with Vikram Griffiths' corpse. I made the decision over dinner the evening after his suicide, but there seemed no point in telling the truth. There is generally no point and above all no merit in telling the truth, I reflect. It was pure madness to speak like that to your daughter on the phone. It was madness to tell your wife the truth, to have her understand that that evening after Vikram had gone I was thinking, while we made love, of Rheims, to have her understand that we made love that night because of Rheims. That man's perverse, she said, as we laughed and made love. It was madness for him to tell us all that, the first time I ever meet him. The perversities of the mind are best not discussed, I tell myself. It may even have been, it occurs to me, that your truthful observation to Vikram, in the coach, that he didn't give a damn about Europe triggered some destructive train of thought which ended in his suicide. Who knows? Luìs said we lectors should have dinner together on our own. We should take stock, he said. We should ask ourselves if we could have prevented it, if we were responsible. And in some sort of bistro in the suburbs – four small metal tables pushed together – it was Barnaby Hilson, the Irish novelist, who immediately said that we shouldn't have just voted him out like that. There seemed to be general agreement. I was sitting next to *her*, she had chosen to sit next to me, everything was ambiguous between us, and next to Colin, who shook his head. Vikram was totally wrapped up in this Europe business, Colin said. He took some chewing-gum out of his mouth and folded it in a napkin. We were selfish not to see that. Not to see what a blow it would be. The Avvocato Malerba wasn't there, I noticed, disappeared with Plottie presumably. The wine was red, in two carafes. As Dafydd the dog had likewise disappeared. Dimitra said, We should have looked for some kind of compromise. I mean, let Vikram speak and then Jerry. Jerry was brilliant, Heike said. People smiled at me, wanly. I filled my glass. The waitress brought lamb. But Dimitra said she was the one who had been most determined to get him out. It made her feel terribly guilty now. Perhaps he thought we did it because of his colour, she said. We all felt guilty, Luìs said. We had all failed to notice that he was in real difficulty, Heike said. And sitting beside *her*, wondering at the way *she* and I seemed to be back together somehow, I felt this was true. You in particular spent the whole of last night obsessed with your own personal problems, I thought, while Vikram Griffiths was preparing to kill himself. Which amounts to criminal neglect, I told myself. It was criminal neglect really, Colin was saying. We laughed at him, Luìs said, I spent the whole of yesterday thinking about the exchange rate. Doris Rohr confessed that she had always thought Vikram an insensitive, bullying person, she had never realized how much he must have been suffering. But then the opposite might perfectly well have been true, I reflected,

245

vaguely aware that *her* leg was touching mine beneath the cramped bistro table. Vikram Griffiths, I reflected, might perfectly well have spent the whole of last night obsessed with his own personal problems while I planned my suicide. Nothing could have been more likely, I thought, now acutely aware of that leg. And even assuming you had understood, I told myself, and certainly you had an inkling, you did see how morose he was beneath the apparent razzle, even if you had understood, how could you be expected to help him with such a deep and long-established misery? How could Vikram Griffiths be expected to help you? And why shouldn't Luìs rejoice over the fact that the Lira has plummeted? It is in his interest. Really, in what way, I wondered, wondering if that leg were touching mine on purpose, is it incumbent on each of us to seek out another's misery? Or was it just that the tables were cramped? Do I want anyone to seek out mine? Especially if we can't really do anything to help. Every man is an island, I told myself, sitting at the cramped bistro table, keeping my elbows close to my body. That he is not entire unto himself does not make him part of the main. Terrible, Heike was saying, crushing breadcrumbs with her thumb, I sat on his knee and did nothing but make snide remarks all evening. That is the paradox, I thought, that one is not entire unto oneself, and yet still not a piece of the continent, still not a part of the main. Psychiatry is the least successful of medical disciplines, I thought. Donne's was a false dichotomy. Awful, Barnaby Hilson agreed. You could no more have saved Vikram Griffiths, I told myself, than he could have saved you. Heike said, I always thought of him as just a rampant hetero. You know? The others nodded and drank. Always trying to get his hand up your skirt. And looking up at the altar that is not an altar, here in the Meditation Room, thinking back on last night's dinner, its chorus of *mea culpas*, then last night's embraces, I am suddenly convinced that all this collective

246

guilt with regard to Vikram Griffiths' suicide, with regard to our not having noticed that Vikram Griffiths was suicidal, whatever that might mean, was quite ridiculous, was another piece of theatre, another opportunity for waterwords. One always waits for the bell to toll, it occurs to me, before reflecting that someone was a piece of the continent. When he was missing, Colin said ruefully, I thought he must be off a-shagging. Christ! he said. He clutched some hair in his hands. It is as likely, I reflect now, thinking that any cubic affair in the centre of a quasi-religious space must somehow imply an altar and that every altar implies a crucifix, or a first-born child, or a fatted calf – it is as likely, I reflect, that Vikram Griffiths committed suicide because we voted him out or because I made some disparaging comment to him on the coach, as that the Son of God was put to death because Judas kissed him on the cheek, or because Pontius Pilate washed his hands. We should have tried to get him to stop drinking, Doris Rohr said, rather than just voting him out. The Son of God was looking to die, I reflect. As was Vikram Griffiths. Most probably the idea came to him – the European Parliament, his suicide – and then he just couldn't get it out of his head. He felt destined. The point is, we excluded him, Barnaby said, rather than discussing things with him. Most of us are obsessed with the notion we have some destiny or other. We prefer calamity to routine. We should have put it to him frankly, the Irish novelist said. It is ridiculous, I reflect, the way the Bible invites us to share the guilt of Judas Iscariot and Pontius Pilate, as if they were really responsible. Vikram always got off on referring to himself as damned, on claiming that he bore the mark of Cain. He had the idea, and then it just overwhelmed him. This sense of destiny. If it be your will, Father. He received a message, perhaps he dreamt it, or an intuition, this *mise en scène*, but the wrong message, the wrong intuition. And he just couldn't escape it. Despite the excellent company his dog provided. The cup wouldn't pass. True, we betray with kisses, I tell myself, true, we wash our hands, but that hardly makes us key players. If I kill myself this morning, I tell myself, here in the Meditation Room, so called, *she* would not be responsible. Not even after last night. Perhaps the problem, Luìs said, very earnestly, was that we didn't explain what we valued in him, and what we did not value. No, especially not after last night, I reflect. We gave him the impression we didn't value him at all, Luìs said. The prime movers are these intuitions, these passions, I tell myself, and for some reason I find this an immensely clarifying reflection. Even if it doesn't quite solve anything. We pretty well washed our hands of him, Luìs said. Dimitra hid her face in her hands and began to cry. She would keep the dog if it was found, she said. Then, sitting next to me, *she* said, Oh, if only I'd at least kissed him when he asked me to. For God's sake! If I'd given him a bit of a cuddle. But this was the last straw. Her leg was definitely pressing against mine. I spoke more loudly than I need have:

You didn't kiss him because you didn't want to, I announced. You don't have to have sex with people to stop them committing suicide. And then you didn't kiss him because you spent most of the evening screwing Georg.

I had spoken rather more loudly than I need have. Perhaps it was the wine, perhaps the effect of having her knee against my thigh as she expressed remorse for not having cuddled Vikram Griffiths.

Were you screwing Georg because he would have committed suicide if you'd refused? I demanded, far more loudly than I need have. Because the mother of his child was dying again? The situation around the four small bistro tables was cramped and intimate.

Would you fuck me, I demanded, if you believed I would commit suicide if you didn't?

Colin said, Jerry, please.

Vikram was just one of life's victims, I announced, setting down my knife and fork beside the lamb. He was a victim of circumstance and his own psychology. There will always be people like that, I said very loudly. None of us could have helped him, I said. I pushed my chair back. His analyst didn't help him at all, I said. Just gave him fancy explanations for his state of mind. Vikram Griffiths was on another planet, I said. You all heard him tell his life-story. He was looking to be voted out, I told the party at the four small bistro tables. Otherwise why would he have been drinking so much at ten in the morning? Why did he need to trail his dog around everywhere? I stood up. It's absurd our baring our hearts like this. Vikram was mad, I said. Likeable, but mad. I liked him, I said, but he was crazy. I walked out. And walking out I was acutely aware that I had been describing myself. You too, I thought, are in a vicious circle of psychology and circumstance. I had described myself perfectly. You too are beyond their help, I told myself. Vikram Griffiths' death was your own future death, I thought. Perhaps. Perhaps he did kill his fiancée, I thought. After all, I could hardly believe I'd hit *her* sometimes. Vikram Griffiths was more likeable than myself, though. More the clown. More charismatic. And I told myself, *You must change.* If the world has changed, if *she* has changed, then you must change too. *You must not go back on the coach*, I told myself. That would be fatal. You must not go back to Milan with them.

She was calling my name. The night was blowy, but not raining. Dark. I was walking at random. She caught up with me. Her arms round me. Her cheek against mine. I wasn't with Georg last night, she said. She started to kiss me. She would never have gone with Georg last night. I asked why not. Spend the night with me, she said, and I'll explain. Please, she said. I thought: The Rheims routine. I'll explain,

249

she laughed. She insisted, Of course I wasn't with Georg last night. How could you think that? I notice at least you're admitting you have been with him, I said. This conversation in French perhaps, perhaps in Italian, though I remember it here in the Meditation Room in English. When we kiss, it is so wonderful, I thought, and yet my resistance is enormous. Why wouldn't you go with him again? I said. After all, it's none of my business. Or Vikram's. However suicidal we may be. For old times' sake, she said, spend the night with me. I'll explain. Something's happened. All this on some blowy suburban street in Strasbourg, France. Very little recollection of the surroundings. We can find another hotel, she said. You are not going back to Milan on that coach, I told myself. She had a smart velvet jacket, the black dress, the soft glow of her neck and cleavage. I love a woman who loves to be a woman. To *play* the woman, I thought. I love the things that are dangerous about her. And there was the smell of her breath and the old old cocktail of scent and skin. For old times' sake, Jerry, she said. Watching pornography, when the knickers come down, Colin invariably says, I can already see my bald spot. Please let's not let it end so badly. She pulled me into a kiss again. And what he means is, between those legs. Rheims. Please. I can already see my bald spot, he says. He laughs. All whoring surfs on an undertow of melancholy, I thought. On memories of Rheims. We found another hotel. Exactly similar to our own. Small modern rooms with over-size beds. But spared the reproductions of the great painters of our time. Spared Picasso. Mass-produced. Spared Klimt. She showered. Tell me first, I demanded. Why are you doing this? Because I like you. It was you left me, she said. Retrospective jealousy is mad, she told me. Tell me about Georg, about something's having happened, I said. Tell me first. I showered. She spoke again about not wanting it to end badly. Which were more words taken from myself. My phone-calls, my attempts to arrange happy valedictories that were really new beginnings. But everything is taken from somewhere else, I thought. Tell me, I demanded, between kisses. If you must, she said. It was you said something had happened, I said. Otherwise I wouldn't be here. She broke off. Pulling herself back to sit against the pillows, she fished for her handbag, lit a cigarette, looked at me down its narrow length, inhaled, exhaled. So theatrically, I thought. The big dark eyes. So naturally theatrical. Whereas I just don't seem able. Except that speech perhaps. What a theatrical gesture it was on Vikram's part, I thought, to hang himself in the European Parliament. He saw the *mise en scène* and then just couldn't get it out of his mind. A sense of destiny. I've made a sensible decision, she said, leaning back on the pillows. I also took a cigarette, and here in the Meditation Room it occurs to me now that one sign of when things have truly changed, when I will have truly changed, will be when I stop taking other people's cigarettes. For taking it I saw myself taking cigarettes on a thousand other occasions. From drinking companions, from tottie. Whereas before I met *her* I hadn't smoked for years. I hadn't smoked for years before we became lovers. Smoking reminds me of her, that's the truth. Smoking reminds me of my addiction to her. I must stop taking cigarettes, I thought. She was naked against the pillows. I've decided to go back to my husband, she said. I want to have another child. Before it's too late. It's the sensible thing to do. Emotionally and economically. Sometimes I can't understand why we ever split up.

You said you hated him, I reminded her. You said he was a dick. You said money took up too much space in his life for there to be any room for you. You laughed at him. You said he was crass, stupid. You said he had no culture whatsoever. You said the only reason you married him was because you were still young enough to be over-awed by fast cars and business suits. You said living with him was hell.

She said I had said much the same sort of things about my wife, but both of us knew deep down that I loved my wife and should never have left her. Especially having Suzanne. Suzanne's so wonderful, she said. And I have Stephanie. It's good for her to be with her father.

And that was the reason why you couldn't have been with Georg last night? Because you're back with your husband.

She nodded.

But you can with me?

It's different with you, Jerry.

I put on my clothes and left. As I dressed she was saying, For Christ's sake of course it was different with me. There was no need to go to bed with Georg again. Because that had just been fun. Just creature comfort. There had been no hard feelings. But she wanted to take this opportunity to sign off happily with me. I stubbed out my cigarette and found my socks. Don't be such a baby, she shouted. Georg had loads of women, she said. She wanted to clear things up. You know I love you, she said. I want you, I don't want things to be so unpleasant. And she wanted to tell me to go back to my wife. You really ought to go back to your wife, she said. We could still see each other if we felt like it. We could still go to bed even, occasionally. Why not? She's fucking you to tell you to go back to your wife, I thought. I put on my shoes. Hit me, if you must, she shouted. She got up and tried to grab my arm. *Frappe-moi!* I dressed and left. Nor would I go back to Milan on the coach with them. I found the stairs. Nor would I take any more cigarettes. I crossed the lobby, pushed through the swing doors and caught a taxi someone else had just got out of. It hadn't meant anything, I thought. The words 'in vain' came to mind, sitting in the dark at traffic-lights. The taxi-driver drummed on his wheel. Who had used them? She did. About Vikram. She was going back to her husband, I thought in the back of the taxi. *To her husband.* All the words spoken over all those months, years of love-making had been entirely in vain. Thucydides and Benjamin Constant and Chateaubriand and Plato, all entirely in vain. My husband is so crass, she used to say, so ignorant. Rheims, in vain. Pensione Porta Genova, in vain. A thousand phone-calls. She was going back to her husband. *As if nothing had ever happened.* Something's happened, she said. She was always telling me I had to make something happen in my life. I've taken a sensible decision. But what she meant was that nothing had happened, ever. Nothing has happened, she said immediately before I hit her the first time. That was the turning-point. What difference does it make if I went to bed with him? she said. Nothing has really happened. My mind darkened and I hit her. And the moment I hit her I was lost. Turn round, I told the taxi-driver. I'll show her what it means to say something's happened, I thought. *Retournez.* Go back. This morning in the foyer of the European Parliament, I bought a copy of *The European.* The headlines were deaths in Bosnia, the decisions of the Bundesbank, the collapse of the Lira, but on the inside pages it told how Indian Welshman Vikram Griffiths, feckless fragment of British Empire, hanged himself in the lavatories of this very building with a petition pinned to his tweed jacket. And it said: After this tragedy, the Italian Government will have to introduce measures to resolve the position of fifteen hundred European nationals who continue to live in conditions of the utmost precariousness. Assuming it does so, and assuming this brings to light the urgency of such cases in other countries, then perhaps this death will not have been entirely in vain. It was then, in a daze, with nothing in the world to do, that I saw the stylized plastic sign that indicated this Meditation Room, this pseudo-chapel, with its polished quiet, its indifferently dusted redundancy, as if waiting for someone to need it, perhaps with a copy of *The European* in his hand, perhaps with the words 'in vain' ringing in his mind, her words, her briefing, as I looked over Vikram Griffiths' body on the tiled floor of the institutional toilet. The relationship that entirely changed, destroyed your life, was just a brief hiatus in hers, I thought in the taxi, a brief parenthesis in her marriage to a successful Italian businessman with a small factory producing picture mouldings, perhaps of the very variety that frame mass-produced reproductions of modern masterpieces in cheap hotels. She laughed when we read the *Odyssey*. I'd forgotten Helen went back to Menelaus, she said. That's so bizarre, isn't it? After ten years and all the deaths. *As if nothing had happened at all*. She laughed her very light, very French laugh. *Retournez*, I told the cab-driver. I'll make something happen. Vikram Griffiths' suicide has nothing at all to do with the lectors' crisis, I thought, reading *The European* when I first stumbled into the Meditation Room. And it could not be in vain because all it was intended to do was to *stop* the voice in his head. No other results were intended. I will stop this somehow, I thought, as I stumbled back into the lobby of the hotel, having paid the driver fifty francs to bring me back to where I'd started. Making sure not to glance at the proprietor speaking on the telephone, I headed for the stairs, so as not to have to wait for the lift. Narrow stairs. I was aware that I could not remember which room it was. Which number. The proprietor had given the key to her. I had been in such a daze of scent and skin. I knew it was on the fourth floor. Four panting floors of narrow, carpeted stairs. I am doing something at last, I thought. *I am doing something I don't want to do*. But did Vikram really want to kill himself? And sitting here in the Meditation Room, as I have been for three hours now, bowed forward in this attitude so close to prayer, without quite being prayer, as this place is so close to being a chapel, without quite achieving that, going over and over the events of the last two days, as if at some point I might ever be satisfied that they had been explained, going over and over these events, and in particular going over this moment when I started to run up the stairs to the fourth floor of that hotel, not even knowing the number of the room, but knowing that once there I would find it, the last red door on the right, and above all remembering how I told myself, *You are doing something that you do not want to do,* but madly determined just the same, as Vikram Griffiths perhaps had been madly determined to do something he would rather not have done, in the Meditation Room here with its quiet vocation, however anachronistic, for offering refuge (I could no more go back to the church than I could go back to my wife, I reflect), in the Meditation Room, remembering the charge up the second flight of stairs, the third, remembering the voice whispering, exulting, *You are doing something you don't want to do,* it occurs to me now that half of philosophy hangs on this, on this wondering why we did what we did, why we did what we clearly did not mean to do. Myself, Vikram Griffiths. Why hadn't I said okay two years ago, when she obviously did want to come back to me, when Georg proved *not at her level in bed*? Why didn't I accept her offer last night of a return to my wife with continued affair? God knows it's a scenario I have fantasized often enough. My home, my mistress. Everyone happy. I scrambled up the fourth flight. Had something chemical changed in me? Is that possible? That disillusionment brought about a chemical change in me, making it impossible for me to accept what she had done? Last door on the right, I told myself. Responsibility is a myth, I reflect, sitting here in the Meditation Room. Illusions lost, an enzyme slips. You find yourself charging up four flights of stairs in the heart of Europe, determined to do something you don't want to do, determined to beat some sense into life. There is no alternative, I thought, perhaps as Vikram Griffiths did. But I had stopped in the corridor. The carpet was crimson. The impetus wavered. Perhaps another, deeper chemistry orders you to consider yourself responsible, I reflect, here in the Meditation Room. Perhaps this is what obsession means. Two chemistries at loggerheads. Two conflicting processes. A negative fizz of implacably opposed substances. Thus my mind, here in the Meditation Room, there in the crimson corridor of a hotel whose name I didn't know, approaching a room whose number I didn't know, overwhelmed by the notion that all had been in vain, that for her nothing had happened, as mythical figures go back to their husbands after ten years of atrocities and sit happily together at table, in Sparta, in Milan, welcoming guests and telling stories. *I would make something happen.* Thus my mind, bent on doing something I didn't want to do, yet still aware that I would be responsible, that I would feel responsible. I would *want* to be responsible. We seek responsibility even where it is denied to us, I tell myself in the Meditation Room of the European Parliament. Why else the crucifix that somehow presides here despite its absence, why else the *mea culpas* over Vikram Griffiths, the endless pictures of Rwanda, the self-flagellation over Bosnia? We establish elaborate machineries *as if we were responsible*, I tell myself. Why else the European Community? Our mental processes are interminably engaged in weighing up our responsibilities. This is no bad thing, I thought. I started to walk along the corridor. I walked with one hand steadying myself against the wall. It is no bad thing to imagine oneself responsible. Yet when the mind darkens, I reflect, when the hand lifts, when the fever of that chemistry is upon us . . . My hand reached a door frame and I noticed the number. Forty-one. How could I not have fallen in love with her, invented my love for her? Forty-two. How could the structure of marriage hold? I began to walk more quickly. One might as well resist a flood, I told myself. Responsible or not. Forty-three. My dreams were all of seas and floods in that period, I reflect. I remember that. I attributed it to Jung. Ground giving under foot and animals tossed on the surf. People have the dreams they read about, I reflect. That fatuous period when I imagined myself an interesting subject for analysis. Forty-four. The European Community would be helpless against such a passion, I tell myself. When the mind darkens and the hand lifts it will be pointless to talk about negotiated identity and pooled sovereignty. We don't plan to do what we do, I tell myself, here in the Meditation Room with no idea where I shall go when finally I get to my feet. When will I get to my feet? I have been here four hours. No political solution could have stopped Vikram Griffiths from killing himself, I reflect. I saw the room number was 45. What message could be clearer than that? Even if it was the wrong message. Vikram's age a red herring. Our passion was always the wrong passion, I told myself. That's clear now. The handle turned. All that remained was to end it. The door was unlocked, as I had left it. 45. Determinedly I pushed. She wasn't there. I looked in the bathroom. There was nothing of hers in the room. But then we had brought nothing. I lay on the bed. She would come back. Ten minutes, half an hour. If she had checked out, the proprietor would never have allowed me to come up. An hour. At least there were no modern masterpieces in the room. Nietzsche went mad at forty-five, I thought. Whereas *she* was serenity itself. Our passion has left no mark on her. She has gone back to her husband. I could no more go back to my wife, I reflect, than I could go back to the church. Or live in the natural state, swinging from tree to tree. Footsteps approached along the corridor, I stiffened. She never left the church, throughout our long adultery. They slowed down. Perhaps she never really left her husband. They stopped. This was her. But it wasn't her. There were keys in the door across the passage. Perhaps she wasn't coming back, I thought. Suddenly I felt relieved. Perhaps she isn't coming back.

Suddenly, very slightly, the chemistry shifted. I should call my daughter, I thought. I felt a growing sense of relief. It's her birthday. And I actually began to dial. Until it occurred to me that my daughter would be enjoying her eighteenth birthday party, a big party, taking place in my no doubt much-censured absence. And I did not want to spoil my daughter's coming-of-age party with stories of suicide and unhappy passion. God knows how my voice would sound. Let Suzanne have a happy birthday party, I thought, wondering should I stay here, in this hotel room, or should I go? Wondering why I had come. Perhaps I should have made love to her and enjoyed it, I thought. Why do you never do the sensible, practical thing? Had she left and paid? In which case why had the proprietor allowed me to cross the lobby and set off up the stairs? Why was the room unlocked? I turned on the TV. The mind produces its own tranquillizing effect sometimes. I got into bed with the remote control. The mind decides when you've had enough. I found a football match. It grants a lull. Watch football, I told myself. You always loved football, and as always I began to root for the losing team. There were two beers in the small fridge. You swore you would never use physical violence, and then you hit her, I told myself, watching some-one from my own team being sent off. Paris St Germain nil, Bayern Munich one. Yet what could have been more creditable than my good intentions? What could be nobler than the project of a United Europe, I thought, watching players exchange insults? Had she managed to leave without checking out? What more splendid than the dream of a perfect love? The referee was pushing someone in the chest. Even if you don't believe in such things. I opened the second can of beer. Did I have enough to pay? Would they take my credit card? Was I creditworthy? You have no better religion to offer than Christianity, I thought. A man made the sign of the cross as he stood up to take a penalty. You would never wish for Rheims

258

not to have been. The European Cup. Perhaps one should subscribe to such things, even in scepticism, I thought. We should enchant ourselves with such things. Thus Socrates, on myth. As I recall. *We should enchant ourselves even in scepticism.* And I remembered the students dancing together in the main square by the floodlit façade of the cathedral, singing *Sei un mito, sei un mito,* You're a myth, you're a myth. I saw Sneaky-Niki's face. Tittie-tottie's face. The extraordinary promise that men and women hold out for each other, I told myself, is the opportunity for inventing a myth together. For enchanting ourselves, reciprocally. All invented and all dissolved, I said out loud with remarkable equanimity, and remarkably I fell asleep in front of the television, to be woken eight hours later by the sound of jets over Bosnia. Perhaps three seconds passed, waking in this strange hotel room to the sound of the TV, three passable seconds, before the nightmare returned like a hammer, it returned like a flood, it returned like the roar of aero-engines sudden over the brow of a hill. It filled my whole mind. *She has gone back to her husband.* The whole thing, my whole life, was a farce from beginning to end.

You must phone your daughter, I thought, standing up quite suddenly from my seat in the Meditation Room. One sits down for hours, I reflect, and then inexplicably one stands up, without having decided to stand up. My time in the Meditation Room was over. The coach would be somewhere round Geneva by now. You were very lucky last night, I thought. Last night could have gone a great deal worse than it did. I phoned from the foyer of the Parliament. She answered immediately. I apologized for not having phoned on her birthday. Not to worry. She spoke in her childish English, which is so endearing. We missed you at the party. Something terrible happened, I said. And I explained that Vikram Griffiths had killed himself. Vikram Griffiths, I repeated. He hanged himself. You remember he came to dinner once, ages back. There was a long silence at the other end of the phone. I watched a franc slip by. Our phone-calls can be measured in any currency, I thought. It was a very long silence and, afraid somehow I might not be believed, I started to say how awful it was and how it had put it quite out of my mind that it was her birthday. I had forgotten to call. Everybody had been so upset. There were so many practical arrangements to make. Especially seeing that the wife didn't want to come and handle it herself. They were divorcing, I explained. But now I realized that my daughter was speaking. I saw him last week, she said. She spoke in Italian. Her voice was choking with shock. Standing in the foyer of the European Parliament with its expensive polished woods and marbles, its news-stand, its messages of solidarity, I jammed the receiver to my ear. What? I often used to see him, she said. She could barely get the words out. Baby-sitting Stephanie. He used to drop by. With Dafydd. Or in the Tre Arche. She named a bar. I can't believe it, she said. There was another long pause. She was fighting back tears. He was so funny. He always cheered me up. Oh, I can't believe it, my daughter was weeping. This year's been such shit, Papà! O Papà! I ran out of money. Suzanne, I said, but the line had gone. My daughter had been seeing Vikram Griffiths, I thought, leaning against a pillar of the European Parliament. I couldn't believe it. There was only one reason why Vikram saw women. There is only one reason why I see women. Your daughter's very beautiful, *she* said. She bought her underwear for her eighteenth birthday. The kind of underwear she removed herself to take a shower last night. Razzled though she may very well be. Her tottie-tackle. I shook my head in bewilderment. Papà! Suzanne hadn't called to me like that since I left eighteen months ago. What shall I do, I asked myself, standing in the great foyer of the European Parliament? What shall I do, now I have decided not to go back on the coach with them, now I have decided not to return to my job? For I suddenly realized that I had decided not to return to my job. How do these decisions happen? I asked myself. I felt completely disorientated in the busy foyer of the European Parliament. I was leaving my job. Suzanne had been seeing Vikram Griffiths. Half philosophy hangs there, in the chemistry of decisions, I thought. *She* had gone back to her husband. In understanding volition. What shall I do? Wait for some enzyme to shift? For a moment I was seized by anxiety. Could it be I'd left my bromazepam in the hotel? I opened my bag, then and there on the polished wood floor of the busy foyer. Where? My clothes spilled out. Underwear, crumpled shirts. In my wash-bag? Yes. But did I need any? Make a phone-call first, I told myself. Phone Georg. I bought another phonecard at the news-stand, but Georg was out. His wife was better, the mother said. Crisis over. Opera-tottie was out. My wife's phone was engaged now. Who was Suzanne calling to tell of her lover's death? No, his suicide. I did need a bromazepam. At least it might be possible for us to talk now, I reflect. At least my daughter is definitely *in* life, up to her eyeballs. At least we don't need to speak about *Black Spells Magic* and such-like silliness. Unscrewing the child-proof cap, I called the Welsh MEP's Yorkshire secretary-tottie. Had she seen the petition? I'd brought it earlier. She had. I was staying behind to look after the red tape, I said. Perhaps she knew of a better hotel, cheap, central, near the main police station, the town hall? The death had to be registered. She'd look one up, she said. Call back in half-an-hour. But there was something else, I said, swallowing the bromazepam. Immediately I took it, I regretted having taken it. It'll sound crazy, but I'd like to have a chat about the possibility of working for the Parliament. I find the whole thing so exciting. I waited. Perhaps, I don't know, perhaps we could eat together this evening. Seeing that I'm here. Amazingly, she said yes. Yorkshire-tottie and I like each other, I thought. We like each other. Sneaky-Niki would already be somewhere south of Geneva. I regretted taking the bromazepam. *She* would be safe and sound, watching a video perhaps. It wasn't impossible, Yorkshire-tottie said, to find work in the European Parliament. I liked her accent. Particularly if you spoke a few languages and were willing to accept lousy conditions. Nobody will give you a permanent contract here, she laughed. Forget that stuff. I liked her laugh. Not to mention the pay! A lot of MEPs' staff were taken on on an entirely temporary basis, she said, depending on how many people anybody needed at any one time. Your speech was very good, yesterday, she said. Very personal and professional at the same time, if you know what I mean. Owen noticed it. She meant the Honourable Owen Rhys. She laughed. Perhaps he could speak to somebody on the Petitions Committee. Perhaps you could spend the night with her, I thought. She was telling me to call back in half-an-hour for the name of the hotel. Perhaps the rest of your life. All invented, I thought, putting down the phone, and looking around the grand sweep of the foyer: the languages, the flags, the brave inscriptions, brave waterwords. Safe and sound on the way back to her husband, I thought. Beyond the glass and concrete, the flags flapped bravely in alphabetical order. Europe. As yesterday, the sky was a liquid drift of clouds and stabbing light, changing changing. Such a scandal. And a speck of dog was barking at the wind. One woman's worth another, I thought. One man. *Egalité*. I wish I could speak to Georg now. I wish I could talk to Vikram. What had become of Dafydd? Of Welsh poetry? But tonight might be fun. Then it occurs to me I don't even know her name. You don't even know the name of the woman you are inventing, I told myself. Inventing your night with, your life with. I laughed. It's quite a privilege to laugh out loud on your own in a public place. Not Christine again, I hope. Not Christine.